"We better get down there. The trial will be starting any time now."

"Wait," Whit asked. The boy complied, checking the walkway on the wall again. "Give me an idea what's about to happen."

Miles took a few breaths, then wiped angrily at the tears in his eyes. "The church bell down the road will start ringing, tolling the death knell, and then all the other church bells will join in, too. That'll bring out anyone who hasn't heard what's going on. They . . . like a big crowd for these things.

"Procurator Fowler, General Macowmber and Reverend Sharkey will come out on the palace balcony that overlooks the square. The Procurator's counselors will call for witnesses. Some guys from the Coal Man's Bar, who have been bribed, will give testimony. No one survives a trial here, innocent or guilty. Then they'll take your friend to the platform and lash her to the rings on that big post. Last night they threw a lot of ethanol on the logs below the platform, so everything's ready for action. The Reverend will come down and say a sermon full of fire and brimstone, and end it by throwing a lit torch on the wood. It will take about an hour from start to finish and the smell won't leave this town for a month."

Whit stared at him, aghast at the detailed description. "You've seen this happen before."

"Yes," he whispered, his shoulders slumping.

The possibility that she was going to see the person she loved most in the world burned alive descended on Whit like an avalanche. A swift, racing wall of white was slamming into her. For a moment, she thought she might faint. Willing herself to maintain a grip on self-control, she struggled to breathe.

Visit

Bella Books

at

BellaBooks.com

or call our toll-free number
1-800-729-4992

WIZARD OF ISIS

JEAN STEWART

Bella BOOKS

2004

Bella Books, Inc.
P.O. Box 10543
Tallahassee, FL 32302

Printed in the United States of America on acid-free paper
First Edition

Editor: Anna Chinappi
Cover designer: G.V. Shea

ISBN 1-931513-72-4

As ever, this is for Susie Hart.
You are the love of my life.

And for my Mom, Henrietta Stewart, who taught me to read and to love.
You are the star I navigate by.

✧✧✧

Thanks to Jackie Murray, Ginger Dunn, Paula DeFusco,
and Linda Baaken
for all the dinners, laughs and encouragement
during a tough couple of years.
I love you guys!

Thanks to Lori Lake, for trading writer chats with me on the net.
You're a great writer and even greater friend.

Last, my gratitude to my editor Anna Chinappi,
to Linda Hill and Terese Orban,
and everyone at Bella Books.

Prologue

Once, there was land called America. A vast and varied land, it rolled from the Atlantic Ocean to the Pacific, and it was populated by an energetic, hopeful people. For more than two hundred years it was a haven for liberty, a land of free men and women.

Then came a virus called AIDS. For several decades after it was first discovered, the disease existed in certain groups of people, but most of America was unaffected, and so it went ignored. Then, around the year 2000, the AIDS virus mutated and bonded with a virus called Genital Herpes. As AIDS had, in America, for unknown reasons, nestled into gay male and then poor minority populations in preference to others, so did AGH seem to make its chosen home among heterosexuals.

The mutation went unnoticed until about seven years later, when large numbers of young, sexually active heterosexuals contracted odd forms of pneumonia and reproductive tract cancers. Throughout the medical world, research and drug development efforts were mobilized, but a cure was not found. By 2009, AGH was well on its way to becoming the worst plague since the Black Death of the Middle Ages. Young heterosexuals were dying in record numbers. In the midst of the resulting panic, America took extreme measures.

Societal behaviors which had developed during the AIDS crisis became driving forces. Instead of trying to cure AGH, people blamed the victims.

In June 2010, a select group of white men, The Aryan Procurators, joined forces with a group of religious zealots called the New Order Christians. They convinced the U.S. President that something radical had to be done. He issued the Laws of Public Safety. Originally conceived as a temporary measure, the Laws of Public Safety ultimately superseded the U.S. Constitution. Liberty and personal freedoms gave way to a code of strict regulations, and democracy was crushed by fundamentalist interpretations of the Bible. Not surprisingly, the Aryans and New Order Christians ended up with all the power. They called the new nation Elysium, the Greek word for paradise.

Then, they began to kill. At first, it was just AGH carriers, but soon it was anyone who wasn't wanted: anyone who wasn't white, heterosexual and an avowed fundamentalist Christian. A tide of refugees came racing west. The states in the middle of the continent, already swamped with their own health emergency, were simply overrun. By 2011, people were dying so fast that the highways were clogged with abandoned cars, with nothing but corpses at the wheels. Orphaned children ran in small herds, raiding supermarkets for canned food, and even eating rodents when packaged food was not to be found. Eventually, rumors of cannibalism were heard everywhere.

Once affluent, pristine suburban towns became armed forts, cut off from humanity. Yet, when the plague struck enough of the towns-people, those forts became ghost towns, littered with debris the vandals created as they passed through, tossing discarded loot crazily among the decomposing bodies.

The far western states, meanwhile, had rebelled against the Laws of Public Safety. Their leaders met in Las Vegas to plan a resistance, and sent a cable to Washington, D.C., stating that they were a "free land." A civil war, later called the Great Rift, erupted. America had split in two, into Elysium on the east coast and Freeland in the west.

In 2013, the Elysians eliminated western resistance by dropping a hydrogen bomb on Las Vegas. The introduction of radiation made the spread of AGH even worse; anywhere the wind blew the fallout became a death zone. Anyone left alive near Nevada, fled. The entire center of the continent became an unpopulated wilderness. In the east, AGH killed two in ten people, but in the west, AGH killed two in three.

AGH went on to ravage the world. More than one third of the global population was gone by 2017. By 2030, the United Nations, or what was left of it, met in France and announced that more than one half of the world's population was dead and many more were dying. In the hardest hit areas—Russia, India, Brazil, China, and much of Africa—the plague meant annihilation. Contact between countries was reduced to a tribal affair and, out of fear of encountering some new mutant strain of the virus, contact was, for the most part, shunned.

In keeping with this sentiment, in 2013 the Elysians used the best minds of their military-industrial complex to create an invisible photo-electromagnetic shield. An oval of light beams controlled by NASA satellites in space, the Border rose out of the Atlantic Ocean. Impenetrable on land and sea, it fell across the Gulf of Mexico and the center of the continent. Like a huge, unscalable wall, the Border sealed Elysium into its own world, so that no one came in, and no one went out. After they'd hunted down and exterminated every AGH carrier they could find, the Elysians were sure they would be safe.

It was not to be. No matter how many AGH carriers were executed, the disease continued to move through the populace like a foul smell. Finally, the Elysian leaders began to understand they could not stop the plague with their extermination program; they were also beginning to understand the importance of having a productive workforce, even a sick one. There were jobs to be done and no one to do them. AGH-free women were turned into Breeders and kept in penitentiaries (called "breeding pens") because there were no longer enough healthy women to assure a future Elysian civilization. Other AGH-free persons were allowed to become citizens in the walled, feudal towns that were erected outside of the polluted, corpse-filled city centers. New York City's elite class relocated to West Point. The leaders of Washington, D.C., moved out to Bethesda, Maryland. In the east, large cities were abandoned and left to ruin. Laws were created making AGH victims serfs, to be posted on farms in rural areas, far away from "normal" people. They were doomed to slaving away their remaining years, providing food for their oppressors.

Meanwhile, in Freeland, only one group of people survived in vast numbers. These were the ones who were not heterosexual. When the plague emerged, some women in the Pacific Northwest had had the foresight to organize. Via mass e-mailings over the Internet, lesbians were encouraged to prepare for the worst, to turn their savings into supply stockpiles and then relocate to communes hidden deep in the national forests. Among stands of century-old trees, they set up sperm banks, medical clinics and water purification works. Carpenters among them built small but sturdy structures for housing. As the Great Rift began, lesbians throughout the west seemed to disappear. There was too much else going on for the authorities to worry about a network of crazed survivalists camping in the national forests.

After the Border went up in 2013, lesbians resurfaced and began asserting their presence. Mounted troops of well-trained, armed warrior women came out of the Cascade, Olympic and Sierra Mountains. For the next decade they methodically gathered up survivors, and subdued the packs of vandals that had become a more likely cause of death than the plague. The vandals were given a choice: leave the life of preying on the weak behind, or die. Faced with that inspiration, many of the vandals became model citizens, while others found unmarked graves near the villages they tormented. Throughout it all, new settlements were built, new life created. Civilization survived. Patriarchy, however, was gone for good.

Fierce women, later called "The Mothers," kept civilization alive by bringing new generations into the world. They spent their lives contributing without reservation to the welfare of their city-colonies. They developed inventive methods of food production, expanded medical resources, organized schools. Women took on back breaking tasks, had large families, and passed on the concept of woman-strength to their daughters and sons.

Some of the sperm banks had no categorical descriptions attached to the sample. A woman bore a child and it was considered good fortune, the gift of a future. Racial hybrids were the norm. Other women chose to preserve their ethnicity. They searched the sperm banks until they were able to match the donor sample with their own heritage. Since the Elysians were promoting Aryan purity, it seemed essential to some that the Unwanteds be cultivated, too. Japanese, Navaho, African, Vietnamese, Hebrew, Mexican—the differences were prized and preserved.

After witnessing the Murder of the Unwanteds and other acts of terror sanctioned by Elysium's Fundamentalist Christians, many in Freeland turned away from Christianity. New and old religions came into practice: Buddhism, Wicca, and belief in the Native American Great Spirit, among them. However, after the horrific example of Elysium's intolerance and its consequences, religious tolerance became the overriding cultural maxim. Gradually, once-common Christian names were forsaken for the names of amazons, ancient goddesses and ethnic heroines. A culture once centered on Judeo-Christian beliefs and trappings slowly redefined itself. The Christians who remained steadfast were not fundamentalists, but rather people who lived by the loving and forgiving example set by Jesus.

At first, survivors congregated in tiny villages. Then, in an effort to marshal the meager populace that was left, seven city-colonies were formed. Arranged along the western coast and the southwestern edge of Old America, the city-colonies were Artemis, Boudica, Harvey, Morgan, Susan B. Anthony, Lang, and Tubman. While Artemis and Susan B. Anthony, and years later, Isis, adopted women-only mandates structuring separatist societies, the other city-colonies were populated by a mix of male and female, lesbian, and heterosexual peoples. All were matriarchies, with the exception of Harvey, which drew a majority of gay males. No city-colony was larger than 50,000 people, and a development program was created to publicly fund the founding of new city-colonies when growth demanded it.

The seven city-colonies were governed by the U.S. Constitution, although the clause regarding the executive branch was altered. A bitter lesson was learned when the American President caved in to special interests during the plague panic that preceded the Great Rift. No longer would so much power reside in the authority of one person. Instead, Freeland's executive branch was defined as a Council of Seven Leaders, each one the elected leader of a city-colony.

As time passed, Freeland out of necessity entered a technological revolution. The Mothers began collecting machines—all kinds of machines. At first, they were merely salvaging usable pieces from a unit that no longer functioned in order to build another unit from scratch. But, as the ranks of hungry children grew, demands for increased productivity had to be met. With two-thirds of the population gone and distribution systems in ruins, there were simply not enough people left to do the necessary work. Manual labor could not plant, harvest or process all the food they needed; could not grow, pick or weave all the cotton they needed for cloth. The Mothers began designing new machines, machines run by computer programs instead of human beings. Computerized hydroponic sheds, computerized cotton and clothing production, computerized manufacturing processes providing a wealth of necessities, from soap to construction materials. Within a few decades, Freeland was moving out of the shadow of the Great Rift.

Just after the Border went up, a Seattle doctor, Dr. Kea, assembled an intensive research team. In one series of experiments, she had consulted with Native American healers to obtain an herbal mixture that had immunostimulator properties. While the active ingredients remained unknown, the extract had been used for years in the treatment of various infections and was known to enhance T-cell activity. The research team found that a vaccine derived from dead AGH virus particles, when used in conjunction with the herbal immunostimulator, had a profound protective effect on bone marrow and ultimately resulted in elimination of the virus in the infected patient. After the doctor died, a plague victim herself, her research assistant, Dr. Satrina, eventually perfected the treatment.

Once the three necessary medicinal plants involved in producing the immunostimulator were successfully introduced into a farming and harvesting regimen, only the actual production of the mixture became a problem. The laboratory preparation was time consuming and needed a team of botanists and analytical chemists to attain desired results.

A young woman named Maat Tyler created the computer program that automated the preparation of the immunostimulator. The vaccine was manufactured and dispersed throughout the small but ecstatic populace of Freeland. By the end of 2058, within a decade of Maat's contribution, AGH ceased to exist in Freeland.

Meanwhile, in Elysium, officials ended funding for public education. Illiteracy and ignorance became as destructive as the AGH plague. Soon, the only knowledge in Elysium was what was passed down from father to son. Simple medical procedures were lost, computer skills disappeared. Eventually, no one in Elysium knew how to control the Border they had so painstakingly erected. The wall they had built to keep out the world now imprisoned them.

In Freeland, Maat Tyler turned her attention to solving the mystery of how the Border worked. After years of study, Maat at last rediscovered how to coordinate the satellite beams that kept the shield dome in place. Then, she had taken the design one step further and developed a means of breaking the light beams at certain points. She called the weak spots "Bordergates." For a while, it had become stylish for the more daring Freeland warriors to go undercover in Elysium and gather information, coming and going via these Bordergates.

Then gradually, Freeland had become convinced of the steady dissolution of whatever threat Elysium posed. Elysium was clearly destroying itself, strangled by its feudal caste system, sexist doctrine, scientific ignorance and religious fanaticism. A gestapo-like police force, called Regulators, enforced the law, controlling the Elysian populace with storm trooper tactics. And the AGH virus that had provoked it all was still spreading quietly among them, evading all attempts at quarantine.

Freelanders, meanwhile, had learned to cherish the differences in race, religion, and sexual orientation that enabled their mutual survival.

Now, in the year 2095, eighty-two years after the Border was first erected, the satellites that control the photo-electromagnetic shield have been replaced, and the near catastrophe of the loss of the Border has been averted.

However, while the Border was not stable, the Regulators have attacked and destroyed the city-colony of Lang. Soon, Isis, too, was once more under attack. The Leader of Isis, Tomyris Whitaker, and her wing woman Danu Sullivan, have chased two Elysian fighter jets across the Border and into the land inhabited by Freeland's mortal enemy, Elysium. They are about to meet their neighbors, and discover things about themselves and Elysium they never knew.

Chapter 1

"Stay up, stay up," Whit muttered to her crippled jet.

She peered into the odd, amber-colored clouds enfolding her aircraft. Whit knew that somewhere just ahead, the first in a long series of mountains lay between her and her goal. She was about to fly over the Allegheny Highlands, a remote wilderness that made up the center of the Appalachians. The altimeter before her confirmed her instincts. Her Peregrine was steadily dropping lower and lower.

Can't bail out, she told herself. *Not before I've gotten a better GPS fix on Danu.*

As if in a surreal dream, leafy tree tops suddenly emerged from the fog below and seemed to reach for her. Whit gasped and jerked up the nose of the fighter jet. She felt the wings catch a helpful updraft and rode the swell of air along a ridge. Heart pounding, she cleared the long, forested crest beneath her. Almost immediately, the craft lost the supportive slipstream and dropped lower.

The thick cloud cover became vaporous wisps, then cleared altogether. Surprised, Whit gazed into a vivid blue sky. Below her, miles of lush, verdant deciduous forest stretched out in almost fairy tale splendor. This wasn't the sickly pale yellow of the sparse ground cover she had seen on the other side of the Appalachians, where decades of clear-cutting, agricultural over-production and pollution were causing the ecosystem to implode.

How has this place escaped?

Her eyes drifted to the thickly wooded mountains lining up in the west.

Damn, there's not a place to land in sight.

Nervously, she glanced left at the bullet holes in the wing. Less than five minutes ago an Elysian F-24 had strafed her during a dogfight over the Shenandoah River Valley. A clear, gleaming stream of cold fusion fuel was flowing across dark, radar-proofed metal, emptying into the sky behind her.

Whit checked her GPS gauge. She was nearing the section of Old West Virginia territory where Danu Sullivan's radio transmission had originated only a few moments ago. Danu had tersely stated that her own Peregrine was going down, and Whit had ordered her to bail out.

Keying open her helmet microphone, Whit called, "Lieutenant Sullivan. Do you read me? Over."

Whit searched the forest below for some sign, almost afraid to admit that she was looking for the blue-green flames of a cold fusion fire; it would probably be all that was visible from the air if Danu's fighter jet had crashed. Steeling herself, Whit slipped her jet sideways into a convenient current of air. The jet glided forward, banking on a wind running along the length of the next mountain ridge.

Whit's engine chugged several times, signaling that her fuel was dangerously low. Quickly, she reached under her seat and disengaged the emergency packet stowed there. Jerking open the zipper of her insulated flight suit, she shoved the packet inside, and zipped herself up again.

"Danu, answer me!" Whit snapped, her professional manner gone in a rush of anxiety. The young pilot was a good friend, and as the one who had drawn Danu into this sortie, Whit battled a wave of guilt and anxiety.

Earlier that morning, Whit had led the team of Peregrine pilots that had taken to the skies, defending Isis from an Elysian sneak attack. The battle had played out on the western flanks of the Cascade Mountains in Old Washington state territory. Though badly outnumbered, the Peregrines had fought the Elysians and their ancient F-24s to a standstill.

Then two F-24s had broken away from the fight. Whit had been sure that one of the two F-24s was carrying a small thermonuclear weapon. Ever since a rogue F-24 had made it as far as Lang, another Freelandian city-colony, a few weeks earlier, it seemed as if the Elysians were determined to take advantage of the abnormally weak Border and do as much damage as possible. In the space of a few minutes, Lang had been transformed from a thriving agricultural center into particles of radioactive dust. When Whit had seen the two F-24s break away from the fight near Isis, Whit had immediately surmised that the F-24s were trying to evade the Peregrines and find another way to approach and attack Isis.

Whit and her wing woman, Danu, had chased after the escaping Elysians. Unable to shake their tail, the two F-24s had quickly given up on going for Isis, instead settling into a long retreat back to Elysium. Whit and Danu had continued to chase them across the breadth of the American continent. At last the four jets had simultaneously reached a gaping hole in the shimmering, photo-electromagnetic Border that divided their conflicting nations, and Whit had made a ruthless decision. Even if it meant sacrificing her own life, she was determined that this particular bomb was never going to leave Elysium again.

One F-24 had swung back to run interference, leading Whit to believe the other F-24 carried the nuclear weapon. Whit had ordered Danu to handle the interference while Whit pursued the craft that was still trying to flee. Two separate one-on-one dogfights had erupted in Elysian airspace roughly fifty miles apart. Apparently, she and Danu had each won their confrontation, then had encountered difficulties keeping their craft airborne in the minutes afterward.

Where are you, Danu? Whit wondered, her eyes straining for some clue as they swept over the wooded landscape beneath her jet.

Ahead, halfway up the mountainside, she saw a flash of incongruous gray and white amid the texture of green leaves. Whit peered harder. As she came closer she realized that what she was seeing was a parachute rippling from the branches of a tree. Whit noted the small waterfall below, marking the area in her memory.

Her jet sputtered, and then the sound of a struggling engine was replaced by the quiet rush of wind against the wings.

"Shit!"

She released the seat belt, then punched the canopy retraction lever as the jet began to drop. The plexiglass top shot back and the sudden force of air knocked her flat against the flight seat. A second later she was powered upwards into the sky in the automatic ejection sequence. As she triggered her parachute she saw the small, black Peregrine scoot over a hill and disappear into a shadowed hollow. A spectacular blue-green flash appeared, telling her the jet had crashed even before the reverberating roar came.

The Peregrine was history. Whit knew she had new troubles to deal with as she manipulated the chute lines. Below her there was nothing but trees and more trees. The only clear space was the channel of a river, but seeing the churning white water, and the plentiful dark, round rocks, Whit knew she couldn't chance landing there. She tried to steer closer to where she'd seen Danu's chute, but the wind was taking her in the opposite direction.

When she was no more than two hundred yards from the ground she glimpsed a small meadow sloping up from a bluff just above the river. Purposefully, she steered for it. The ground quickly grew closer, then seemed to rush up at her. She dropped into tall grass and blue cornflowers with a thump, her feet and legs collapsing beneath her. Immediately she rolled, then came smoothly to her feet. Breathing hard, she began gathering in the billowing white and gray paneled chute. Suddenly, she froze.

There, twenty feet away, in the middle of the clearing, were the rusted and charred remains of what looked like an Elysian heli-jet. Grass and weeds obscured the sides and tail, and a wild tangle of brambles grew over the top, but below the thick vines the long blades that had once powered the aircraft through the air were still rigid and unmistakable. Whit instantly knew that this little empty patch existed in the miles of forest surrounding it because a few years ago the heli-jet had crashed and burned here.

Get outta sight, Whit told herself. She bunched the silken chute material into a haphazard ball and broke into a run, moving through knee-high grass toward the cover of the dark wood.

Racing under the tall, big-trunked maples, she pushed her way through the underbrush, moving deeper into the forest. Within ten meters, the thick blueberry and rhododendron bushes growing along the periphery of the wood gave way to low scrub. She dashed a few strides farther and found the scrub giving way to a smooth, even carpet of peat moss. Whit's boots sunk into the soft earth up to her ankles. Glancing up, she saw a cathedral roof of limbs arching high above her. Whit realized the greenwood ceiling was too tall and all-encompassing to permit much life-giving light to penetrate. This was truly a forest primeval, a forest such as the first Europeans had found while exploring the eastern seaboard of America back in the sixteenth century.

Puffing, Whit dropped to her knees and dug a hole in the moist loam left by a hundred autumns. She unbuckled her chute pack, freed herself from the straps and unceremoniously shoved the chute into the hole. After a moment's hesitation, she slipped off her flight helmet, placing it on top of the soft material.

The radio feed in the helmet isn't any good without the Peregrine's unit to link with, Whit told herself. *Lighter I travel, the faster I can move.*

She pushed the soft, dark dirt over the evidence of her presence, then rose to her feet. Briskly brushing the soil from her hands, she jogged back to the meadow again. She hesitated near the edge of the wood, her eyes restlessly scanning the sky as she cocked her head and listened for the tell-tale whump-whump sound of an Elysian heli-jet.

All she heard was a wood thrush singing on the other side of the meadow.

Mother's blood, I'm down in enemy territory. She unclasped the ponytail tie at the back of her head, then repeatedly ran a hand through her dark, shoulder-length hair. *Kali is gonna kill me.*

Sighing, she pulled the small laser pistol out of the leather holster on her right side, checking the firing gauge and making sure it was set as high as it could go. She slipped the weapon back into place, then retied the ponytail. Still watching the sky, she reached into a cargo pocket on her thigh and drew out her long-billed warrior's cap. The gun metal gray matched the flight suit she wore; and she hoped the color would provide camouflage in the deep shade of the woods. Deftly, she tucked her hair up under the hat, out of sight.

Even in this Freeland Warrior's uniform, it's best to look as much like a man as possible, she told herself. *A woman in Elysium is nothing but a target.*

Staying beneath the cover of the broad-limbed maples, she jogged toward the rushing river she heard off to her right. As she moved through the tall trees, she tried to calm her racing thoughts and make a plan. She would use the river to backtrack to the little downhill stream with the waterfall, then hike up the mountainside to where she'd seen the parachute. When she found Danu, they would have to get out of this section of woodland as soon as possible. The Peregrines were radar invisible, but after two dogfights and possibly four crashed jets, the Regs would certainly know they were here. It was only a matter of time before the hunt was on.

I'm sorry, Kal, Whit thought. Even though Kali was telepathic, she knew Kali would never hear her from this distance. *So much for my promises not to be reckless.* Feeling flustered and chagrined, she realized Kali was probably crazy with worry by now.

Whit resolved to get out of this mess as fast as she could. She stepped up her pace, glancing up through the occasional gap in the leafy canopy above, searching the skies for the Elysian aircraft that would eventually come.

Thousands of miles away, on the western side of the American continent, the mica-flecked granite walls of the Isis Leader's house glinted in the midday June sunlight. Surrounded by a wide expanse of lush lawns and rose gardens, the imposing three-story structure sat squarely in the center of the city-colony. Freelandian diplomats and Isis politicians were coming and going from the lower floor entrances and exits, as noisy and lively as commancheros patronizing a popular cantina. Upstairs, however, in the private residence of the Leader and her life partner, a less obstreperous meeting was underway.

Kali hurried across the private suite she shared with Whit. She marched into the large walk-in closet, then paused. Thoughtfully, she selected a few T-shirts and some sturdily made hiking pants, then tucked the folded clothing under one arm. Spotting her calf-high brown boots, Kali leaned over and grabbed them. In the half hour since the news had come of Whit's disappearance in Elysium, Kali was already enacting a plan of her own.

"Come over here a moment," Lilith called. "You need to see how this water purification unit works."

Kali nodded and moved toward her, dropping the articles she'd gathered on the bed as she passed it. Wiping a hand across her moist brow, she felt the first squirm of nausea. *Oh Gaea, not now.*

Lilith's silver haired head was bent over the canteen in her hands. "See?" she said, unscrewing the lid from the metal receptacle and fitting the tiny filtration cap in place on the mouth. "You dip the canteen into an available water source and the internal crystal drive zaps any bacteria present while the sieve filters out everything else." Lilith made a motion like she was dipping the canteen. "Then the miniature crystal drive will do a sweep, killing any bacteria in droplets on the mouth or external part of the canteen." She detached the water purification unit, put the lid back on the canteen, and handed it all to Kali. "Simple enough, right?"

Kali swallowed hard.

Lilith's perceptive blue eyes focused on her with concern.

Carefully, Kali placed the tiny water purification unit and the canteen on the dresser.

"Are you all right?" Lilith asked. "You're very pale all of a sudden."

Kali nodded and walked slowly back to the bed. She pushed the piles of clothing and supplies out of her way, crawling across the quilt, and then sinking down, exhausted.

She felt the bed move as someone sat on the edge. A gentle hand smoothed over her back. Kali knew it was Lilith, but as the hand moved into her long blonde hair, sifting through the strands, Kali let herself drift into a wistful haze, imagining that it was Whit who was comforting her.

"Kali, this is madness," the no-nonsense voice above her asserted.

The sweet vision of Whit effectively banished, Kali gave a small, disappointed moan.

"You're three months pregnant and sick every afternoon! To say nothing of what you've been putting your body through these last few weeks—working twelve hours a day while the satellite crisis was going on!" Taking an indignant breath, Lilith finished, "I know you want to help find Whit, but honestly, the last thing you need to be doing right now is joining a search and rescue team and trekking through Elysium!"

Kali rolled over and made eye contact with her only remaining parent. "Lil, I have to go," she said quietly. "I can find her. They can't."

"They have the last GPS locations Danu's and Whit's Peregrines sent, and they'll be using state-of-the-art heat-seeking equipment!"

Kali sighed. "Those GPS locations were sent by their aircraft before they went off-link with the satellites. Gaea only knows where Danu and Whit really ended up."

"Even so—" Lilith began.

"Listen to me," Kali interrupted. She gazed up at Lilith, trying to find words to explain. "Lil, it's like Whit is part of me." Her voice quavered with emotion and Kali took a deep breath, trying to master it. "I feel her like I feel my right hand at the end of my arm." She flexed her hand in front of her, gazing at it with a bemused expression. "I could find her in the deepest part of a forest, in the middle of the night."

Lilith adopted a firm tone. "I have an intelligence report that says an F-24 crashed near Andrews Air Force Base and apparently set off a mini-nuclear bomb. There's an eighty mile blast zone in Maryland."

Kali met her eyes, and said in a tone just as firm, "Before she left for Boudica, Styx told me that the wind was blowing northeast—away from the last GPS readouts for Whit and Danu."

Lilith looked away, her annoyance evident in the way she tightened her lips before she rapped out, "Isn't it bad enough to have Whit lost in that hellish place? Must you go tearing into Elysium—recklessly placing my unborn granddaughter, to say nothing of yourself, at risk?"

Slowly, Kali took Lilith's hand in her own. "Lil, I'm not a prize brood mare in foal," she answered, her voice very quiet.

Startled by the comparison, Lilith's gaze snapped back to her.

"I can't stay home, safe in the paddock," Kali said softly, pouring her soul into her warm, brown eyes. "Whit needs me. You know I have to go."

They sat there watching each other, until Kali grimaced, curling into a ball as another wave of sickness came.

Exhaling her exasperation, Lilith leaned over and rubbed Kali's back again, murmuring, "You always were more Maat's than mine, Bean Sprout. A more stubborn girl I never knew."

Kali mumbled into quilt, "My genes are as much yours as hers."

17

Refusing to debate the point, Lilith said, "You'd end up having to have some sort of adjutant. Someone assigned to just be your second, to haul your pack and protect you when you're unwell."

"That would be Tor," Kali stated, her voice coming out of the bed covers with amazing clarity. "I've already asked her and she's agreed."

Lilith raised her eyes to the ceiling. "Oh, Kali. Be reasonable! She's going to be as physically challenged by this venture as you are. She still hasn't recovered from that expedition up to Hart's Pass."

Kali rolled over again, her pale face earnest. "She's regained much of her strength this past month, and she's got the heart of a cougar." She ignored Lilith's incredulous head-shaking and plunged on. "Besides, she has some sort of vibe with Danu that I can't explain, but I can follow it—maybe even track Danu with it."

Now Lilith was frowning.

"Look, Lil, you know this crazy mage energy is getting more unpredictable as my pregnancy goes forward. Whatever power I've still got I want to be able to control and wield as best I can. Certain people, like Tor, boost the strength, increase the sensations I feel. I don't know whether it's her background in Zen studies and channeling ki, or if it's just that she believes in me . . ." Realizing she was beginning to sound like a Wiccan raving in the wildwood, Kali wound down to an abrupt close. "Is any of this making sense?" she asked faintly.

"I live with Styx, remember?"

Kali half-laughed, nodding. Styx, Lilith's partner, had spent her youth studying with Baubo, one of Freeland's most eminent Wiccan scholars. Styx was also incredibly intuitive, and had helped Kali sort out a variety of psychic growth spurts in the past.

"I need Tor. We can take a small troop of warriors if the Council insists—which to tell you the truth I expect—but all those rough, tough fighters combined will be no substitute for what Tor can do."

"You realize, of course," Lilith interjected gently, "that it will be the Isis Council, and not you, who will choose the members of this search and rescue team. There are going to be a lot of volunteers. The best of the best. You may not be allowed to say Tor goes, even if you are Whit's handfasted partner. You, yourself, may not be selected."

Outraged, Kali flashed, "I'd like to see them try to keep me out of this!"

"It's well known in the colony that this pregnancy has . . . well, that you've been having a hard time of it," Lilith stated.

Kali sat up, her hand on her stomach. "What a bunch of meddling gossips!"

Lilith rubbed her forehead.

Glancing around the bed at the piles of clothes she had chosen for the mission, Kali wondered, "How can I cram all this into a single backpack?" She bit her lip, then asked Lilith, "You know, I'm already taking the laser pistol, but do you think I should take a laser rifle, too? Or some detonation grenades?"

Lilith stiffened, then abruptly left her seat on the bed and glared down at her daughter. "For the love of Hera, I don't know why I bother! Even when you were little you never listened to me!" With that, she stalked over to the door and disappeared into the hall.

"Better take both the rifle and the grenades," Kali muttered to herself. She grabbed the pack and began slipping things inside it. "Whit can get into so much trouble."

Running along what seemed to be a narrow deer path, Whit stayed beneath the shadow of the trees and followed the river's edge. Eventually, she came to a place where the path ended. She climbed over an outcropping of rocks and saw a stream intersecting the wider white water of the river. Flowing swiftly down the side of the mountain, surrounded by thick huckleberry bushes, the stream was larger and louder than what Whit guessed from the air. Craning her neck, she peered up the mountainside, trying without success to spot both the waterfall and the parachute she'd seen earlier.

Taking quick, shallow breaths, she began trotting uphill. She impatiently pushed through the huckleberry bushes, snagging a few ripe berries as she passed and popping them in her mouth. She was thirsty, but unwilling to stop long enough to dig her canteen out of the emergency pack tucked inside of her flight suit. Gradually, she slipped away from the stream and again found less underbrush under the cathedral roof of the large trees. Smoothly, she jogged over the soft, dark soil and a variety of ferns. The higher she went, the larger and older the trees became. Amazed, she realized she was weaving in and out of trunks that would take three women to encircle. She was used to the giant firs and cedars of the Pacific Northwest, where lumber women could not put a dent in the massive forests taking over the mountain lands. But she had never seen deciduous trees like this—so tall and broad and elegant in the dim sunlight. As she ran beneath them, she lifted her knees, using her arms to pump as the hill became steeper. She could hear her breathing starting to labor. Purposefully, she leaned into the effort.

Finally, she had to stop and catch her breath. Hands on her knees, she stood on an exposed ledge of rock, listening to her ragged gasps. After a bit, she raised her head and looked around. She could hear the roar of a waterfall somewhere past the thick shrubbery off to her left. She hoped that meant Danu's parachute was attached to a tree somewhere just ahead.

Recovering, Whit chugged forward, lifting her eyes to the trees. She was automatically searching for the bright white cloth, counting on it to lead her to Danu. By now, sweat ran in long, fluid lines down the sides of her forehead. There was a strong, early June breeze riffling through the leaves high overhead, but down on the forest floor the air was still and humid. She trampled over a thick patch of ferns, turning her head and trying to listen for the sound of incoming aircraft. The waterfall was downhill, now, and the primary sounds were bird trills and the persistent rustling of leaves.

Then, Whit heard a different noise: the soft, silken ruffling of fabric. Overhead, between the branches of high tree limbs Whit spotted the bright white and gray of a parachute. She quickened her pace and moved toward the beech tree, then recognized the limp form suspended above her.

Danu!

Her heart thundering, Whit raced closer.

On the other side of the continent, in Isis, Tor was standing fretfully in the middle of a healer's office.

"Yeow!" Tor cried, leaning away from the cold metal tool.

"The calibrator pinches like that because your body fat is way too low," Neith told her sternly.

"I've gained five pounds this month—all of it muscle!" Tor blustered. "That protein supplement you gave me and all the weight lifting I've been doing—"

"Save it," Neith interjected. "You're out of your mind if you think I'm going to give you clearance for active duty."

"Aw, c'mon, Neith!" Tor pleaded. "I'm fine."

"You're better than you were a month ago, I'll grant you," Neith allowed, "but you're still underweight, and your heart rate was erratic during that cardiovascular stress test last week . . ."

"*Neith, please!*"

The healer bent her head, deep brown fingers pinching the bridge of her nose. Tor stared helplessly at the tight, black curls.

"Tor, I've seen the comline coverage," Neith said. "I know Danu's Peregrine went down over Elysium this afternoon."

"Then you also know that if you don't sign the forms I can't get a place on the rescue team!"

Neith raised her head and gazed at her with compassionate dark eyes. "You shouldn't *be* on the rescue team."

Tor whirled from her, grabbing up the shirt she had taken off earlier in the examination. "Great. Just great," she muttered angrily. She yanked the red tunic over her head and shoulders, settled it brusquely in place, then grabbed up her belt and fastened it around her slim middle.

"Tor, be realistic," Neith began, then shook her head. "A warrior medical panel will be reviewing anything I sign. For the love of Sappho, Tor, you aren't just recovering from a serious wound—you came back from the dead! For over four minutes up there at Hart's Pass, you had no vital signs, and then Kali somehow resuscitated you! You're incredibly lucky to be alive!"

Turning to face her, Tor took a step closer and hissed, "Danu's lost in Elysium! What use is it being alive if she—" Tor whirled away, gulping down the words. "I have to go!" With a snarl, she reached over to the keyboard on Neith's desk, stabbing hard at the key she knew would close the medical clearance forms page displayed on the comline screen. "I've got to get Danu out before the Regs find her! I don't give a flaming shit about anything else! Nothing else matters."

"She's my friend, too, you know," Neith defended quietly. "I know how you feel and I wish I could help—"

"Sure," Tor interrupted, already heading for the door. "Don't trouble yourself on my account," came floating back, in a tense, angry voice.

It didn't surprise Neith when the door slammed.

Whit slowed as she got to the bottom of the tree.

Danu was still secure in the parachute harness, dangling about twenty meters above from some chute lines that were snagged on limbs higher up in the tree. Whit squinted up at her, trying to make out the details, registering primarily that Danu was not moving and there was something dark on one side of her bowed head. As Whit moved underneath her, a splash hit her cheek. Whit touched a finger to the spot and found herself gazing at blood.

"Danu!" she called in a urgent tone.

She thought she heard a faint groan in reply.

"Danu, can you hear me?"

"Tor," Danu's voice slurred.

Okay, Whit decided, *she's hurt.*

Whit began scanning the tree, looking for a way up.

It was a smooth, gray-barked beech, and the closest branch was possibly two and a half meters off the ground. Moving back to give herself an approach, Whit dashed toward the tree and used her momentum to leap as high as she could. She snagged the branch, then swung a leg up and pulled herself to a straddling position. The forest around her went quiet as Whit stood and carefully began climbing from branch to branch.

Whit closed in on Danu. As she had guessed, the young woman was hanging from the twisted parachute lines that had caught on branches as Danu fell through them. Glancing up, Whit saw the gray and white of the chute still fluttering on the thin ends of the uppermost branches. However, the cloth was ripping with each passage of the light but constant breeze. Whit knew it wouldn't be much longer before the chute blew clear of this tree, removing the marker it provided.

Good, Whit decided, hoping the chute would blow clear off the mountain. *I want to get us out of here before the Regs see that big flag up there and come right for us.*

Whit returned her gaze to Danu and knelt, then straddled the thick limb. Carefully, she levered herself along the branch, maneuvering through chute lines, to a position directly above Danu.

Suddenly, Whit had a good view. Clotted blood coated Danu's short, red hair and covered one side of her face in red streaks. *Gaea, please let her be all right*, Whit prayed.

She surveyed the scene for a few moments, considering the fact that not all of the lines were supporting Danu's weight. Hoping her idea would work, Whit pulled her boot knife from its sheath. She raised herself up a little on the branch, then began sawing one of the looser chute lines that ran by her. When the line parted, she yanked and tugged until the length above her came free and dropped. Whit gathered the rope up, then scooted through the lines that did bear Danu's weight. Pausing directly over her friend, Whit tied a series of knots, fastening one end of her freed piece to a line supporting Danu.

Each of these chute lines is designed to take the weight of what would be considered an average warrior.

She passed the length around the limb once. Carefully, she checked her work for possible error. The makeshift pulley system had to work on the first try. Once she cut the remaining support lines, she had to depend on this line to safely lower Danu to the ground.

Whit threaded the rope behind her back, settling it around her waist, then wrapped her left hand and elbow in the guideline she had created. Her left foot was planted on her pulley rope, and the right foot was tucked up against the underside of the tree limb. Knife firmly gripped in her right hand, she began sawing the first supporting line. Over the next few minutes she cut all five weight-bearing lines, eliminating one by one the lines that held Danu captive. The muscles in Whit's arm felt as if they were on fire by the time the last rope parted with a resounding snap.

Whit dropped her knife. Danu plunged straight down. Abruptly, Whit's guideline lost its slack and Danu stopped with a jerk that nearly took Whit over the side of the branch. Cursing and sweating, Whit braced her boot against the rope carrying Danu's weight and gripped the rope with both hands. Then, using every muscle in her body to hold her precarious position, she slowly lowered her friend to a gentle landing on the forest floor.

Whit's cramping hands released the rope and it fell to the ground after Danu. Quickly, Whit moved backward along the branch, then retraced her path, climbing cautiously down the tree. Her muscles were quivering from the intense exertion and she reminded herself to actively guard against a fall. She reached the last low branch and swung down, landing with a hop that sent her toward Danu. She spied her knife and scooped it up as she passed, tucking it back into her boot.

The young woman was lying in the crumpled position her body had assumed as she came to rest on the loamy ground. Studying the bloodied face, Whit knelt beside her. Methodically, she took a pulse count from the young woman's carotid artery, then leaned her cheek over the freckled nose to check her respiration. When she realized that Danu's vital signs seemed fairly normal, Whit gingerly moved aside strands of red-gold hair. She found a long, shallow gash along the top, right side of Danu's skull. Beneath the blood, a large lump showed.

"Hecate," Whit swore said softly. "Took a good crack, didn't ya, kid?"

Her hands automatically began checking the rest of Danu's body, looking for fractures. When she found nothing except a few more bumps, Whit straightened Danu's limbs into a relaxed, stretched-out position. Quickly, she cut free the long line she had used to lower Danu, and coiled it into a slim, lightweight rope bundle.

"Never know when I'll be in need of this again," she said to herself, as she opened her flight suit, and shoved the bundle of cord in beside her emergency kit.

"Whit?"

Surprised by the faint comment, Whit leaned back and met Danu's half-lidded gaze. The young pilot blinked several times, then her brow creased. "Ohhh, damn, my head hurts. What happened?"

Whit was trying to think of a fast explanation that wouldn't tax whatever reserves of clarity or strength Danu still had, when she realized something had changed.

The forest had been quiet before, but there had still been an occasional bird song, and the repetitive racket of distant locusts shaking their carapaces. Now, even that had ceased. The forest was as silent as a Quaker prayer meeting.

Nervously, Whit looked around, expecting to see a troop of Regs quick-marching through the trees toward them.

Picking up on Whit's sudden alarm, Danu whispered, "What's wrong?"

Whit held her index finger against her lips. Slowly, she stood, then placed her hand on the laser pistol she wore on her belt.

"Don't," a commanding voice ordered.

Whit's hand froze on the stock. She turned and saw a woman step from behind the same beech Whit had been climbing just moments before.

The woman reminded Whit of an illustration she had once seen: a pencil sketch of a Shawnee Indian, circa eighteenth-century America. The woman wore the same style of clothing: deerskin leggings and a long-sleeved deerskin shirt cinched around her middle with a colorfully beaded belt. The difference was the tawny-brown hair that was cropped at her collar, and shining with blonde strands even in the filtered light of the forest. Whit had a moment to realize she was attractive, even though her light-colored eyes seemed cold and hard. Then Whit focused on the old-fashioned Winchester rifle the woman carried waist-high, the barrel pointed unerringly at them.

"Get your hand off the weapon," the woman ordered.

Whit lifted her hand and held it away from her side.

Swiftly, the woman moved in, lowering the rifle barrel to point menacingly at Danu. Whit went rigid, aware of the silent admonition. The stranger darted forward to grab Whit's pistol from its holster and then jam it beneath her beaded belt. She ordered Whit to take out her sheathed boot-knife and toss it from her. Seething, Whit complied. Smoothly, the woodswoman retreated, then circled Danu, approaching her from the opposite side. When Whit took an instinctive step to shield her friend, pale blue eyes flashed a warning. Then, as if reading Whit's concern, the woman stated, "I'll not harm her."

Whit nodded.

The woman kept the rifle on Whit as she knelt beside Danu and slipped the laser pistol free of its leather holster. She shoved the gun in her belt, then fished out Danu's boot knife and tossed it aside. Slowly, she stood and moved away from them, whistling a bird call.

Other deerskin-clad women came scurrying quietly through the trees, some carrying hardwood crossbows, others carrying what appeared to be a variety of twentieth-century hunting rifles. Whit gaped at them, amazed. There were small, silvery coins braided into the tresses of some of the longer-haired ones, while bits of smooth-edged, blue or green glass were strung along leather thongs and hanging from several necks. All of them wore thigh-length deerskin shirts. Blue and green embroidery decorated the sleeves and collars, and even the sides of some of the leggings. Thick-soled moccasins graced their feet, and half of them were wearing what seemed to be long loincloths. As they milled around, staring at her and Danu, Whit counted sixteen altogether. All of the women appeared incredibly fit and fierce.

The first woman, who seemed to be their leader, came closer to Whit and jerked a thumb at her. "Bind her, Florey," she told one of her party.

A huge, husky woman lumbered closer, pausing to scoop up Whit's and Danu's discarded knives as she came. "Sho, Colonel," Florey said, taking a length of rawhide from a waist pouch and motioning Whit to extend her hands for the tying.

Whit took another quick look around, briefly considering trying to run for it. The colonel narrowed her eyes, watching her. Angrily, Whit glared back at her, accepting the frustrating reality of the situation. *I can't leave Danu. I'll just have to go along with this and see if I can get both of us away later.*

Slowly, Whit straightened her arms out, keeping her wrists together. Florey eyed her nervously, before stepping closer. With a brisk efficiency, she tied Whit's hands, then attached a long leather thong. As Florey backed up, stringing out the thong, Whit understood that she was going to be on a lead.

A small, wiry youngster came near her and patted her down in a quick search, finding the slight bulk of the rope bundle and the emergency kit. With a shy leer, she unzipped Whit's flight suit and pulled out the two articles. The youngster tossed the kit and rope to the colonel, who caught them in midair. The tawny-haired woman spent a few minutes checking the contents of the small leather bag, then shoved the kit and the rope in a deerskin slouch bag draped across her torso.

Excited and triumphant, the younger women in the group began to give high-pitched yips, pumping their crossbows and antique rifles over their heads.

From her reclining position, Danu remarked hoarsely to Whit, "Who the hell *are* they?"

Whit's reply was a low growl.

Chapter 2

As twilight fell over Isis, the Council was still grinding through an interminable emergency meeting. Within the gleaming, massive, hewn log structure that was the Cedar House, a dimly lit balcony known as "the gallery" ringed the Council chamber. Several hundred interested citizens seated there were afforded a close-up view of democracy in action.

Fidgeting restlessly in the middle of the whispering crowd, Kali tried to ignore the watchful eyes she felt on her. She had submitted her plan to the Council about two hours ago, and now she was forced to sit here, above the assembly, listening to the endless debates about what to do.

Each woman on the Isis Council was interacting with a crystal plate flush with the pine table and situated before her. The plate was a computer monitor, allowing the member to see and read the specifics of each rescue mission plan under review. On the large wallscreen located on the opposite side of the Cedar House, a bulleted version of the plan was displayed for the benefit of the gallery. Around the chamber, numerous small cameras were documenting events for the live comline broadcast underway. Any city-colony in Freeland was able to access the events underway, and across the miles, in the midst of their usual work or quiet evening routines, many citizens were keeping one eye on their wallscreens.

After all, Kali reflected, these weren't just any two Freelanders lost in Elysium; this was the Leader of Isis and her wingwoman. Whit wasn't just a Leader, she was a warrior reservist, an ace, who had without hesitation shed her civilian duties and jumped into a fighter cockpit to defend their home. Danu wasn't just a nineteen-year-old pilot, she was the Think Tank genius who had designed and supervised the building of Isis itself. Their exploits as part of the Scramble Squadron alone would have guaranteed them a place in herstory. The largely civilian squad had fought off the overwhelming Elysian numbers trying to sneak attack Isis. However, there had been a more ghastly threat involved in that Elysian incursion, and Whit and Danu had sniffed it out and hounded it back to Elysium itself. Whit and Danu had stayed one-on-one with the two Elysian F-24s that had broken away from the action. Denied an end run around the dogfight they'd encountered approaching Isis, the Elysians had retreated. Whit and Danu had herded them back through the Cascades, back across the Wilderness. Then, while the Border was still down, they had somehow shot down those F-24s over Elysium itself. Even with the scant surveillance reports available, the news was leaking out; everyone now knew a small thermonuclear bomb had detonated over the Elysian military headquarters, Andrews Air Force Base.

And the only one who truly believes you survived that holocaust is me, Whit.

Kali pressed a hand against her stomach, willing her rebelling system to calm down. She glanced at the jacket she had placed on the chair to her right, wondering for the hundredth time where Tor was.

Looking over her shoulder self-consciously, she noted again how packed the gallery was; women were standing all along the back, pressed against the log wall. She was on the end of a row, with an empty seat to her right. Whenever she looked around, she found eyes on her that skittered nervously away.

So this is what it's like to be possibly widowed, she thought. *I'm making everyone uncomfortable. They don't know what to say to me.*

Kali returned her focus to the Council session, agonizing over how much time this was taking. She felt as if precious hours were being squandered in the typical Freelandian preoccupation with talking every problem to death. Glumly, she found herself studying the thick, dark red wooden beams that arced like wings from the walls, supporting the high roof. Colorful banners graced the walls, declaring victories at this inter-colony intellectual contest or that athletic event. The Freeland flag, a deep purple cloth with a leaping dolphin in the green circle at the center, hung from a rafter over the empty Leader's chair.

In a sudden glimpse of the past, she recalled daydreaming like this when she was twelve and forced to sit here while her mother, Maat, presided over long-winded Council sessions. Lonely and bored, she had often hidden her palm computer in a pocket, then once abandoned to the gallery, she had found a shadowed corner. When she was quiet long enough, the adults forgot about her, and she'd sneak out the palm to play Amazing Amazon, the video game she loved. Fondly, she thought of Cooper, the tall, pale-eyed, tawny-haired hero who led a band of women and through wit and skill, vanquished every enemy. Kali smiled. In one game the opposition was ancient Greek Argonauts, in the next it was Roman soldiers, in another the foe was the Persian caliph's army. There was even a program that allowed Kali to fight Elysian Regs. Smiling to herself, Kali shook her head.

Cooper was a mania for me. Guess I've always had a thing for warriors.

As the Leader's daughter, she had been surreptitiously watched, and her lack of interest in the proceedings invariably reported. In those days, she was considered a willful, if not incorrigible, brat. She had not taken her mother Maat's divorce from Lilith well, nor Lilith's subsequent retreat from her life. Maat had finally given up on trying to manage her by stern talks, reminding Kali of the dignity of the Council chamber and Maat's position in the community. The palm computer and the Amazing Amazon programs had been taken away and locked in Maat's desk. More bored than ever, Kali had simply sat in the Council gallery and made up Amazing Amazon action sequences in her head. Early in life, she had learned the art of looking interested while her mind was somewhere else entirely.

Sighing, Kali allowed her gaze to follow the long sweep of the oval table below. The ribbon of light pinewood led her eye to the clean Shaker lines of the empty Leader's chair, where Maat had once sat, where Whit should now be.

Kali bent her head and covered her eyes with her hand. *Damn, Whit! If you survive this I'm going to—*

Someone touched her shoulder, and she glanced up to see Tor standing in the aisle. Kali moved her knees aside and gracefully, Tor took the seat Kali had saved for her. "You okay?" Tor asked, concerned.

Kali nodded, then shot a glance around her and saw a host of eyes skip away.

"Don't mind them," Tor told her, following her gaze. "Bunch of" —she paused and pointedly raised her voice—"damn busybodies!"

Kali couldn't help the burst of laughter that escaped her. Below, she saw a few Council members turn from the proceedings to glare at them as disruptive children, but it felt good to find humor in something. With the pregnancy hormones raging and her usual wide-open psychic bond with Whit completely shut off, Kali felt stressed to the limit.

"They're still at it, huh?" Tor asked, nodding at the Council members.

Kali whispered back, "As ever. I think there are at least eight different rescue proposals on the table."

"Hmph," Tor responded. "Which one are you favoring, so far?"

"My plan, of course." Her blonde-brown eyebrows furrowing, Kali answered, "The one that has you, me and ten warriors going into West Virginia territory in two small Kestrels."

"Uh . . . make that you and ten warriors," Tor said quietly.

Kali huffed. "Surely Neith—"

Tor touched her arm, forestalling her. "I started with Neith," she said, grimacing unhappily, "and then worked my way through every healer I know in Isis. That's why it took me so long to get here." She stared unhappily down at the Council session. "No one would approve me for duty."

Kali gripped Tor's hand. "Then I'll just appoint you to my party and make it a team leader's mandate," she said firmly.

Seeming very discouraged, Tor just gazed back at her.

"What?" Kali asked warily.

Then all at once the psychic link tore through her.

In her mind, she saw Weetamoo, the colony's most prestigious and ill-tempered healer, as she had been seen through Tor's eyes only a short while earlier. As Tor had pleaded for Weetamoo's help in her effort to join Kali's rescue mission, Weetamoo had given a deprecating laugh. "I've already sent the Council a comline message," Weetamoo explained. "Lilith asked me to send them Kali's fitness evaluation—you know, standard procedure when a mission force is being assembled. I told them that Kali Tyler ought to be the last person in Isis considered for a place on that team. And as the Leader's household healer, my assessment will be final. I'm afraid you'll both be sitting this adventure out, Lieutenant Yakami."

Shocked and angry, Kali clenched her hands into fists. "Fucking Hecate!" she hissed, then jumped to her feet.

Below, the Council had finally wound down its discussions and the various rescue mission plans were coming up for the official vote. In the pinewood table, crystal slates shifted color, glinting purple in the lamplight, signaling that each of the sixty-odd Council members had the go-ahead to cast their ballot.

Someone farther back in the gallery called to Kali, "Hey! Down in front!"

Kali whirled and dashed up the aisle, heading for the door. She moved down the wooden stairs from the gallery and ran through the short hallway that led to the Council chamber. A sentry posted by the entrance began to block her, then recognized her as Whit's partner and hesitated. It was all Kali needed. She pulled open one of the large, oaken doors and slipped into the Cedar House. Purposefully, she marched forward, up to the pinewood table. She lifted her legs and quickly scooted over the table's surface, too impatient to trigger the receding gate. Once inside the oval ribbon of wood, she let her momentum and fury carry her right to the space before the empty Leader's chair.

On what would have been Whit's right-hand side, Lilith sat in the cushioned Deputy Leader's chair. Her bright blue eyes had watched Kali's progress across the Council chamber. Once she felt the full force of Kali's accusing look, she lifted her chin and took on a culpable, but still coolly defiant expression.

Her suspicions confirmed, Kali turned, her hard gaze finding the face of one supposed friend after another. Few of the Council met her eyes, and some of them actually flinched.

Kali's hands went to her hips. "So it's true," she pronounced. "I've been set up. You let me go through the motions of presenting a rescue plan while you all conspired to keep me here!"

"Kali, it wasn't like that . . ." Lilith began wearily.

Incensed, Kali jabbed a finger toward the Leader's chair, while she scanned the women around the table. "The woman who sits there is my partner. She's *mine*." She drew a ragged breath, trying to master her rage and utterly failing. "Not yours. *Mine!*" Tears rushed into her eyes and she tried to hold them back. "No one else could be better at finding her." She shook her head, feeling overcome. "How dare you," she finished, her voice breaking.

She ran, jumping up and sliding over the conference table again, then continuing to run all the way out of the Cedar House. She knew they would send someone after her, someone she knew and loved who would be sent along to reason with her. To elude that distasteful probability, she ran faster. Lifting her legs, she plunged into the knee-high grass and wildflowers of the mountain meadow that surrounded the Cedar House.

It's bad enough that they think I'm a fool, she decided. *I'll be damned if I'm going to sit and listen to whatever feeble excuses they come up with!*

Using the blue-gray light of the three-quarters moon above, she churned across the wildflower meadow. The field grass was already wet with dew, and her pant legs below her knees were soon soaked. A half mile later she was moving from the grasses into the edge of the huge fir forest that encompassed Isis.

She ran past the rhododendron thickets that edged one of her favorite hiking trails and plunged up the hilly path. Huge Douglas firs rose in the darkness on either side of her, causing the moonlight to fall in long, slanting angles. She breathed in the astringent scent of the pine needles underfoot, while the rhythmic drum of her steps sounded in her ears. Still angry, she made herself slow, settling into her usual pace. She was a habitual runner, and had kept up the exercise, undaunted by her three-month maternity. She knew a good run would help her bleed off her surging emotions, but she wanted to do it right and not cause any strain on the baby.

Two-thirds of the way home along the four-mile route, she came to the section that led into the city. She jogged past the rambling cottages that made up the outskirts of the colony, past the vegetable and rose gardens that graced the country plots. Overhead, the lights of an incoming flight caught her eye. Musing thoughtfully, she watched the dark silhouette pass against the backdrop of stars, trying to guess what kind of aircraft it was.

It wasn't a grain transport. Kali knew they were fat cows of a craft—wide and immense—unmistakable, even at night. The Cormorants, too, were big-bellied and large, though about half the size of a grain trader. Cormorants were jet-propelled troop ships, and had the capacity to land and take off vertically.

No, Kali knew the plane she had just seen had been small. Possibly even a Kestrel.

Tor can fly a Kestrel, Kali remembered.

Intrigued, she found herself altering her path, jogging across an intersection to a road that didn't lead to the Leader's House. She was suddenly running along a road that led to the Isis Airfield. A plan was hatching in the recesses of her brain. Feeling justified in stooping to something underhanded, if not downright illegal, Kali found herself wearing an evil grin.

Maybe it's time someone showed them what a pregnant woman can do, she thought.

In the strange half-light of moon shadows, Whit, too, was running. Mindlessly, wearily, she followed behind the deerskin-clad woman called Florey. They were not on anything resembling a path. There were only trees and bushes and hillsides, now. Every once in a while, she did not manage a patch of uneven ground as well as the band ahead of her. She'd stumble, lose her balance, and the resulting tug on the lead attached to Whit's bound wrists would jerk her forward. Four times now she had fallen flat. Four times she'd been dragged upright by Florey, and told, "Ya gotta keep up."

All the same, by the behavior of the group, Whit did not think the tempo was meant to humiliate or harm her. Rather, it was as if they were intent on fleeing the area where Whit and Danu had crashed. To Whit's mind, it was as if there was the possibility of pursuit by something the band of women did not want to meet.

Whit squinted ahead and saw the litter where Danu rested. By her friend's quiet stillness, she had the feeling Danu was only barely conscious. Remembering how Danu had fainted when a few over-exuberant members of the band had obeyed their colonel's orders and pulled Danu to her feet, Whit realized things could definitely be worse. It had surprised Whit when the band hadn't summarily abandoned Danu. Instead, the two young women who held Danu had carefully lowered her to the ground and then tended her head wound. The colonel had snapped off a series of succinct orders, and several other women had scrambled for materials. Soon the women had created a litter from the nearby strands of parachute rope and a couple of rapidly pruned tree limbs.

Whit still wasn't sure who these women were. She had no idea if they were the wives of local farmers, escapees from a breeding pen, or AGH victims who had quit their serfholders. Or maybe they were just the best shots, and so the local men tolerated the fact that females made up this hunting party—that would certainly explain the way they were all armed. Then she doubted the last guess almost immediately. Obsessed with maintaining control, Elysian men didn't allow their "inferiors" to carry weapons. Whit fuzzily knew her lack of information should be bothering her more than it did. Tired and hungry as Whit now was, the one certain thing seemed to matter the most: they weren't Regs.

The group slowed, then chugged to an abrupt stop on a ridge overlooking the next valley. Squinting to make out what was going on in the dim moonlight, Whit saw the women congregating just ahead of her. They were having a hushed, yet heated discussion. Whit noticed that a new woman had joined the band. Even in the obscure light, Whit could see the newcomer's lean face was dripping with sweat, and she was gasping as if she had run hard for a long way.

Taking advantage of the fact that Florey had dropped the lead, Whit inconspicuously edged over to the spot where they had settled Danu's litter.

Crouching down next to Danu, Whit placed a hand against her cheek. "Hey. How are you?" she asked.

Danu's eyes opened and, as if disoriented, she blinked at Whit for a moment. "Uhm," she began, then ran the tip of her tongue over her lips. "I think I'm kind of out of it. The last thing I remember is dogfighting an F-24. Where are we? What's going on?"

Whit tried for a reassuring grin. "Welcome to Elysium. The bad news is we crashed our very expensive Peregrines, so at some point we're gonna catch hell from Warrior Command." Motioning with her head toward the women about twenty meters away, she said, "The good news is we've been picked up Jemima Boone and friends."

After struggling to lift herself onto an elbow, Danu peered over at their captors. Her eyes shifted back to Whit and fell on the rawhide strips binding Whit's hands.

"That's right," Danu said, remembering. "I saw them do that. What do they want with us, Whit? Where are they taking us?"

Whit shrugged. "Not much talking going on, so I haven't had a chance to figure out what they're up to. We must have covered more than fifteen kilometers since this afternoon. By the moonrise, though, I think we've been traveling primarily west. This is only the third rest stop they've taken."

Danu slumped back onto the pallet, looking worried. "Do you think they're gonna turn us in to the Regs for a bounty or something?"

"I'm not sure," Whit told her honestly. "Like I said, so far it's been a marathon with big hills." She blew out a breath. "Thank Gaea I've been running distances with Kali in the mornings, or I'd have dead-legs by now."

The women on the ridge ceased their quiet argument and turned toward Whit and Danu, silently studying them. Decisively, their colonel pushed by the others and strode over to stand before Whit.

Reaching into the leather pouch on her waist, the woman brought out Whit's laser pistol. She tensed, as if expecting Whit to try to grab the weapon, and appeared to show it to Whit while carefully keeping it clear of her. "How do you make this work?" she demanded.

Whit slowly eased out of a crouch, rising up to her five-foot-nine-inch height and looking down at the captain. "I saw you trying to fire it while your friends were building this litter," Whit answered, lifting her jaw toward Danu's conveyance. "Why didn't you ask me then?"

An exasperated snort answered her. "Because I knew you wouldn't tell me." She eyed Whit. "You were lookin' a mite bad-tempered 'bout then."

Laughing softly, Whit said, "Oh, I was." She sobered, watching the women milling beneath the trees farther away. By their restless body language she could see they were upset about something, and more than a little anxious to get going. "What's wrong?" Whit asked. "Why do you suddenly have to know how to fire my weapon?"

For a moment, the colonel's face closed, and Whit thought for sure the woman was going to stonewall her. Then, she blew out a tight breath. She half-turned from Whit, as if trying to hide her features.

"A scout came for us . . . she brought word." The woman paused and swallowed. "A Reg raidin' party tried to hit Seneca—that's our village. My clan fought them off before they got beyond our first picket . . . but as the Regs was leavin' the area, they came across some kids. They were outside the defenses . . . out berry-pickin' . . ." The colonel's shoulders drooped. "They're jes little girls—ten years old and younger. And now they're on their way to pleasure markets and breedin' pens."

For an instant, looking at the strands of blonde on the bent head, Whit was reminded of Kali. Her hair had the same way of catching the moonlight. When the woman raised her head, it struck Whit that the colonel's face held the same plucky willfulness Whit had often glimpsed on Kali's face.

Whit shook off the sensation. "See the gauge on the right side of the stock?" she asked, pointing at the laser pistol the woman held. "That's the power designator. Stun, knock-out or kill. Your choice."

Eyebrows lifted in surprise.

Quietly, Whit said, "You'll have to let me set it up for you, in order for you to be able to use it." Shrugging, she clarified, "It's geared to read my DNA code."

The woman frowned at Whit, obviously not understanding.

"Trust me," Whit said softly.

39

The woman stepped closer, warily offering the right side of the stock. Whit pressed the small depression that activated a "users all" capacity, then checked the codes to be sure the laser was still at its maximum setting. During her last stay in Elysium, Whit had learned that you did not stun a Reg, or leave a Reg knocked out. Not unless you wanted to have to deal with that same fearsome, bloodthirsty menace a few hours later. Regs were rapists and killers. For Whit, giving a Reg a quick, clean death was as good as they deserved.

As the colonel took the pistol back, studying the weapon, Whit asked, "What's your name?"

The woman looked up at Whit, and the silence dragged out interminably. At last she said, "Jamie Rexrode."

Behind her, the murmuring fighters overheard the exchange and went still.

"There is a price on my head," Jamie Rexrode offered, then warned, "I would advise you against tryin' to collect it while you're travelin' with my militia." She indicated the party in the distance. "We're freedom fighters. Now who the hell are you, 'cause I gotta tell ya I ain't seen nothin' like ya'll in my life." She cast her gaze up and down Whit's form-hugging gray flight suit for emphasis.

Whit lifted an amused eyebrow at the young woman. "Tomyris Whitaker, Major, Freeland Warrior Reserve." Over the gasps and quiet exclamations from the band on the ridge, Whit remarked, "And I'm willing to bet there's a bigger price on my head than on yours."

"Shit—she's the one!" one of the younger militia women called to Jamie. "The one that snuck into Reg Headquarters three years ago and hacked into the mainframe!"

Without turning around, Jamie gave a brisk wave that demanded quiet.

"Freeland warrior, huh?" Her expression unreadable, she regarded Whit for another moment, before saying, "We thought Freeland was a myth. 'Til we heard 'bout you messin' with their computer surveillance and dumpin' the data on outlaws they'd been keepin' for years. Freed us up to run wild for a time there."

"Oh yeah?" Whit commented.

"There was Wanted Posters everywhere," Jamie informed her. "And now that you mention it, I see the resemblance." A small grin. "You're a helluva lot better lookin' in person, though."

From her position flat on the ground, Danu began a soft laugh that ended in a groan. Concerned, Whit knelt down beside her. "Take it easy. And hey . . . I was trying to look unappealing," Whit told both Danu and Jamie. "I needed male attention like I needed a case of dysentery."

Jamie nodded, then called softly, "Florey. Get these bonds offa her."

Florey hustled forward, bringing out the knife Jamie had confiscated from Whit earlier. Carefully, she cut the rawhide straps.

Thanking Florey, Whit shook out her hands and rubbed her wrists. Florey handed Whit the knife, and she slipped it back into the sheath in her boot.

"And who is this?" Jamie asked, indicating Danu.

"Lieutenant Danu Sullivan," Danu answered, placing a hand on her heart in salute.

Whit placed a hand on Danu's shoulder. "If I don't miss my guess, I think we're about to be parted here, little sister." She raised her eyes to the woman standing beside them. "I think most of this band is gonna try to chase down the Regs, while a few muster you out to the village." Watching Jamie, Whit asked, "Am I right?"

Jamie gave a terse nod.

"Okay if I go lend them a hand?" Whit asked Danu. "They probably need anyone who can fight." Again she glanced at Jamie for confirmation, and again Jamie nodded.

The militia leader moved away then, quietly informing her band of the change in plans.

Danu frowned at Whit. "You gonna be okay?"

In answer, Whit gave a wicked grin. "Chance to chase some Regs? What do you think?"

Wrinkling her nose, Danu complained, "You always get to have all the fun."

"If it makes you feel any better, while we were running up the last mountain, I was wishing my butt was the one being hauled on a litter."

Danu laughed, and once more it ended in a groan. "Go," she told Whit. "Hopefully I won't be ready to barf all over you next time I see you."

Leaning over, Whit kissed her forehead. "Stay down and rest up, Danu. Please," she urged. "I have enough to answer for already."

Danu gripped her hand and held onto it. "I'm here because I want to be, Whit. Don't you dare blame yourself." With a determined smile, she finished, "And I can get into my share of trouble without your help."

"True," Whit agreed, remembering Danu's crazy one-woman assault on Arinna Sojourner up at Hart's Pass. "But if I'd known my hare-brained scheme would cause this"—she cast a rueful glance at Danu's horizontal form—"I'd have never tried it."

Disbelief rich in her voice, Danu returned, "Yeah, right."

It was Whit's turn to laugh.

Jamie crossed to stand near them. "We have to get movin'," she told Whit.

As Whit stood and stepped back, Jamie squatted down beside Danu's pallet. "Ya'll will be reunited, Lieutenant. My word on it. Meanwhile, my braves will get you to our village, where our doc will tend you."

"Braves?" asked Danu, not sure she had heard correctly.

"Amazon braves—that's what Fowler calls us. He's the Procurator of this fine state of West Virginia," Jamie said, grinning, her pale blue eyes flashing with pride. "We scare the shit outta him."

Danu laughed.

Still grinning, Jamie stood and handed Danu's laser pistol to

Whit. As Whit hurriedly re-keyed the weapon to her own DNA code and checked the power settings, Jamie asked, "Ready to run, Freeland Warrior?"

"Lead on, Amazon," Whit replied.

Signaling her band, Jamie set off through the dark silhouettes of huge trees. Whit and the majority of the fighters fell in place behind her, moving off in the dusky moonlight.

Three of the younger militia women approached Danu.

One of the women offered water, and Danu drank thirstily. "It's still a fer piece," the woman said. "Why don't you close your eyes and try to take it easy. We'll try not to jostle this rig too much . . . okay?"

"Okay," Danu answered.

The women lifted her and with shuffling steps, set out in the opposite direction from the others. Danu relaxed into their jogging motion, and gradually, she fell into a doze. At length, she dreamed of Whit. Wearing deerskin leggings and a long-sleeved deerskin shirt, Whit ran in the moonlight through the big-trunked oak trees, a Freelander among freedom fighters.

Meanwhile, in Isis, Lilith waited in the private residential suite of the Leader's House.

Arms crossed, she sat on the sofa before a small, cheerful hearth fire. It was hours since the scene Kali had made at the Council session, and Lilith was both annoyed and mildly alarmed.

Kali seemed to have effectively dropped out of sight after she'd fled the Cedar House, and Lilith was worried. She had told the Council she would track Kali down and settle matters with her. Instead, Lilith had been left cooling her heels while Kali was off doing Gaea knew what. Bristling silently, Lilith just knew Kali was up to something. The girl was too much like Maat to be foiled by the Council's fondness for procedure.

The door on the other end of the large room opened, and Lilith got to her feet with all the dignity of her sixty-five years. Regally, she turned, intending to pin Kali with a hard gaze. However, instead of Kali, she found Styx crossing toward her.

"Damn, Lilith," Styx declared. "I go down to Warrior Command in Boudica for a few hours to discuss borrowing a Cormorant for the rescue mission, and while I'm gone you get into a pissing contest with your only child!"

"That's not what happened—" Lilith began hotly.

"The hell it isn't!" Styx flared. "No sooner had I climbed out of the Swallow than I got an earful. They say you had Weetamoo deep-six Kali with a medical report listing her as a major risk."

Lilith proclaimed, "Weetamoo filed a routine health evaluation for a candidate being considered for the mission. There was no conspiracy—no matter what Kali or anyone else thinks!"

Styx shook her head, and her long black-and-silver-threaded braid fell forward over her shoulder. "Even so, Lilith," she said. "You knew that report was going to be filed, and you surely suspected what it was going to say—and you didn't warn her?"

Lilith defended herself, saying, "I tried. It did no good. She won't see reason when it comes to things like this. It's not enough for her to contribute ideas and submit a plan of action—she has to go do it herself!" Frustrated, she looked away and declared, "She's always been mule-headed!"

Turning from her, Styx murmured, "Yeah, the apple doesn't fall far from the tree."

"What?" Lilith demanded.

"Oh, you heard me." Moving by her, Styx swept her eyes over the backpack, bedroll and laser rifle lying on the wide bed at the far end of the suite. "Sure looks like she was ready to head out, Lil. She must be plenty mad."

Ignoring Styx's observation, Lilith pronounced, "Have you noticed that the longer Kali lives with Whit, the more unmanageable she's becoming? It's like a marriage of mavericks!"

"Lil," Styx sighed.

44

"Styx, I'm serious," Lilith said, following her partner across the room. "I fear for them both. Since they met they've been involved in one calamity after another. They're never content to stay safe at home like any normal married couple—they're always rushing off, trying to save someone, or the whole damn colony—or Freeland itself!" Drawing a deep, tremulous breath Lilith finished, "It seems like I'm forever on the brink of losing one or both of them."

As Lilith stood in the center of the suite, bracing against tears, Styx came slowly back to her side. Embracing her, Styx whispered, "And that's your problem, dear heart. Not theirs."

Lilith clung to her, while Styx moved a hand soothingly over her back.

"They are strong women, Lil," Styx reminded her gently. "Both blessed with the Goddess's own courage and the will to use it." Quietly she stated, "They are just not the sort to stay safe at home. You know that."

Impatient with herself, Lilith scrubbed her face with her hand, wiping away the watery betrayal. "I know," she whispered. "I know. But I still can't help trying to . . . change things."

Her voice mild, Styx observed, "It's called 'meddling,' Lil, and there's a reason why it's not appreciated."

"Oh! So I'm a meddler, am I?" Lilith said sharply, pushing free of Styx.

"You may call it 'acting as a counselor,' if you wish, but with a grown daughter—"

"All right! Enough lecturing." Rubbing her forehead, Lilith confessed, "How can I fix things with Kali? She's so angry with me."

Placing a hand on her shoulder, Styx steered Lilith over to the large desk that helped separate the living quarters section from the bedroom area. On the cherry wood surface, Whit had an assortment of chip boxes and archaic printed-paper books stacked side by side.

Styx pulled a few pieces of paper from a pile there, and a pen from the little wooden box, placing them on the pad in the center of the desk. "Write an old-fashioned note of apology," she encouraged

Lilith. "And include an invitation to brunch tomorrow morning at our house. Tell her you want to go over the latest satellite scans of West Virginia with her."

Pursing her lips, Lilith contemplated the paper and pen. Then she took the pen and leaned one hand on the smooth blotter surface. Swiftly, she composed a note, then folded it and took it over to the bed, leaving it on Kali's pillow.

"Now," Styx said, extending her arm, "let's go home."

As Lilith slid under her arm, enjoying the feel of it settling on her shoulder, she asked, "What if she stays out all night just to spite me?"

Styx laughed. "C'mon, she's not fourteen anymore. It's been a long day. She's gotta be tired. In fact, I'll bet she's out there right now, watching the back entrance where you and I came in. Once she sees us leave, she'll scoot up the back stairs and go to bed." Cocking her head at her lover, Styx finished, "If she's avoiding you it's only because she's been treated enough like a recalcitrant child to act like one."

"I only want what's best for her," Lilith retorted, beginning to fume again.

"Well, you won this round," Styx answered, "so content yourself with the victory and come home with me."

"Hmph," Lilith responded.

Her back stiff with indignation, Lilith nevertheless allowed herself to be led out of the room.

From the shadows of the rear garden, Kali watched Lilith and Styx leave the Leader's House and climb into Lilith's electrobile. Humming quietly, the sleek little car rolled past the rose gardens that buffered the front of the large granite structure, then made a left turn onto Cammermeyer Street and disappeared from view. Kali knew Lilith and Styx were probably headed toward their house, about a mile away. She could finally go up to the private residence and be alone.

Sighing, Kali walked into the bright halogen lights of the court-yard. She met the startled eyes of the two warrior sentries stationed by the rear door, who clearly hadn't known she was back there among the dark hedges.

Excusing herself, she offered, "Didn't feel like company."

One young sentry opened a door for her. As Kali passed through it, the sentry muttered, "Sorry about what's happened to Leader Whitaker, ma'am."

Kali answered quietly, "Mmm, well, I'll have her home soon enough."

Baffled by the reply, the sentry closed the door behind Kali and took her parade rest position again. "What do you think she meant by that?" the sentry asked her companion. "I heard there's a good chance Whitaker's toast. And they say the Council won't let Tyler be on the rescue party."

The other sentry was an old veteran. Rocking forward and back on her heels, she answered, "Don't ever count Whitaker out, kid. And it sounds to me like the Council ain't in charge of certain par-ties."

"Think we should report it?"

"Nah," came the certain answer. "We're here to protect her, not to rat on her. 'Sides, there's no one in Isis that loves Whitaker more than that one—and that's enough for me."

"But she's pregnant—and instead of using the Delphi Clinic, she's carrying!" the young sentry protested. "Kinda barbaric."

Chapter 3

The first rays of sunlight cast an ethereal glow through the morning mist rising over the Allegheny Highlands. Moving at a brisk pace, thirteen Amazons emerged from the tree line, jogging down the mountainside. Silently, they clambered over a rock fall that had piled up six meters above a narrow, fast river. Whit chugged along behind the Amazons, following in their wake.

The river below was a loud, constant noise as it flowed over gleaming rocks and partially submerged logs. Whit eyed the rapids, trying to catch her breath in rasping gasps as she wondered how the Amazons intended to cross the river.

During her long run through the night and the woods, she saw more of West Virginia than she had ever wanted to see. She realized it was a country of long, forested ridges and steeply sided valleys. It was also a place where streams invariably threaded through where the land was lowest. She had crossed more than one strategically placed fallen timber last night, had soaked her boots wet in more than one shallow tributary. But more than anything else, it was the trees Whit noticed. They were everywhere. The only open ground she had seen was where a moldering town from the last century stood. Even there, in the middle of disintegrating streets and collapsed buildings, large trees were slowly reclaiming what centuries of progress had once tamed.

The Amazon militia leader, Jamie Rexrode, was making a series of hand motions to her band. Whit interpreted the basic military signal codes: Rest. Eat. Drink.

Relieved to oblige, Whit collapsed against a boulder, stretching her legs out in front of her. She took deep, settling breaths and rubbed her hands over the aching muscles of her upper thighs, trying to ease the quivering weakness. Around her, the Amazons were taking up positions behind an outcropping of pale sandstone rocks. Sharing hunks of jerky and passing water skins, they rested their assorted weapons on the stone surfaces before them. There was an old, crumbling macadam road down below them, portions of it recovered by high grass. The women were taking furtive glances at it every now and then. Whit suddenly suspected that the Amazons were mounting an ambush here.

Jamie came to Whit's side and crouched down, handing her a skin bag. As Whit accepted it, she wondered where her emergency kit was. The Amazons had taken it from her during a search just after her capture. She knew there was a canteen in there, fitted with a micro water purification unit. She glanced at Jamie and saw the tension in her face, then dismissed the thought of asking. While Whit had qualms about how hygienic the water in Jamie's bag might be, she was simply too thirsty to refuse the offering.

"It's spring water," Jamie stated, obviously reading Whit's hesitation. "Pure as pure can be." With a ghost of a smile, Jamie finished. "I use it in my still."

Embarrassed, but relieved, Whit squeezed off a long drink.

Jamie began talking quietly in her soft West Virginia drawl. She explained that the long, dark shape in front of them was Jack Mountain. Pointing over the rocks to the road that wound by the river, Jamie informed Whit the old road led through Moyers Gap, and it was the only flat, still relatively paved route out of Amazon lands.

Florey called in a stage-whisper, "Whitaker!" When Whit turned her way, the big woman grinned and tossed Whit a piece of jerky.

Waving back gratefully, Whit pushed the food into her mouth. She had not eaten in over twenty-four hours, and she was famished. After watching how quickly Whit consumed the small handout, Jamie pulled a cloth bag out of her travel pouch. She motioned for Whit to lean closer to her, then opened the cloth bag over Whit's left palm, dumping three squares. Whit sniffed the little cakes, recognizing that they were some sort of honey, oatmeal and nut concoction. Her mouth watered.

"I can't take this," Whit said, meeting Jamie's light blue eyes. "Someone made this for you. A treat, right?"

Jamie ducked her head, but Whit caught the dour expression. "G'wan. I cain't eat."

Whit thanked her, pondering the troubled look she'd seen. She took a bite and closed her eyes, savoring the cakes with a soft groan.

Half-standing, Jamie squinted into the distance. "I'm gonna send out some scouts . . . get the trap set up. The Regs don't know the hills like we do, so they stick mainly to the roads. We took a short cut and got here ahead of them. I s'pect they'll be bringin' the girls along any time now."

Whit frowned and used the back of her hand to wipe oatmeal crumbs from the corner of her mouth. Her eyes caught on the fog rising in drifting threads from the trees on the hillside. "Why are the Regs on foot?"

Jamie went very still.

"Why no heli-jets?" Whit persisted. "They should have been criss-crossing the sky since five minutes after Danu and I went down, but I haven't seen one yet."

Slowly, Jamie turned, staring at her. Her lips were a tight line. "And why is it so green here?" Whit asked wonderingly. "The rest of Elysium is an environmental nightmare, but here it looks like . . . Gaea's own garden."

Jamie gave a short, nervous sigh. "Secrets. Not mine to tell." Lowering her gaze, she finished, "So please . . . please, don't ask."

Whit watched her, recognizing the tightening of the skin around her eyes. *She's afraid.* A hundred other questions instantly clamored through Whit's mind, demanding speech. Carefully, she chose the most important. "Who *can* tell me?"

"You'll probably meet her later," Jamie said, still avoiding Whit's eyes. "Let's get through this mess first, okay?"

"Okay."

During the next few minutes, Jamie called the women over and pointed to various places along the heavily wooded slope. Two by two, the Amazons moved away to take up hidden locations. Whit surveyed the place. There was a river on the left side, a sharply inclined wooded hill on the right. A wall of dark gray rock flanked the far side of the river, going straight up to a high cliff. The Regs were going to come down the old macadam road and be caught between the Amazons and the river. They would be forced to run a gauntlet into a steadily narrowing gap.

The colonel knows combat strategy, Whit couldn't help thinking.

As the last women scurried away to their assignments, Jamie knelt by Whit's side and peered at the road. Whit could read the tension in her posture.

Calmly, Whit asked, "What can I do?"

Jamie sat down, leaning her back against a boulder. "We're gonna be seriously out-numbered. And they'll be totin' fully functional M-28s." She scratched behind an ear, appraising Whit's tall, well-built form, following the lines of the body-hugging flight suit. "You much good in a scrap, Freeland Warrior?"

Smiling slightly, Whit saw the challenge in the woman's eyes. "I can take care of myself," Whit answered mildly.

Jamie gave a dismissive sideways motion of her head, as if to say *Yeah, yeah*.

Whit's brows raised in surprise as she realized that Jamie had her doubts. Feeling a flush of irritation, Whit suspected that Jamie had just decided to stick her somewhere largely out of the action to keep her from fouling up the ambush.

"In some parts," Jamie was saying, "the Regs are havin' trouble stayin' properly outfitted. Since the insurrection started, they've been losin' supplies they cain't replace. But we here in Pendleton County was first to secede, and so they make us pay dearest. The Regs that come agin us are usually armed to the teeth."

Secede? Whit's mind repeated in shock. *Insurrection?*

"Jes stay up here behind the rocks and try to pick off as many of 'em as you can," Jamie said. She brought out Whit's pistol and ran her hand over the metal surface. "How much kick does this thing have?" She glanced up at Whit expectantly. "What about clips—you got any extra?"

Though she felt like barraging the woman with another round of questions about what the hell was going on in Elysium, Whit held her tongue. They were about to get into a fire fight with a far superior foe. She could pump Jamie for details about Elysian current events later. Now she had to focus on the moment.

She watched Jamie gripping the Freeland pistol, and suddenly realized the woman thought she had a conventional cartridge-loaded weapon. Whit cleared her throat. "There's no kick. It shoots a laser ray."

Jamie's eyes searched Whit's. "A what?"

"Like a little lightning bolt," Whit said. "And there's no need to reload. It's crystal-powered. That crystal plate on the barrel absorbs and stores the sun's energy. The bolts will fly as long as you squeeze the trigger." Then Whit leaned back, a sensation of unease pouring through her. She suddenly felt as if she had just handed a Napoleonic soldier a machine gun in place of a musket.

For a long moment Jamie sat staring at the weapon in her hand. Whit knew the woman was comprehending what her Amazon band could do with a few more Freeland pistols. Softly, Jamie uttered, "Sheee-it."

"Yup," Whit agreed.

In an incredulous voice, Jamie asked, "Ya'll thought this up and made it?"

Rubbing the back of her neck, Whit nodded, feeling sheepish. "We may be more technologically advanced than Elysium, but some of Freeland's most marvelous creations are killing machines. Guess some things never change, huh?"

Jamie gazed back at her, then shook her head ruefully. "When you're fightin' off them that just want to catch ya and sell ya, moral concerns about killin' the bastards jes don't come up."

Reflecting on that, Whit pulled out the laser pistol she'd borrowed from Danu and checked the settings again. *It would be damn stupid to get captured*, she told herself.

Amid the sweet birdsong filling the chill dawn air, a series of hawk whistles sounded.

Jamie's head snapped around. Roughly, she grabbed Whit's arm, pulling her lower. They both hunkered down behind the wall of rock, breathing faster.

Carefully, Jamie raised her head to peer over sandstone. Seconds later, Whit joined her.

Helmeted storm troopers in deep green jackets, black pants and boots advanced down the road. With the exception of the Reg walking point, they were laughing among themselves and not paying much attention to their surroundings. Whit counted six Regs in the front and six in the back. In between them was a line of five girls, who were tied to a length of rope like a string of prize ponies. The youngsters stumbled along in single file order, their faces tear-streaked and dirty. The four men walking beside the children were alternately prodding them with their rifles or directing sneering remarks at them. One man in particular was smiling an ugly, gap-toothed leer as he reached out and stroked the almost-white blonde hair of the third child in the line.

"Wait for my signal," Jamie told Whit in a soft but commanding voice. "When I give the hawk call, I'll need you to pick off the six Regs in the front."

Jamie's face was mere inches from Whit's. In the steadily increasing morning light, Whit found herself gazing into her clear, crystalline blue eyes. "And what are you going to do?"

"I'm goin' down there," Jamie whispered. "Gonna separate the kids from the Regs, before the Regs try to use 'em as shields."

A one-person frontal assault? Whit asked herself. Barely audible, she commented, "That's suicide."

Jamie looked away from her. "The third child on that slave line is my niece."

The little tow-headed girl, Whit thought.

"Her name is Weezy and she is seven years old."

Frowning, Whit bent her head. She thought of her own child, safe within Kali, far away in Freeland. She lifted her eyes and met Jamie's, nodding in understanding.

Jamie waited until the Regs were only about thirty meters away, then cupped her hand around her mouth and sent out the high, piping sound of a bird of prey. In answer, the quiet morning air was shattered by the staccato report of single-shot rifles firing from the woods. Several bullets ricocheted off the left side of the macadam road. In barely disguised panic, the Regs spun, all of them facing away from Whit and Jamie, yanking their M-28s from their shoulders. Jamie used the distraction to scramble over the sandstone boulders in front of them.

Whit gripped her pistol in two hands and went to one knee, leaning her arms on the rock. The six Regs in the front of the slave line turned back toward them. As Jamie dropped over the edge of the rock face out of Whit's line of fire, Whit snapped off six blasts. Six Regs were tossed backwards, fist-sized red holes burnt through their chests.

Jamie was racing forward, unimpeded.

Two Regs were down at the rear of the pack. The little girls huddled on the roadway, while the remaining eight Regs were shooting their automatic weapons nonstop at the forested slope to their left. The single-shot Winchesters continued to crack from the woods. One Reg hollered out orders, gathering three others to him in the rear. In a disorganized charge, he led them toward the trees, as if determined to root out their adversaries.

Whit watched Jamie keeping low as she scurried forward, closing on the slave line. Jamie's laser pistol flared, taking out first one, then two of the four Regs flanking the captured girls. The third Reg whirled, laying down a sweeping spray of rifle fire. Jamie dropped flat, disappearing in the high grass, then scrambled behind a small boulder.

Whit saw one of the two Regs still near the girls reach for Jamie's niece. Aiming carefully, Whit squeezed off a shot. The horrified Reg staggered back a step, then screamed, waving the scorched stump that remained where his hand had been. Seconds later a crossbow bolt zipped out of the forest and plunged into his neck. The line of girls loosed shrill screams and shrank away from him as he toppled.

The little blonde, Weezy, hunched into a ball with her arms over her head.

Get those kids outta there!

Without making a conscious decision to move, Whit found herself clambering over the rocks in front of her and dropping to the ground. She was sprinting straight for the single Reg still close enough to the slave line to grab a hostage. The M-28 began swinging her way and suddenly everything went into slow motion. As if watching a series of still camera shots, she saw the sputtering flash at the end of the barrel and knew the Reg was firing without pause. She was weaving from side to side, hearing the zipht-zipht-zipht of the bullets passing only centimeters away. She felt a burning slice across her right arm and dove, rolling in the grass closer to the river. In a smooth continuation of the roll, she came to her knees. It was a maneuver she had preformed a million times in battle exercises. With easy precision, she found her target and shot. The blast hit him in the upper torso, spinning him around and throwing him off the road. Whit saw him crash limply into a landscape of tall, green grass.

She kept low as she rushed forward, very aware that the Reg had fallen while still holding the weapon. She glimpsed Jamie going by, heading straight for the little girls whimpering fearfully behind her on the roadway. As Jamie was caught in Weezy's near-hysterical embrace, Whit saw the Reg rise up on an elbow. He raised the M-28, aiming at Jamie and the child.

Whit yelled, "Jamie, *down!*"

Before the M-28 could fire, Whit squeezed off two shots, finishing him. Rigid with tension, she strode over to the smoking torso and kicked the weapon away from him.

Women began streaming from the woods, hurrying to join them. Whit looked around, counting green-jacketed bodies in the road and on the edge of the hill, not lowering her weapon until she realized they had killed all sixteen of them. Swallowing hard against the bile pushing up at the back of her throat, she surveyed the bodies surrounding her. Deliberately, she turned her gaze from the ungainly poses of death.

"Whitaker."

Whit looked over at Jamie.

The deerskin-clad woman rose from the road, holding Weezy tight against her chest. Tears shone in her fierce blue eyes. "Thank you," she uttered, her breathing ragged.

Unsure what to say, Whit gave a tight nod.

Then, feeling incredibly weary, Whit watched the Amazons freeing five frightened little girls. Amid the crying and the hugs and the worried reunions, Whit noticed two of the Amazons moving among the Reg bodies, collecting M-28s.

At the same moment in Isis, Kali cruised Whit's motorcycle along a service road that bordered the back of the Isis airfield. Removed from West Virginia by a three-hour time zone, the pre-dawn darkness still hung over the broad expanse of tarmac, cloaking the mountains that ringed the city-colony.

Slowing, Kali halted the motorcycle by a storage building, thankful that the decibel squelch system on the engine made the cycle a near-silent means of transport. She waited patiently until the sentry assigned to this side of the airfield strolled by, then waited a little longer before chancing the long open ride across the tarmac.

Kali stashed her long blonde hair under a gray Warrior's cap, with the bill pulled low over her face. Shrugging her shoulders, she resettled the heavy backpack. She glanced down at her traveling apparel: hiking boots, loosely fitted field trousers, a soft pullover and a waterproofed anorak. Everything was a muted shade of green or tan, as close to camouflage coloring as possible, and she hoped it would suffice.

What if I'm making a mistake? Self-doubt and anxiety squirmed through her gut. Firmly, she clamped down on any traitorous thoughts and reached into her memory, stirring up again the outrage and resentment she had felt as she fled the Council meeting. *I have to go get Whit. I have to.*

Before her, the big halogen lights were all on, as they were each night, illuminating the airfield in daylight-like radiance. There was little activity at this early hour, and if the sentries didn't observe her passage, she knew she'd be home free.

She gunned the engine once, then opened the throttle. The only sign the engine was racing was the vibration of the cycle barrel rattling against her knees. In a sudden burst of speed, the motorcycle zipped across the well-lit airfield, closing on the structure where the Kestrel was parked.

The hangar door was open, so Kali scooted inside and jammed on the brakes, coming to a stop that caused the back wheel to make a brief, sudden squeal.

Tor stood by the Kestrel. "Shhhh!" she urged, making a sharp, downward wave of her hand.

Fired up by how close she was to actually pulling off this act of defiance, Kali broke into a helpless laugh. Impatiently, Tor whispered, "Hurry up!" Kali steered the cycle into the shadows at the far side of the hangar, then killed the engine. In a fluid motion she dismounted and set the kick stand. As Kali approached her, Tor continued to load articles into the open door on the side of the small heli-jet.

"Did you delete my message from your comline port?" Kali asked, her tone hushed.

After nodding an affirmative, Tor gave a slight snort. "Like they're not gonna eventually notice that a Kestrel that logged a flight plan down to Morgan disappeared into thin air." Giving a slight shake of her head, Tor finished, "Lilith is gonna figure it out, Kali, and she's gonna be really pissed!"

After biting her lip, Kali admitted, "Yeah. I'm guessing we have about six hours before they link a missing you and me to a missing Kestrel."

Tor snickered, "Sure will teach them all not to mess with a hormonal mage!"

"Oh, like that's the point of this whole thing!" Kali hissed.

Tor pulled off Kali's cap and affectionately ruffled the shining blonde hair. "Don't get snappish, fearless wonder." Kali rolled her eyes, and Tor stepped behind her, helping Kali out of her backpack. "You feeling jittery?"

"I haven't been throwing up recently, if that's what you mean," Kali muttered. "I've been working my way through an assortment of herb teas Cimbri sent me, and tonight I found one that's working like a charm. Got it packed up in quantity."

"So, no chance on a last-minute change of heart?"

"No." Kali snatched her cap back from Tor as Tor stepped by her and placed the pack in the Kestrel. "My heart is dead set on going."

Tor smirked, then leveled a steady, measuring gaze on her. "We're ignoring the Council's dictates, stealing a military aircraft— to say nothing of a mess of weapons and supplies—and sneaking off into enemy territory. My career as a warrior and any plans you might have had to emulate your mother's stellar political ascent are ending as we speak." It was her last attempt at reason, and Tor went silent, waiting as Kali fidgeted with the cap.

Taking a deep breath, Kali settled herself. "Whit and Danu need help. Now. Anyone who doesn't understand what I'm doing can just kiss my ass." Determined, she pulled her cap back on. "Let's go, Tor. You want to do this as much as I do."

"Oh, yeah," Tor responded. Turning, she nimbly climbed up into the Kestrel and headed for the pilot's seat. "Just wanted you to be clear. Technically, this is almost an act of piracy."

"Where's my eye patch?" Kali cracked, hoisting herself into the Kestrel.

Tor flashed her a grin, then concentrated on keying the onboard computer and running through the pre-flight checklist. Behind her, Kali was closing the door and throwing the pressure locks. She moved to the co-pilot seat and fastened the harness of the seatbelt.

"Here's the search data I snitched from the Watch Room computer," Kali stated, holding up a box of crystal chips. "I copied the heat-seeking readouts and aerial photographs from the satellite sweeps made over Old West Virginia territory before the Border was restored. The electromagnetic screen was shockingly thin, then, but it still caused some interference in the surveillance. I did hyper-reads on the Watch Room crystal drive—you know, boosting the program to fill in the blanks with logical fill from the comline data banks. Then I analyzed and organized the results. We can load this in the onboard unit and check it out while we're on our way. Should be enough to get a location on those two within about a fifty-mile radius."

Tor flipped the engine start switch and the Kestrel rumbled to life. "That's still going to be a lot of area to cover."

"The dirt bikes onboard?" Kali asked, leaning around the flight seat and craning her neck to see into the dark recesses of the cargo hold behind them.

"Yep. Crystal drive batteries charged and ready to roll," Tor assured her. "But it will still be like looking for a needle in a haystack."

"Which is where I come in," Kali stated firmly.

"The Wizard of Isis," Tor cracked.

Kali flung her fist out sideways and delivered a light smack to Tor's shoulder.

"No hitting the pilot," Tor warned. "We gotta move fast, now." She pushed the accelerator handle forward. The Kestrel began rolling toward the hangar door.

Kali dutifully radioed the airfield tower. "Kestrel 420 en route to Morgan." She had purposefully lowered her voice, trying to disguise it. Whit had often told her that she had a very singular tone. She wasn't sure who was on duty in the tower tonight. If it was a warrior who had been posted as a sentry at the Leader's House, they might hear the transmission and recognize the Leader of Isis's handfasted wife. "Requesting permission for departure."

Tor cleared the hangar and the small heli-jet moved across the tarmac. Beneath the bright airfield lights, the Kestrel coasted fluidly into the center of large yellow circle. Once there, Tor brought the Kestrel to a stop.

The radio announced, "You have permission to take-off, Kestrel 420."

Tor keyed the computer to start the lift-off jets. "Here we go," she told Kali.

The Kestrel rose steadily straight up, hovering over the airfield. Kali leaned over and looked out the plexiglass window on her side of the craft. Below them, the bright halogen-lit tarmac fell away. As their distance from the ground rapidly increased, she saw the rows of hangars and then the street lamps marking the roads leading to the airfield. Moving her hand across the flight console, Tor flipped a switch, and the rotating engines shifted from vertical to horizontal mode. Then the heli-jet slipped forward, over the sleeping city-colony.

Kali could see the illuminated granite of the Leader's House nestled in a green clearing, could see the large pinewood proportions of the Warriors barracks and the long hydroponic sheds on the outskirts of town. Her eyes followed the streets lamps leading out into darkened neighborhoods, noting how small the city looked. Beyond Isis, it was all a blur of black-gray forest and ebony mountains. Tor directed the craft toward the eastern horizon, into the shimmering suggestion of a sunrise that was another two hours away.

"Love you, Lil," Kali whispered. "Forgive me."

Even though Whit's eyes were focused on the trail, she stumbled coming down the stone strewn path. Beside her, Florey grabbed an elbow.

"Sorry," Whit muttered, embarrassed, managing to keep moving as she cast Florey an apologetic look.

Florey's wide, round face split with a grin.

Jamie turned from her position ahead of them on the trail. Her pale eyes focused on Whit with concern. She stopped and shifted Weezy's sleepy head from one shoulder to the other, waiting for Whit to come abreast of her.

"We're almost there."

Whit merely nodded. *Probably thinks I'm a real cupcake*, she thought.

Though no longer running, the other women were moving along at a fast paced march, their gaits loose-limbed with fatigue but their heads held high. Whit noted the way their alert eyes scanned the old growth forest on either side of the trail, peering past the late morning sunshine and into the shadows. Yawning until her jaw cracked, Whit realized she wanted nothing more than to lie down in the soft ferns by the shady edge of the woods. The desire to sleep was becoming overwhelming. Frowning, she realized she had not felt this physically exhausted since her days at Warrior boot camp, years ago.

A wood thrush called quietly in the distance, and Whit paid no attention to it until she heard Jamie echo the call. Whit looked over at her.

One side of Jamie's mouth edged up in a half grin. "Jes tellin' the look-out to pay no mind to them strange clothes you're wearin' and stow the arrow she was considerin' plantin' in ya."

Whit gazed down at the scuffed and dirty flight suit. The gray uniform had held up to being ripped by countless branches and brambles, suffering only a few tears. Still, it was designed for the kind of cold a person encountered while traveling in a high altitude jet. Tramping along in the increasing heat of a summer day, the flight suit felt incredibly hot and uncomfortable. She wanted it off, and soon.

The trail approached a rocky cliff face. Glancing up, Whit saw a dozen women spring from hiding places behind the boulders and thick shrubs that sprinkled the rough, uneven surface. Weapons were being waved in the air by jubilant, cheering Amazons.

Ahead, Whit saw the narrow entrance to a canyon. A slim figure darted from the rocks and ran ahead of them, winding through the gap in the rock wall. Whit could hear the girl shouting, "They're back! They have all five kids!"

Whit concentrated on keeping pace with Jamie as they left the sunlight behind and passed into a narrow canyon. Side by side, they marched through the startling darkness of the shade there, traveling deeper into the narrow gap. They had walked approximately thirty meters into the black slate seam, when the trail began climbing up and over a small ridge. They came around a bend as the trail curved to the left, and Whit heard drums. The trail curved to the right. Once more, Whit and Jamie passed into daylight.

Momentarily blinded, Whit stopped. There were suddenly women yelling and rushing by them, women jostling her, searching, anxiously calling out names. Whit squinted, trying to regain her vision. A woman with fair hair seized Jamie and hugged her, before relieving her of Weezy. Within seconds, she was sobbing helplessly into Jamie's shoulder. Jamie soothed her with quiet words, then began shepherding the woman and Whit forward. Weezy's mother glanced once at Whit, looking fearful, before Jamie murmured, "She's all right. Whitaker saved Weezy's and my life." Still weeping, the woman stared at Whit, then Whit, too, was crushed in an embrace.

All around them, mothers claimed their offspring in tearful, noisy jubilation. Then, they all moved off together, down a steep slope, like a spontaneous parade. Whit shook off her weariness and forced herself to look around, taking note of her surroundings out of long habit.

An assortment of horses, cows and goats grazed in a sage-green pasture and the animals were turning to watch the noisy little crowd of humans go by. Down below, in a plain of meadow between two rolling, tree-covered mountain ridges, Whit noted with surprise the thatched roofs of an array of small houses. Once they came closer, Whit could see the houses were mostly log cabins. However, she also saw a few structures that seemed to be a jumble of ancient plastic containers set like bricks in concrete walls. With a wave of nostalgia, Whit remembered the little home she'd seen near the northern Bordergate almost two years ago, where Kali had lived as an Elysian outcast.

The drums she'd first heard in the narrow slate canyon became louder as they approached the village, quickening Whit's blood. It felt like some sort of tribal welcome. A small delegation of staid-looking Elders met them at the entrance into what seemed to be the dusty main road. Younger women came pouring out of several barns, some shops and even a forge, while others came running out of the lush crop fields that bordered the rear of the town. Unlike the Amazons who were in the rescue party, Whit noticed that these women were not dressed in deerskin leggings and tunics. Instead, they wore butternut homespun, or well-worn linen dyed in a variety of colors, crafted into skirts, trousers, shirts and scarves. Laughing and shouting, women were singling out certain members of the rescue party and grabbing them possessively, greeting them with hugs and kisses. It was obviously a lesbian community.

Reflecting on the warmth of this homecoming, Whit smiled, blinking her burning eyes against the dust and heat. She followed Jamie down the dirt road a little farther and then a small, gray-haired Elder was before them, clapping Jamie on the shoulder.

"'Bout time ya got back!" the Elder said gruffly, then passed a hand over Jamie's brown-blonde hair, pulling her into a hug. "Ya did us proud, sweetpea!"

As the Elder saw Whit, the vivid blue eyes narrowed. "And what's this I hear 'bout Freeland warriors traipsin' around in our woods?"

Jamie grinned as she faced Whit. "Granma, this is Major Tomyris Whitaker." Whit gave a small bow, and Jamie continued, "Major Whitaker, my grandmother and the Chief of our village, Irene Rexrode."

"Welcome to Seneca." The tanned, wrinkled face only came to Whit's shoulder as Irene Rexrode stepped closer, touching the arm of Whit's flight suit and examining the fabric. Slowly, she circled Whit, looking her over, her eyes lingering on the rough, rust-colored bandage on her right arm. Then she peered up into Whit's face with a keen, almost intimidating blue stare. At last, the woman allowed, "Them wanted posters had yer likeness, all right. Ceptin' ya look a mite flashier in these duds."

Whit couldn't help smiling. She sent a swift glance around. "Is Danu here? Is she okay?"

"The redhead?" Irene barked, then gave a soft laugh. "Yeah, she in the healer's hut, sleeping off the potion the good witch gave her after she worked on her last night."

Witch? Whit's mind caught on the word, uneasily turning it over. "Can I see her?" Whit asked, needing to ascertain Danu's health status for herself before she sought out a place to collapse.

"Sure," Irene pronounced, leading the way toward the far end of the rustic village. "With that wound, the healer should see ya any-ways. Then we'll get ya a place to sleep."

"It's just a scratch," Whit began. "I don't want to put anyone out. Maybe Danu and I should just move on."

Irene shushed her. "The Rexrode clan has been fightin' the Regs and the New Order since 2010! The victories are few and far between, let me tell ya!" Irene pronounced. "So ya'll stay with us here in Seneca. Hell, we're plannin' on a big celebration, Major! So don't go gettin' all noble and messin' things up!"

Smothering a yawn, Whit nodded. "Whatever you say, Mother Rexrode."

At that, Jamie and her grandmother looked at each other, then burst into wild laughter. Whit watched them, bemused by their response to a customary Freeland term of honor.

Far away, Danu heard drums, and then a wave of cheering voices. The sound of a child's gleeful squeal tugged at Danu's slumbering curiosity. Making a great effort, Danu opened her eyes.

Disoriented, she took a moment before she comprehended that she was looking at the wooden cross beams of a low ceiling. There was a wall beside her that was made up of smooth logs and some sort of earthen wattle. On the opposite side of the room, morning sunlight was penetrating buff-colored window curtains. Rows of colorful pottery containers graced the shelves by the fireplace, and an old-fashioned hardcover book was open on the wooden table in the center of the room.

I remember them carrying me in here last night.

Carefully, she took stock of herself. Her mouth was dry as dust. Her head still ached, but it was nothing like the all-encompassing pain that had punished her yesterday and last night. She raised her head a bit, then lifted the woolen blanket that covered her and peeked down the length of her body. She frowned, confirming the dim memory of someone peeling the flight suit off her. A large, clean, off-white shirt covered her upper torso, draping down to her mid-thighs, and beneath that there was nothing.

"Well, at least I'm not naked," she commented to herself, settling back weakly into the soft bed by the wall.

Slowly, Danu eyes tracked over the room, then focused on the large pewter pitcher that rested on the table by the open book. Beside it was a pottery cup. *Water*, Danu thought, remembering being given a cool-tasting drink last night, when she awoke feverish and restless.

She frowned, trying to recall the features of the woman who had held her, touching the cup carefully to her lips. It seemed odd, but she drew a blank. There had been a candle nearby, and a strong fire in the hearth, both casting a golden hue over the room and the woman. The young Amazons had carried her in, transferred her from the make-shift travel pallet to the bed, and then shifted away. A hunched figure in a plain brown hooded monk's cloak had entered. The mysterious figure had knelt beside Danu, and then slowly but surely had given her a knowledgeable going-over.

Her hands felt so good, Danu mused.

There had been a tingling sensation as the healer had touched her. Worn out by the pain and the late hour, Danu's eyes had closed against her will. She'd been left with a muddled impression of shadowed face and long, wiry white hair peeking out from the hood. Those strong hands had eased over her body, gently checking for fractures, carefully combing over muscles. Then they had sifted into Danu's short, red hair, coasting over her scalp. There had been a brief, hot pain, and then nothing.

Perplexed, Danu moved her tongue in her mouth. She focused again on the gray metal pitcher on the table. *Shouldn't be that hard to just stand up and walk over . . . get myself a drink.*

Carefully, she maneuvered herself onto an elbow, then pushed herself upright. The dull ache in her head became a full scale pounding. Danu pressed a hand against her forehead and groaned.

"Lord, girl, what the hell are ya doin'?" someone exclaimed.

Feeling breathless, Danu lifted her eyes. A young woman emerged from the bright light of the open door, bustling into the cabin and placing a bowl on the table. She dropped a hand on Danu's shoulder.

"Lay back down," the woman ordered.

Dressed in beige homespun, a calf-length skirt and a round-necked blouse, the girl was slim, with light brown hair and eyes. A smattering of freckles graced her nose and cheeks.

Danu studied her, thinking, *Is this the healer?*

She was a pretty girl, with an oddly appealing look in her russet brown eyes as she smiled. As Danu registered her loveliness, she thought of Tor with a soul-wrenching ache. *Goddess, she's probably so worried about me.*

Aloud, she said, "I'm okay." The pain was fading now that she had been upright for a bit. "Have you heard anything about Whit?"

"Is that the tall one?" The healer asked. She touched a calculating hand to Danu's cheek and pronounced, "The fever's still there, but it's lower, now. Want to try some broth?"

"Could I have some water?"

With a quick nod, the young woman filled the cup and handed it to Danu. After Danu drank it down, she asked for and got several more cups, before the woman admonished, "That's enough. We need to get some broth in ya."

"Um . . . okay," Danu agreed. Her perceptions felt fuzzy around the edges, but she was relieved to realize she felt a lot better than yesterday. Her mind flipped back to the description of height the woman had thrown out, and she asked, "You've seen Whit? The militia made it back, then? Did they save the children?"

"Yes, yes, and yes," the healer answered. She handed her the bowl of broth and a wooden spoon. "The fighters just came in. First time they've come back without anyone badly injured in quite some time, let me tell you—and your friend—Whitaker, right?—seems to have had something to do with that from what I'm hearin' by the cook fire."

"So Whit's okay?"

"Yeah. She walked in here with the rest, all of them carrying a shoulder full of Reg rifles or a little one. They gave the kids back to their mamas, stacked the rifles and right now Whitaker is out there in the street meetin' with Irene Rexrode—that's our Chief. Bet she'll be comin' over to see you once that's over with."

The healer pulled a beautifully constructed wooden chair from its place near the cold hearth. Sitting down, she eyed Danu expectantly until Danu took a spoonful of soup.

"Hey, this is good," Danu stated, eating more enthusiastically once she tasted it.

"Duck soup. Once you've shown me you can keep that down, I'll getcha a bowl with some meat in it. Yer lucky it's Cassandra's week for cook fire. There's some others I can think of that would have slowed yer recovery with their fixin's."

Charmed by the young woman's mischievous brown eyes as she made that remark, Danu laughed. "I'm Danu. Lieutenant Danu Sullivan."

"Kate Ferguson," the young woman answered, bobbing her head. "Dah-nu. Never heard the like of that."

"It's an old name . . . from the Celts. My mother tells me I've Irish blood."

The young woman's face tilted as she considered Danu. "Most of us here are Scotch-Irish. I think the Rexrodes are Germans that came here from Europe two centuries back, but the rest of us are either Murphy or Ferguson clan. Although, there's a mess o' Dilleys, too."

Danu watched her, suddenly understanding that there was a social dynamic at work in this place that she had never come across before. "You're part of a clan?"

The young woman nodded. "Sure. Clans founded all the villages in Amazon territory."

"This is an Amazon village? Like . . . a female society?"

Kate responded to Danu's interested expression with a shake of her head. "Warn't always this way, from what the old ones say. The foundin' of Seneca is a long, sad tale. Best kept for a night by the fire."

Someone blocked the light from the door, and Danu looked over

68

to see Whit's big, rangy form stoop lower to ease below the lintel. "Hey, little sis," Whit greeted her, heading straight over to Danu and kneeling down to enfold her in a firm, heartfelt hug. "How're you?"

Blushing furiously, Danu could barely meet her eyes as Whit released her and leaned back. "Okay. Gaea, it's good to see you, Whit."

Kate spoke up. "What's this?" she demanded, reaching for Whit's arm.

Danu frowned at the dark red bandage wrapped around a large hole in Whit's flight suit.

Shrugging, Whit stood, and gave a huge yawn. "Nothing to worry about."

Kate frowned. "Ya takin' tough-as-hemp lessons from Jamie?"

Whit lifted her eyebrows.

"Come over here and let me lookit that," Kate instructed. Purposefully, she maneuvered Whit to a cot placed at a right angle to Danu's bed.

Whit gazed at the little bed, then with an audible sigh, sank down. Danu suddenly became aware of the exhaustion in her friend's dark gray eyes. Catching Danu's intent stare, Whit scrubbed a hand across her face, then winced as Kate loosened the make-shift bandage.

"You were shot," Kate stated.

"Bullet only scraped the surface," Whit murmured. To Danu, she said, "I field-dressed it with some stuff the Amazons had while we were out there. Still needs a stitch or three. Was gonna ask you to do the honors, Lieutenant Sullivan, but Jamie tells me Seneca has two of the finest healers in the state."

"She told you that?" Kate muttered. She went to the shelves across the room and returned with a small, scuffed black leather bag and a metal basin. "Miz Rexrode happen to mention how many times I've had to test the limits of my craft with her personally?"

Whit gave a quiet laugh and shook her head no.

Experimentally, Danu ran a hand across the right side of her head, wincing as she found a small scab in her scalp by the hairline. "Seneca? That the name of this place?"

"Yep," Kate answered. "And I hear you met the witch herself last night."

"What?" Danu asked, watching Kate take a pair of metal scissors from the old black bag and then begin cutting open the sleeve of Whit's flight suit. "It wasn't you who took care of me?"

"I was out on a midwife call over at the Crickards'," Kate said, arching a mischievous brow. "I'm just the apprentice here. You were tended by my mistress."

Danu dimly recalled the cowl-hidden face of the woman bending over her. "Mistress?" She shook her head, wondering a little at the thrill that term sent up her spine. "She did a good job. I feel a lot better."

Industriously, Kate removed the arm of the flight suit. Whit protested mildly, saying, "Hey, that's the only thing I have to wear." Kate assured Whit that new clothes would be given to her to replace the uniform. Satisfied, Whit shrugged, then yawned. Within a few minutes she was leaning on her other hand. Danu could see the restless energy disappearing, and realized that Whit had been going on sheer nerve and will.

Danu wanted to ask Whit a few of the questions swirling through her mind. *Does anyone in Freeland even know where we are? Have we fallen into a nest of resistance fighters? How long has Elysium been dealing with a revolt?*

Whit's eyes were drooping closed.

Better wait till she's had a chance to rest, Danu reluctantly decided. Then she glanced at Kate. Hiding a smirk, Danu admitted to herself that anything they discussed in front of the sassy healer would more than likely be reported directly back to Irene Rexrode, the one Kate had described as their chief.

For now, Danu made herself stay silent, watching Kate's competent hands cleaning and stitching Whit's wound.

A short time later, Kate had fed and watered both of her patients, then settled them back on their cots for an afternoon of quiet rest. Despite her agitation, Danu complied with the healer's agenda. She had a feeling she and Whit would need all their strength to deal with what awaited them.

Chapter 4

Tor steered the Kestrel steadily closer to the vast, shimmering wall of the photo-electromagnetic screen. "Open 'er up."

Beside her, Kali keyed an equation into the heli-jet computer. The computer took the entry, and a second later the tiny sat-dish mounted flush against the Kestrel bow beamed skyward a signal, relaying a command to the satellite that controlled the northern Bordergate. Moments later, the transmission caused a brief interrupt in the network design over a small area above what was once Illinois.

The wall wavered, reminding Kali of heat vapor coming off tarmac on a hot August day, then suddenly they could see straight through the wall to the shadowed lands beyond the Border. With a slight increase of speed, Tor moved the Kestrel forward. The bright Freeland sunlight was left behind, and they moved into roiling, amber clouds.

Kali knew the clouds were in reality pollution from industrial plants, because for decades now the Elysians had been releasing all kinds of manufacturing waste directly into the air. Many of the poisonous gases caught at the outer edges of the Border and accumulated there, unable to filter through the micro-mesh of the photo-electromagnetic wall. As they flew through the dull yellow clouds, Kali unconsciously held her breath, though she knew the Kestrel had its own air supply. They passed into the dim grayness which marked Elysium, and Kali rapidly entered the sequence command that closed the gate behind them.

Tor shifted in her seat. "Well, if the folks back home haven't already figured out what we're up to, that little hack-job is going to set off every Border security alarm in Freeland."

Kali glanced up from the computer keyboard, feeling her ears heat with a guilty flush. "It will take them a while to get organized enough to do anything about it."

"Think they'll send a troopship after us?" Tor gave a slight chuckle. "I can just see it. A small detail sent to extract Whit and Danu, and a whole battalion of warriors sent to lasso you."

Kali replied by making a face at Tor, then concentrated on bringing up the heat seeking program on the search console.

"I'm going to decrease altitude, now," Tor informed her. "We need to keep under Reg radar."

Kali nodded, watching the Kestrel's altimeter fall as Tor pushed the joystick out, sending the heli-jet into a vertical dive. Kali knew Kestrels were merchant rather than fighter class aircraft. Unlike the Peregrines Whit and Danu had been flying, there was no stealth skin on the Kestrel that would make it invisible to radar detection. The craft dropped down swiftly, wind thrumming over the rotary blade with the speed of their descent. Just as Kali clutched the armrests, feeling as if her stomach were lodged in her throat, Tor snapped the joystick back. Abruptly, the Kestrel pulled up and flattened into a horizontal flight path. They were aimed due east, flying approximately 100 meters above a rippling field of alfalfa that seemed to stretch for untold kilometers into the distance.

73

Kali knew this land had once been a prosperous state called Illinois. Now it was an outlying province of Elysium, where only AGH carriers lived, working the remainder of their lives away as serfs for the Procurators and Reverends that made up the New Order. Kali briefly wondered if the alfalfa rushing below them was as stunted and discolored as the hay that grew in the fields she had tended years ago with Baubo. If the odd, chemical-laced rainfall was still producing outbreaks of previously unknown crop molds, then the answer was probably yes.

Tor reported, "I've set the smart-navigator for the last GPS coordinates Danu's Peregrine sent. Any sign of Regs?"

Kali took a deep breath and focused on the portion of the computer screen that displayed the heat indicator. In the distance, to the south, something caught the program's attention, and an array of small dots were graphically mapped on the topographical representation. A short message appeared on the bottom of the screen, identifying the dots.

Pigs?

That was strange. Meat and poultry were usually raised closer to the governing metropolis, which in this area would have been Chicago. Kali half-smiled, realizing the pigs were probably someone's contraband, no doubt stashed in a thickly wooded copse by a stream, well hidden from Reg foraging parties. The Regs didn't have heat seeking equipment, only radar. During her ten years in Elysium, Kali had used similar tricks, hiding away food, in order to keep Baubo and her from starving.

"I'm getting life-reads, but no people showing up," Kali offered.

"Let me know as soon as something human tweaks the seeker," Tor stated. "I'll adjust our route to maneuver away from anyone who might see us. We'll try to keep out of sight, but after we get through Illinois, we've still got to fly through Indiana and Ohio before we reach West Virginia. Danu disappeared over some mountains in the eastern part of that territory, and Gaea only knows where Whit went down. We've got a long way to travel without being noticed.

Hopefully, the Regs won't have patrol craft out that can get a visual from above us."

Regs! Oh Goddess, what am I doing? Kali began breathing faster.

All at once, memories of her first days in Elysium burst free, tearing through her head in a surreal cascade. Involuntarily, Kali closed her eyes and gritted her teeth.

Regs surrounded her. Their faces were carefully indifferent, as if she were just another serf; only the avid way they watched her betrayed their lust. There were shackles on her wrists and ankles. Over and over, the men made snarling demands that she answer their questions. Time seemed oddly suspended, either due to the drugs they used, or from the shock of seeing most of Isis murdered before her eyes. She felt as if she were in a long fall from the edge of a cliff, unable to believe what was happening, and the bottom never came.

There were terrifying threats hissed by her ear. "Let's try the cat-o'-nine-tails." "No, let's brand her with a cattle iron!" "No, let's rape her."

Then the blows began. A few, well-placed punches, enough to make her stagger and cower away. She was too frightened to speak and her silence infuriated them. The Regs hit her until she couldn't stand, or breathe, and she slid down into black oblivion.

Swallowing hard against a sudden, paralyzing wave of the horror, she opened her eyes and shrank back against the flight chair. *What was I thinking? I'm racing straight back into that!*

"Kali, are you all right?" Tor asked.

She didn't bother trying to lie about it. "I'll be okay," she whispered.

After a long, concerned look, Tor returned her attention to the flight instruments.

Marshaling her considerable mental discipline, Kali gradually centered herself and forced the memories back. *Okay, so I'm scared shitless of the Regs . . . Who wouldn't be after that? But I'm not fourteen anymore. I'm a grown woman and a mage,* she told herself.

Whit's face rose in her mind's eye. Those clear gray eyes and her strong-jawed face; the way one side of her mouth tugged up when she began smiling. *Gaea, I love her.* Just as suddenly, Kali felt the warm, golden glow sweep through her. *I have to do this. I have to get Whit out of Elysium. I won't leave her to those monsters!*

She made herself take several deep breaths, regaining her poise. She caught Tor shooting her a look, and Kali murmured, "I'm okay, really." Sitting up straight, she focused on the heat-seeking program. *I can do this. I just won't let myself think about Regs, that's all.*

The Kestrel zoomed forward, deeper into Elysium.

Lilith marched into the private suite of the Leader's House, her eyes immediately searching out the perfectly made bed and the note on Kali's pillow. The folded white paper was undisturbed, right where Lilith had left it.

"Dammit!" She grabbed the note and crumpled it.

Behind her, Styx was prowling around. "The backpack and weapons are gone, along with the gear she'd set out to wear." She frowned and put her hands on her hips. "Looks like our girl is responsible for the Border breach."

"I knew it—as soon as Captain Razia alerted me!" Lilith spun on Styx. "Has Kali lost her mind? How on Gaea's sweet earth does she think she's going to pull this off? One woman against Elysium!"

Styx muttered, "Anyone check on the whereabouts of Lieutenant Yakami?"

"Oh for love of Sappho!"

By the doorway, five warriors who had been searching the Leader's House with Lilith and Styx snapped to attention and saluted. Two women passed through them, their movement careful and deliberate, as they saw Lilith and headed straight for her.

"Loy! Major Reno!" Lilith greeted them, stunned. "What . . . ?"

Dressed in loose gray fatigues, Whit's Chief Aide, Loy Yin Chen, and Loy's companion on the recent shuttle launch, Major Mika Reno, crossed the room. Loy looked pale, and the sleek black hair near her face was damp with sweat. Reno's light brown skin tone made her state of health harder to guess, but she walked slowly.

Loy grinned unabashedly at Lilith. "Heard the gossip about the big showdown between you and your daughter yesterday, then heard that something set off the Border alarm, so let's just say I put two and two together and got Kali with a wild hair up her—"

Reno smacked a hand across Loy's stomach. "We decided to come see if there's anything we can do." She ended the sentence with a gusty sigh, and bent over to grip her knees.

Gently, Styx took Mika's elbow and steered her over to a comfortable, well-stuffed chair near the hearth. "How is it they even let you out of isolation? You were traveling through space in that shuttle for five days. It takes a couple of weeks to recover, to get your earth legs back after being in microgravity for as long as you two were, doesn't it?"

Mika hunched over in the chair, rubbing her face with her hands, while Loy moved to sit on the plush arm of the chair. "Thank Gaea, Mika outranked everyone at mission control. She made them let us leave." Chuckling, Loy smoothed a hand over Mika's curly, light-brown hair. "Yeah, they told us we'd be ready to faint by the time we got over here, but since when do we listen to reason, huh Mika?"

"Keep it up and I'm going to be sick on your boots."

"That bad, eh?" Loy said it with such an innocent look, Styx had to smother a laugh with her hand.

Loy moved her sharp, black-eyed gaze to Lilith. "So what's the scoop? Whit and Danu are down behind enemy lines and Kali's gone after them?"

Gathering her dignity, Lilith lifted her chin and folded her arms over her chest. "Is the grapevine really that good or is this outcome that predictable?"

Cocking her head for a second, as if considering the answer, Loy simply pronounced, "Yes."

Sudden tears edged Lilith's eyes. She turned toward Styx, lifting her hands helplessly. "What are we going to do?" She shook her head, suddenly feeling overwhelmed. "After her experiences there as a POW, Kali has an almost pathological fear of Regs. She's just gone charging off—how is she going to—" Styx reached out and pulled Lilith into her arms. Burrowing her head into Styx's red cotton sweater, Lilith finished, "I've been so frightened for Whit. Now Kali's there, too."

Major Reno lifted worried eyes. "I want to fill a troopship with warriors and go after them, but, I don't think I can go into action like this."

Leaning over, Loy gave her a comforting hug. "The heart's willing, but the flesh ain't ready for muster."

Lilith stepped out of Styx's arms, her brows rising in surprise. "Oh," she murmured, observing the open affection between Loy and Reno. "You two seem . . . very close . . ."

Smirking, Loy offered, "It was a successful space flight . . . all the way around."

Styx's eyebrows crawled up into her bangs.

Mika gave Loy a nudge in the ribs with her elbow, then sat up straighter and became very professional. "We were completely focused on the mission while we were up there. We just came to an understanding about . . . um, things . . . for when we returned."

"I see," Lilith said. She managed a tremulous smile. "I'm happy for you both."

"Thanks," Mika returned, gripping Loy's hand.

The two women traded a loving look.

Laughing slightly, Styx said, "So back to the topic." She slipped her hands into the pockets of her baggy khakis, moving her gaze from Lilith, to Mika and Loy. "What are we going to do?"

A hurried exchange was heard between someone and the warriors waiting at the door, then Captain Razia dashed into the room, skidding to a stop before Lilith. "The Isis Council is called to emergency session, Ma'am." Razia glanced over at Loy and Major Reno, and hesitated before continuing.

78

"Go ahead with your report, Captain," Lilith said. "It probably won't be anything Loy and Reno aren't already fully aware of."

Razia nodded. "Warrior Command has identified the ship that breached the Border. Sensors traced the sat-dish that sent the command to the Bordergate. The dish is onboard a rogue Kestrel which departed from our airfield at four this morning. After an inventory check of the airfield arms locker, it was discovered two laser rifles and a slew of grenades are missing. Two dirt bikes and several cartons of MREs are gone as well." Razia paused, then announced, "I'm sorry to add that no one has seen Kali Tyler or Lieutenant Yakami since last night."

A long, brittle silence ensued, until Loy remarked, "Well, you have to hand it to them. When they get together, things get done."

Captain Razia glanced at Loy, then looked back at Lilith. "The Council's response will probably be to beef up the officially sanctioned rescue team. You know—add more military might—maybe assign two troopships instead of one. And then send them off as quickly as possible."

Styx added, "Probably with orders to find and arrest Kali, and drag her butt back here whether she likes it or not."

Scratching the back of her neck, Loy laughed humorlessly. "Arrest her? Have all of you forgotten Kali's a talented mage?" She met each of their eyes, then stated, "She's quite capable of evading anyone she wants to, no matter how many troopships of warriors you send, no matter what kind of techno gizmos they use to search for her. She's also probably going to find Whit before anyone else." Loy stood up, going pale again and leaning a hand on Major Reno's shoulder to steady herself. "And Gaea help anyone, Elysian Regs or Freeland warriors, that gets in her way. This is the woman that just last winter fought a psychic battle with a powerful sorceress and won. Remember, Kali blew Arinna Sojourner to smithereens."

Quietly, Lilith replied, "Actually . . . Whit did that."

Everyone looked at her.

Lilith sighed. "If you recall, neither Whit or Kali ever really elaborated on the details of that confrontation. The next thing we knew, rumors took over and the whole of Freeland was saying that Kali outblasted Arinna in a psychic duel." Rubbing her forehead, Lilith grimaced. "It's not true. Kali told me herself that Arinna had her down, had gotten through all her wards and was readying to take control of her. At the last second, Whit slid in front of Kali holding an insulated, highly reflective piece of metal from the nose cone of the space shuttle. Whit and Styx had specially prepared this metal piece to be used like an old-fashioned shield." Shaking her head in wonder, Lilith finished, "When Arinna threw the next bolt of lightning at them, the charge hit the shield and ricocheted right back into Arinna. Kali told me she'd passed out by then, but Whit had said there was an explosion. When the smoke cleared, nothing was left but a scorch mark on the concrete floor where Arinna had been standing."

"Whoa," Loy said. "Wonder why Whit never told me all that?"

Mika shrugged. "As the old saying goes, when the truth contradicts the legend, print the legend." She pushed a strand of curly hair back from her face. "I think Whit understood that Freeland needed a myth. Nothing like believing you have an all-powerful mage on your side to keep hopes up during a national crisis . . . like the Border falling."

Beside her, Loy shifted uneasily from one foot to the other. "So . . . just a scorch mark, huh. How did Whit know for sure that Arinna was dead?"

Wide-eyed, Lilith snapped, "Well, of course Arinna was dead!" Realizing her tone betrayed her own misgivings, Lilith purposefully lowered her voice. "Who could have survived something like that?" No one spoke, but Lilith could have sworn they were all thinking the same unwelcome thought. Impatiently, Lilith began moving. "Enough of this. I've got a Council session to get to."

Captain Razia strode after her as Lilith headed toward the door.

With a solicitous bow, Styx helped Major Reno up from her chair, then extended an elbow to Loy. "Okay, my little space heroines. Let me escort you to your next destination before I get caught up in the save-Kali mission. Do you want to go back to mission control at Cochran Space Center? To the warrior's barracks for a nap? Or perhaps brunch at one of our finer establishments while you're in the heart of Isis?"

With a mock-innocent grin, Reno replied, "Can we borrow your electrobile? I want to pick up some take-out, and then there's this bet I need to collect on." She fixed Loy with a simmering look. "I think Loy's cabin on the South Mountain Road is just the place to do it."

Styx saw the red stain begin at Loy's neck and shoot up into her face.

"Must've been some bet," Styx answered, then commented, "Loy, I don't think I've ever seen you blush like this before."

"I am not blushing," Loy muttered. "Just too hot in here."

Styx laughed, and kept hold of the two women as they made their way out.

Deep in a dream, Danu heard a compelling female voice calling her name. She was standing at the entrance of a large cave, her every breath filled with a strange scent. There were drums rumbling in the distance and wisps of smoke swirling in the darkness ahead of her. Feeling bewildered and uncertain, she walked slowly forward. As she came around a high rock wall, she saw the slender form of a woman dancing before the leaping flames of a large fire. Wiry, white hair swung wildly as she whirled. The face was lost in silhouette, while arms glistening with sweat reached out to her.

Danu, the low voice called, softly, insistently. *Danu, come to me.*

Danu found herself moving closer to the woman, felt an erotic rush as she realized the woman was naked. Moving slowly, sinuously, the faceless woman undulated before her. Laughing at Danu's awestruck expression, the woman touched soft fingers to Danu's neck, then circled her, taking a position behind her.

Hands and arms slipped around Danu's waist, smoothly pulling her in close. The woman's front slid against Danu's back, and she rocked from side to side, drawing Danu into a swaying motion. Warm breath whispered by Danu's left ear, making her shiver. The woman's hips rocked into her, while the arms held her in place against a moist body. Slowly, purposefully, lips began nibbling the back of Danu's neck, where she was so vulnerable to seduction. Danu couldn't help the slight moan, or the way her breath quickened, betraying her hunger. A hot tongue grazed down to the apex of her shoulder, and hands coasted over her homespun sleeping shirt. Then the hands suddenly plunged down to her thighs and lifted the shirt, slipping beneath it and then over Danu's skin. The woman's fingers seemed to tingle with some electric energy.

This isn't Tor, Danu told herself, feeling a moral inclination to resist. "No," she said, although it didn't sound convincing, even to herself.

The woman only laughed, and nibbled the lobe of Danu's ear.

One by one, those skimming fingers were finding her erotic triggers, causing each one to flare uncontrollably, then moving on, as if mapping her. Danu grabbed for the hands, trying to stop the relentless search. Even as Danu caught them, covering them with her own hands, the woman's fingers reached her breasts. Danu found herself arching back, gasping, as the zinging caress lingered there. Exquisite, delicious sensation shot through her nipples, making them taut. Danu began to twitch like a lab rat caught in a current. It felt so good Danu thought she might swoon.

It's all right. It's just a dream, said the soothing voice in her head.

One hand began a slow, mind-blowing descent down, over her ribs and belly, while the other hand traveled lazily back and forth, between her nipples, keeping her enthralled with that stunning touch. Danu heard herself panting, felt herself writhing helplessly.

Yes, let me do this. From behind, a slippery leg inserted itself between hers, nudging her knees apart.

Without consciously deciding to surrender, Danu felt herself cross some line. Her body was on fire. Whatever this woman intended, Danu had to have it.

I'm going to fuck you, the voice whispered. *And you want me to fuck you, don't you, Danu? You crave my hands on you and in you . . .*

The hands grasped Danu's arms and lifted them. Leather cuffs slipped around her wrists. Blinking unsteadily, Danu saw that the cuffs that held her were attached to two separate light but sturdy steel chains that rose over her head and attached to pulleys fastened into the rock ceiling.

"This is just a dream," Danu said aloud, trying to reassure herself.

Yes, the voice said in her mind, *A dream of desire and need . . .* The woman was suddenly laughing.

Still behind her, the woman moved up and down, drawing back Danu's wandering attention. *You have what I need, Danu . . . And I have what you need,* the voice whispered.

Reaching around Danu, the woman took hold of her nightshirt and tore it open. A rain of buttons fell across the rocky floor. The front of Danu was completely exposed and open to exploration. Those irresistible fingers came to her again, sweeping over the entire length of her, making her cry out, making her snake and twist in a wanton display of asking. She could barely keep her footing. She dangled from the leather cuffs, swinging and arching, completely at the mercy of the woman playing with her body.

Oooh, that's it. So ready for me . . .

The woman behind her pulled Danu in tight. One hand slipped over her belly, hesitated in the hair at her mons, then in one slow, relentless push eased between Danu's legs, into the thick wetness. Danu cried out, desperate for it now. With delicate, tantalizing fingers, the woman circled her clitoris, never quite making contact, teasing Danu until she was utterly consumed with need.

Chuckling, the woman caressed the lips at her entrance, bringing Danu to the brink. *You like this, don't you? You like being taken from behind. You like being chained and hung up for me to savor . . . my delicious meal . . .*

Danu felt the sweet power building, spiraling inward, the blood rush surging through her body in a fiery glow. Whispering, *Now you will be mine*, the woman's fingers slicked over her soaking cleft in long, deliberate strokes. A strangled whimper tore out of Danu's throat. She had never felt anything like this. Each deepening stroke was thrumming with some inexplicable, captivating power, reducing her to raw, open lust. Danu's head dropped back and she went rigid. *Yes, that's it* . . . The woman's touch became almost preternatural, giving Danu exactly what she wanted, as she yearned for it, and gradually bringing Danu to a level of erotic pleasure she had never experienced. She had lost her footing. She had no idea how she was being supported, except that she was riding that commanding hand on her sex, and jerking in the leather cuffs like a marionette.

Let me have you . . . Dazed and panting, Danu realized her voice was ringing through the cave, rich with her enraptured enslavement. Then came one long note, full-throated, an aria of release.

The orgasm ripped through her, obliterating any sense of self, any concept of separateness from the being behind her. Shocked, she felt some other foreign energy sink into her, passing through her skin, flowing right through muscle, blood, and bone. She felt this other inhabiting her flesh, reveling in the life force rocketing through them. They were one, awash in an ocean of bliss.

Yeeessss . . .

Whit's eyes snapped open and with a jerk, she sat up in bed. Blinking against the sunlight slanting through the room, she peered at Danu, who was lying on a cot less than five feet away. The young woman was visibly twitching beneath the blanket, and screaming as if she were dying.

"Hey," Whit called, scrambling out from underneath her cover. "Danu!"

She dropped to her knees on the smooth, wood plank floor and reached for the convulsing body of her friend. "C'mon, wake up!"

As Whit's hands made contact with Danu's shoulders, Danu seemed to launch up from the thin, straw filled mattress. Instinctively, Whit caught her, and with a guttural groan, Danu fell back, completely limp.

Carefully laying her down, Whit moved her hands to either side of Danu's face. "Mother's Blood!"

Danu's fair lashes fluttered, then the bright blue eyes came into view. The young pilot looked disoriented. "Whit?" she said weakly. She closed her eyes again. "Goddess, I must have been dreaming."

"That was . . ." Whit leaned back and placed a hand on Danu's arm. "That was more than a dream. I think you were having a seizure." Agitated, Whit stood up and moved to the open cabin door, looking for help.

Kate was standing outside the doorway in the late afternoon sunlight, her hands clenching her apron and a pained expression on her face. Surprised to see her there, and wondering at her apparent hesitation to enter, Whit opened her mouth, then abruptly closed it.

"I'll see to her," Kate murmured as she brushed by Whit.

Kate went to Danu's side and swiftly checked her vital signs. Throughout the exam, Danu was flushed. Her eyes were at half mast, and she seemed too tired to speak. Kate at last stepped back, appearing satisfied. Carefully avoiding Whit's eyes, Kate went to the pewter pitcher and poured water into a pottery cup. Gracefully, she brought the cup to Danu. She helped her sit up enough to take a long drink, then eased her back into the rumpled sheets and pulled the blanket to Danu's shoulders.

"Rest, now," Kate told Danu. "Everything's fine."

Trustingly, Danu's sleepy eyes closed.

Whit watched as Danu's breathing deepened and slowed. Kate rose from her kneeling position and placed the cup on the rough wooden table. Nervously, Kate glanced at Whit, then away. She smoothed her hands over the sides of her beige skirt repeatedly. Frowning, Whit checked Danu, confirming that the young redhead had drifted quickly back to sleep.

Staring hard at Kate, Whit growled, "What the hell was that?"

Shrugging, Kate offered, "Maybe the head injury, or a stress reaction—"

Whit moved closer, her voice rising. "She was seizing and screaming at the same time! Is that physically possible?"

"I guess so, if you just saw it."

"What's wrong with her?" Whit yelled. "Look at her—it's like she's drugged—she's out like a light—not even hearing us!"

"She's been feverish off and on . . ."

Whit grabbed the pitcher, lifting it to her nose and sniffing. She took an experimental taste from the edge of the vessel, then dismissed that paranoia. She angrily thumped the pitcher back on the table, making the water inside slosh over the lip and onto the table. Kate's wide brown irises went from the pitcher, to Whit's face, and dropped.

Narrowing her gaze, Whit observed, "Why are you having so much difficulty looking me in the eye?"

Kate lifted her chin and at last returned Whit's stare. Defiantly, she drew herself up to her full height, and still only came even with Whit's shoulder. "You quit tryin' to bully me."

Whit's hands came to her hips. "Something's going on—I can feel it!"

Tossing her hair over her shoulder, Kate countered, "Yer tired, is all. Yer friend took a bad hit on the head, and is sufferin' the effects of it." As if purposefully trying to calm her, Kate went on in a softer tone. "Yer both in a foreign land at the mercy of strangers. It's only natural for you to get suspicious." She smoothed her hands over her skirt again, looking away as she concluded, "The people of this village will not hurt you."

Perplexed, Whit watched her turn and walk across the cabin, disappearing quickly through the open door. For several more minutes Whit stood beside Danu's cot, observing her friend and deep in thought.

There's more going on here than meets the eye, she decided. *And I better figure it out before it bites me in the butt.*

༄

Kali lifted her attention from the search program display, feeling as if her psychic antenna were trembling. Even with the disruptions the pregnancy hormones were causing, for the most part, the bizarre inner awareness functioned like any of her other five senses. It was once again subtly feeding her information.

Beside her, Tor offered, "We're almost there. Old West Virginia territory and the Appalachians are about twenty kilometers straight ahead. Any sign of Regs?"

"Slow down," Kali answered. "There's something . . . something's not right."

Tor adjusted their speed, then tossed her a wary look. "What?" She frowned as she scanned the landscape before the Kestrel. "What are you getting?"

"I don't know."

Kali studied the hazy gray sky and the scabrous, muddy-green of the stunted deciduous forest passing below them. "There's magic—a lot of it. I can feel it humming. Somebody . . ." She stared ahead, letting her gaze go unfocused, reaching with her sixth sense. "There's a huge, multi-layered spell. It's years old, but still as strong as the day it was fashioned." Closing her eyes, she cautiously extended her own mage power, trying to recognize the hidden effect by mind touch. "Give me a minute."

Slowing even more, Tor continued to fly the Kestrel forward, eating up distance. They passed through a series of huge, amber thunderheads, and their view of what lay before the bow was suddenly gone.

All at once, Kali felt something very close. She sent her psychic reach out and was temporarily stunned by the sheer size of what she found. "Gaea, it's like the Border—but it's a spell, not science! It's a wizard's wall!"

"What?" Tor demanded.

"Turn around! The heli-jet can't fly into that!"

The Kestrel lifted up a bit, as if in a gust of wind as it passed through the clouds. Tor was suddenly visibly struggling with the joystick, and then began pumping the floor pedals frantically. The Kestrel lurched sideways and steadily began dropping lower.

"What are you doing?" Kali yelled. "I said turn around!"

"Can't," Tor uttered, "I'm trying to keep us up. Something is overriding the flight controls!"

"This can't be happening!" Kali gasped. "Who in Elysium has ever been capable of working magic?"

Tor leaned over and flipped open a small panel door. She twisted a knob within the recess there, then pushed a lever down until it was flat with the surface. "Interrupting all computer functions. We're on manual override."

The Kestrel straightened, and the lumbering sound from the decibel-squelch engines abruptly quieted. Tor and Kali held their breath, watching the altimeter. They were losing altitude, but it was gradual enough now to be hardly unnoticeable.

"Try to turn us around," Kali said softly.

Tor attempted to execute the aerial maneuver, but the flight controls were locked in their forward flight position.

"I thought you said we were on manual override?"

Tor removed her hand from the joystick, staring at it in disbelief. "I've never seen anything like this. The controls are being operated by something else. I'm not flying this plane."

Kali pushed herself back in the chair. "I don't think this is the Regs." She bit her lip, watching the treetops below them rise and fall like a rolling green carpet.

"What are we gonna do?" Tor asked.

"Don't know about you," Kali muttered, "but if we're not flying this thing I really don't want to stick around to see where it goes."

"So, we better get out!"

Calm, but serious, Kali answered, "Unless we're trapped in here."

"Maybe it's just the flight controls that are affected. Go try to open the cargo door," Tor said. "Maybe we can toss out some supplies, then bail."

"Okay," Kali said, unbuckling her seatbelt harness, then jumping up and heading for the side door.

Taking hold of the first of the two manual handles, Kali pulled with all her might. After a moment of stiff resistance, the lock released. Kali threw the other handle. The door slid partially open, and a strong blast of wind entered the cargo hold. Kali was pushed backward, then steadied herself with a hand on the wall.

She yelled to Tor, "Let's go!"

"Don't hafta tell me twice," Tor yelled back over the wind.

"We should at least try to get the dirt bikes down there," Kali called, going to the two slim, nubby-tired motorcycles anchored securely to the metal wall.

With a nod, Tor joined her. They made quick work of the cargo moorings, releasing the motor bikes, then pushing them closer to the exit and laying them down by the doorway's edge. Kali grabbed up their backpacks and two cartons of MREs, placing the supplies by the door while Tor fished two parachute packs out of a chest behind the pilot's chair. She tossed Kali a pack and both women quickly slipped a parachute on, securing and tightening the harness straps. With a hard shove, Tor fully opened the cargo door. She steadied herself against the rushing influx of air, then pitched out the packs and MRE cartons. Kali moved forward and helped her unceremoniously dump the two motorbikes.

They were flying over a mountain meadow, and bright green grass and blue wildflowers stretched out invitingly.

Kali shouted to Tor, "You go first."

Tor nodded, gave her a rakish grin, then gathered herself and leapt out of the door. Kali watched her fall a short ways, then the parachute popped out and filled, a billowing bloom above the meadow. Kali took a deep breath and jumped out after her.

She fell through the wind, then tugged the rip cord and was yanked upward by the unfurling expanse of gray cloth above her. She looked up, trying to see around the chute to watch where the Kestrel was headed. The small aircraft continued over the next large hill and then the hill itself blocked Kali's view of it. Looking down, she saw Tor landing gracefully in the knee-high grass, taking large running strides and not even having to roll.

Show-off, Kali thought, surprising herself with a laugh.

Moments later, Kali was landing nearby, hitting the ground with a powerful jolt that sent her into a tuck and somersault. She came up with the momentum, scrambling to her feet and pulling on the chute ropes to bring the cloth back to her and out of the grip of the strong mountain breeze she felt swirling by her cheek. As Kali completed her recovery of the chute, Tor was running toward her, arms full of silky gray fabric.

"The bikes went down over there," Tor called, motioning westward with her head.

"Then that's where we go first. Maybe we'll get lucky," Kali answered.

Tor grinned back. "We're due. Let's bury the chutes."

They dropped to their knees and used their knives to dig into the rich dark earth. "Gaea, look at this dense root system," Kali commented. Frowning, she glanced around at the tall grass surrounding them.

Minutes later they had covered the meters of thin fabric and lines.

They waded purposefully through the thick grasses, hiking west across the meadow. Tor looked around at the waving sea of grass, puzzled.

"Look at how healthy this is! Green and lush, just like a meadow in Isis."

Kali answered, "The trees ahead, too. And the air—it's positively sweet."

"How?"

"That Wizard Wall. It's keeping the pollutants out."

"You're kidding!" Tor looked at her, astonishment clear on her thin face.

"No. Someone here is using magic to keep unwanted things away

90

from this place—which seems to be aircraft and poisonous microscopic particles, probably missiles, too. Goddess knows what else."

"Well it certainly has saved this country. It's beautiful," Tor pronounced, looking around at the vibrant blue sky and rustling grass. The late afternoon sun was hovering low in the sky, a hazy yellow-orange ball beyond the two human-made screens.

Quietly, Kali said, "Tor, whoever made that wall we just passed through has more power than I ever thought a person could have." She took a deep breath. "If it's an Elysian, we're in big trouble. We've got to find Whit and Danu and get out of here without crossing paths with that mage."

"Or else, what?"

"Don't know. Got a bad feeling about it, that's all," Kali said. "I don't question it anymore, I just go with it."

Gleaming tire spokes drew their attention to the first bike, caught high in the branches of an oak tree at the edge of the field. They found the second bike on the outskirts of some rhododendron bushes, cushioned from a hard landing by the depth of the shrubbery. Once they had pulled the bike free, they spent a few minutes checking it, making sure it would operate safely. Then Tor mounted the bike and Kali climbed on behind her. They rode around hunting for the supplies they had dumped and salvaging what they could. They found both of their packs, but only one carton of MREs. Finally, Tor pulled over and they secured their provisions for traveling.

Kali consulted her palm computer, checking the GPS map function and determining the best cartographical trail from their current location to where Danu's Peregrine had gone offline. For orienteering purposes, she pointed out to Tor a landmark due east. With a nod, Tor gunned the near-silent engine and they took off across the meadow.

Hang on, Whit, she sent, hoping Whit could hear her now. *I'm a helluva a lot closer now than I was yesterday!*

91

Chapter 5

Whit opened her eyes. Lifting her head, she glanced around and realized with chagrin that she was half-sprawled across the bottom of Danu's cot. She had parked a chair by the cot earlier, determined to keep an informal watch, but the warm, lazy afternoon had defeated her best intentions. Whit smoothed a gentle hand over the shape of a shin beneath the scratchy wool blanket, then surveyed the sleeping woman.

Sitting up, Whit stretched, trying to ease stiff muscles. Between the long run last night and her recent awkward posture, her body was painfully sore. Then she noticed that the room was only faintly lit by natural light. She turned and looked behind her, noting the velvet blue beyond the open cabin door.

Must be just after sundown, she guessed.

Danu stirred, murmuring, "What."

Whit broke into a soft laugh.

Opening her eyes, Danu gazed at her, puzzled.

"Hey. How're you doing?" Whit asked.

"Great." Danu looked around, and seemed to recollect where they were and why.

Growing serious, Whit warned in a low voice, "We may need to hightail it outta here anytime now. What's your actual status."

Shifting slightly on the cot, and then slowly sitting up, Danu seemed to take stock of herself. "No headache, no dizziness. In fact, I feel fine." Her eyebrows rose. "I had some wild dreams though."

Someone came through the doorway and both Danu and Whit turned.

"Get up. We're feastin'," Irene Rexrode told them, "and yer invited."

Whit rose from her chair, laughing softly. "Who could refuse an invitation like that?"

Acting as if Whit hadn't spoken, Irene moved to Whit's bed and unceremoniously dropped the stack of clothing she carried. "Here's some duds for ya both."

"You don't have to—" Whit began.

Suddenly stiff-necked, Irene gave her a hard stare. "There's families in this town that feel they owe you some, Major. You gonna get in the way of their hospitality?"

Whit shifted from one foot to the other. From her two-year tour of duty as an undercover operative in Elysium, she knew how poor these people were, how they struggled to feed and clothe themselves in a post-apocalyptic world. However, the prickly pride she sensed from the small, wiry woman before her was a powerful deterrent to objecting further.

Nodding, as if satisfied with Whit's reluctance to argue, the Chief of Seneca gestured at the clothes. "I think the fit will be close enough. We'll be bringin' in buckets of hot water for ya in a few minutes, so's ya can clean up proper." She wrinkled her nose at Whit. "You in partic'lar are a mite rank."

Whit couldn't help grinning. "Yeah, I'm offending myself."

While Irene and Danu chuckled, Whit fixed the Elder with a considering gaze. "And later, I'll need some answers, Chief. There's a lot I'm seeing here that just does not jive with the Elysium I know."

Irene lifted an eyebrow. "Plannin' on doin' some recon, Major?"

"I'm not your enemy," Whit said quietly. "But I could be the emissary for an allied force."

Irene Rexrode's bright blue eyes snapped with an emotion Whit couldn't read in her expressionless face. It could have been glee, and just as easily anger. "Request for parlay noted, Major Whitaker. I'll have a talk with the heads of the clans, and then git back to ya."

Danu cleared her throat. "Um . . . will there be something to eat at this feast?"

Irene shook her head. "Land's sake, that's the point, girl!"

"Okay!" Danu said vehemently. She pushed her blanket aside and shifted her legs from the bed. Whit leaned down to help her as the young woman stood. "I'm all right," she assured Whit.

Irene moved to the doorway. Two large teenage Amazons slipped through the opening, and walked by her. Each young hand was weighted by a rope-handled wooden bucket full of steaming water. They made their way to the old porcelain clawfoot tub in the far corner, then hoisted the buckets one by one and dumped their load. Before the girls ambled out, they favored Whit and Danu with curious glances.

"I'll leave ya to yer bath," Irene called, tossing her wiry gray hair off her shoulder as she turned back toward them. "When yer both presentable, jes follow the noise and join us." Pausing, she asked, "Yer not adverse to dancin', I hope?"

While several more youngsters laden with steaming buckets filed in, Whit shrugged, glancing at Danu, and wondering, *What kind of dancing?*

Irene gave them a dismissive wave of her hand and continued to the door, "Cause yer gonna be pulled in, like it or not."

Whit could hear her laughing as she strolled down the road outside.

94

Farther west, roughly seventy kilometers away, Tor pulled the motorcycle over to the side of the grass-grown, pot-holed remains of U.S. Route 33. She dropped her feet to the ground, balancing the machine as it stopped. Behind her, Kali mimicked the pose.

Squinting at the faded paint on a battered sign that stood cock-eyed in waist-high grass, Kali was at last able to make out the words. *Welcome To Elkins.*

All in all, they had made good time. They had bailed out of their Kestrel near the crumbled remains of a town called Spencer about seven hours earlier. The roads so far had been awful, more a combination of disintegrated macadam and loose gravel than actual pavement, sewn with saplings that were bravely taking root and occasionally blocked by fallen trees. However, there were still intact and functional bridges on the old U.S. highways. Even pocked with craters, allowing glimpses of the fierce, fast rivers rushing below, a bridge was a bridge. Gliding over the structures, easily traversing the many streams that sliced through this land, had become enough of an incentive to stay on the roads.

Turning in the seat, Tor advised Kali, "It's getting too dark to see. There's no sense in taking chances, or we're sure to hit a hole. The tires are nondeflatable, but we can still dent a rim."

Kali blew out a tense breath and noted the deepening twilight before them. They had agreed hours ago that they would stop traveling at nightfall, since using the headlight would be risky. Now that night was actually coming, however, she felt desperate to go on, no matter what. Impatience to get her hands on Whit was stronger than the edgy exhaustion she felt in her thighs and lower back, stronger than the queasiness squirming through her belly.

Tor wasn't waiting for agreement. Pointing to a small rise off to their right, Tor commented. "Let's camp in the trees up there. We'll have a good view of this road and anyone on it before we take off in the morning."

Sighing, Kali gave a moody, silent nod.

Her eyes soft, Tor squeezed Kali's jacketed arm, seeming to understand. "We'll be the better for some food and rest, don't you think? Then we can get started at first light."

"Okay," Kali said, swallowing her frustration.

"You look pretty pale. Stomach okay?"

"No," Kali admitted. "I think I need more of that tea."

Tor gunned the quiet engine. Lifting her feet, Kali secured her grip on Tor. In a slow, smooth curve, Tor steered the motorcycle off the road and between the large trees that flanked the old highway. The bike's wheels bit into a carpet of loamy earth, slipping sideways a bit before gaining purchase. Tor revved the engine and rocketed them up the slope of the hillside.

As Kali tightened her hold around Tor's waist, she couldn't help wishing with all her heart that it was Whit she held in her arms. *Where are you, Tomyris?*

Skillfully, Tor maneuvered the dirt bike, zig-zagging a path up the steep slope, slowing as they passed between the closer trees. Finally they came over a rise and found themselves in a clearing. Between the smaller, wind-shriveled trees on the crest of the plateau, there was a clear view of the road from both directions.

Tor steadied the motorcycle, then switched off the engine. Wearily, Kali slipped from her seat and instantly felt the hours of riding in the trembling ache of her legs. She leaned over, stretching, while Tor climbed off the cycle and set the kick stand. Kali straightened and watched Tor carefully inspecting the meadow. Shifting her eyes, she gave a small gasp as she beheld what lay below them.

Far into the distance, a series of rolling, blue-green mountains were fading in the turquoise glow of evening. A swell of breeze brought a high-pitched chorus, a thousand voices singing.

"What is that?" Tor asked, tilting her head. "That 'breep-breep-breep' thing?"

"Spring peepers," Kali answered. She smiled gently, remembering. "Years ago, when I was with Baubo, we used to spend early summer traveling around the Elysian countryside in a little mule-drawn cart, on a kind of peddler's circuit. We'd trade her hedge-witch remedies and my vegetable seeds for fabric . . . sometimes it was cotton, but up this way it was usually woollen goods. All the sheep, you know." Looking up, Kali gazed at the sky. "We used to camp out at night like this. We always spent the hour after sunset listening to the peepers." She shook her head a little. "Forgot about that . . ."

Perplexed, Tor said, "What the hell is a peeper?"

"Little frogs. They're in the marshes in the valley below. That song is their love call."

Shaking her head, Tor said, "You mean we're going to be sere-naded all night by a thousand little froggies looking for nookie?"

Kali grinned, and pulled her back pack out of the bike's saddle-bag. "They'll stop after an hour or so."

Tor walked back and went to the opposite saddlebag to remove her own pack. "You mean once they've found their honey for the night."

Dropping her eyes, Kali replied, "Well, at least somebody's finding their honey."

She hadn't meant to sound as wistful and near to tears as she did. She had intended it to be a joke. All the same, when Tor's arms went round her, she felt a small sob emerge from her throat. She leaned into Tor, absorbing the strength of her.

"We'll find them, my friend," Tor whispered to her. "We'll find them."

Feeling raw and overwhelmed, Kali could only hang on to her.

After a moment, they separated. Tor took Kali's pack from her and untied the tightly coiled sleeping bag fastened on top of it. Sheepishly, Kali used her jacket sleeve to scrub the tears from her face, while Tor stomped down the high grass and then unfurled the blanket.

"Sorry," Kali murmured.

"It's okay. You're all done in," Tor responded. "Remember, you've got a little one inside you, probably spinning around like a pup chasing her tail."

The image made Kali half-laugh. She was suddenly so grateful that Tor was here with her.

"Okay. Time to get ready to hit the sack," Tor instructed. "The daylight is going fast."

After a quick trip to the woods, Kali took off her boots, and sank down cross-legged into the thick cloth sleeping bag. A damp chill was entering the air as night fell.

Kali whispered to herself. "Some of that stomach-settling tea and trail grub . . ."

She drank deeply from the pre-made canteen of tea, then rooted through her pack for an MRE. Using the razor sharp edge of her knife, she opened the vacuum sealed pouch. She found her mess kit spoon and began to eat mechanically, watching Tor set up her own sleeping bag right next to her. When Kali was halfway through the tepid beef stew concoction, her exhaustion moved aside and she realized that she was starved. She was shoveling spoonfuls quickly into her mouth, when she glanced up and saw Tor's open amusement.

"What?" Kali asked self-consciously.

"The pouch is biodegradable, but please don't eat it," Tor cracked.

Kali grabbed one of her boots and threw it—and missed.

"Better locate that before you have to hike off for a whiz sometime before dawn," Tor suggested.

"You're worse than Whit!"

"Why, thank you," Tor remarked.

A short time later, boot found and returned to rest with its mate near her sleeping bag, Kali snuggled into her warm bag, feeling full and content. The anxiety and frazzled emotions that had engulfed her just an hour before were gone. Now a heavy lethargy was moving through her like a sluggish summer river.

Overhead, the royal blue night sky was darkening enough to reveal a few stars. Rustling grass betrayed Tor's return. She had gone off a few minutes earlier to bury their MRE wrappers and then stash their packs in the crook of a tall tree. Tor hadn't mentioned it, but Kali realized they both had no idea what kind of wildlife might be nearby.

She heard Tor take a deep breath of the night air, fragrant with sweet grass. "It's so peaceful and beautiful," Tor commented. "Hard to believe we're in Elysium."

"Mmmm," Kali agreed sleepily. "It was always like this . . . the Allegheny Highlands. Always too far out in the boonies for the civilized world to bother with. Protected them."

"Was it like this when you were here with Baubo? So green and clean?"

"No, not like this. Three years ago it was nicer than most places, but the trees were yellowing and the crops were failing." Against her will, Kali yawned. "Sure is like the Mother's Garden, now."

Tor sat down and unlaced her boots, humming a bit. Kali watched her open her sleeping bag and climb inside. A whippoorwill was singing farther down on the mountain. Kali blinked solemnly as Tor settled down and went still.

"Tor?"

"Yeah?"

"Thanks for coming with me. I don't think I could have done this without you."

Tor's quiet laugh came back. "Right."

"Really."

"Uh-huh." Then more softly, "Go to sleep, little warrior."

Kali smiled and closed her eyes. Within the next minute, she was asleep.

Whit and Danu wandered down the main street, following the noise. In the center square of the village, the leaping flames of a blazing fire silhouetted a large crowd of women.

A few fiddlers, an uilleann piper, and a girl with a tin whistle were playing a lively tune, accompanied by several youngsters playing skin drums of varying sizes and tones. Laughing and yelling, women were dancing a reel in front of a large bonfire. Farther back, in the shadows, others were congregated in groups, talking and grinning. Whit noted that many of them were passing jugs.

Sniffing the air, Danu proclaimed, "Something smells good!"

Whit ruffled Danu's hair, carefully avoiding the wounded side of her head. "Well, then, let's find out what."

Whit spotted an area of tables laden with dishes of food and large roasts of meat. She nudged Danu and began moving around the back of the crowd, easing between exuberant Amazons and drawing subtly appraising eyes.

Hurrying to stay even with Whit's long strides, Danu leaned closer in order to be heard above the noise. "These clothes feel great."

Whit glanced down at their outfits. They were both dressed in soft, deerskin trousers and moccasins that laced to mid-calf. The homespun cotton shirts were cinched around the middle with beaded belts, and had long, billowing sleeves. She cocked an eyebrow at Danu, and jibed, "I'd like to see your chances of staying in them more than fifteen minutes once Tor got a look at you."

Laughing, Danu returned, "Like Kali wouldn't be all over you, too!"

Whit threw an arm around Danu's shoulders, giving a quick hug. "How'd we get so lucky?"

Danu fell silent, the mirth abruptly leaving her freckled face.

"We'll find a way back," Whit told her, giving her a gentle, reassuring squeeze before she let go.

Danu glanced up at her, her bright blue eyes unsure, as she followed Whit to the feast tables. They picked up the wooden plates and utensils as they joined the line.

"This looks hand carved," Danu commented, fingering the two-pronged fork she held.

Whit nodded, surveying the food. A huge platter of what looked like roast venison was surrounded by pottery bowls of mashed sweet potatoes and gravy. Next to this were platters of steamed trout, loaves of baked bread, and bowls of buttered yellow and green squash. Nearby, a large wooden tub held fresh baby-leafed spinach, graced with pine nuts and small wild strawberries. Whit squinted at the small pottery dishes beside the spinach, each filled with varying shades of pale liquid. She decided they must be salad dressing.

A warm, womanly body suddenly inserted herself between Whit and Danu, and Whit looked down into Kate Ferguson's brown eyes. "This one is mine. Honey-mustard based," Kate murmured, gesturing to one of the little pots. "Flavored with dill from my own herb garden."

Danu immediately reached for the spoon, and ladled some of Kate's dressing over her salad. Whit tried the unknown bluish mixture right beside it.

Unexpectedly, Kate slipped a hand around Whit's upper arm and with a firm tug, pulled Whit out of the line. Danu, preoccupied by the tempting food spread before her, continued to move along the table, helping herself.

Whit eyed Kate. *Now what? She looks . . . scared.*

"Use any dressing but that one, Major," Kate whispered. "Put the plate down on the table and leave it."

Whit asked quietly, "Why?"

Kate gave her a quick, exasperated glance. "Do it," she hissed.

When Whit didn't obey, Kate huffed, "Suit yerself, then. But don't blame us fer what bein' so ornery earns ya."

Abruptly, Kate moved away, easing into the crowd of women behind them. Whit tore her gaze from the woman's retreating form and uncertainly examined the innocuous green leaves on her plate. Dressing caught the leaping light of the bonfire and gave an enticing gleam. Sensing someone else approaching from her right, Whit turned and found Jamie Rexrode. Without a word, Jamie took Whit's plate from her hand and replaced it with an identical plate of food. The only difference was the ungarnished baby spinach.

"Tell me why?" Whit asked, trying to appear reasonable.

Jamie glowered at her, then as if embarrassed, stepped closer and said in a voice so quiet, Whit could barely hear her, "There's a fertility rite tonight."

Perplexed, Whit replied, "And?"

"Everyone here but you and yer buddy knows to leave the blueberry dressin' alone unless ya got a wish to try fer a child." Jamie gave a brief sigh. When Whit remained clueless, staring at her, Jamie gave an impatient gesture with her free hand. "It makes ya . . . frisky."

Whit's eyes moved to the plate Jamie gripped. "The dressing's an aphrodisiac?"

There was a pause, then making a face, Jamie muttered, "If that means 'it makes ya frisky,' then yeah."

Taking a moment to peer around her, Whit confirmed an observation she had made when she and Jamie had strode through the village in mid-morning. "There's only women here." Her gaze swiveled back to Jamie. "How do you handle procreation?"

Danu joined them, obviously catching the end of Whit's sentence. "I've got a bunch of questions, too."

Whit looked over at bright blue eyes, alive with curiosity.

"Why is the land so green here? How'd you escape the environmental holocaust that's hit most of Elysium? How is it you've obviously pushed the Regs out of here? What kind of government is running things—republic, tribal council, clan chief? Or is your grandma, Irene Rexrode, some kind of warrior Queen?" Danu took a bite from the biscuit she held. Around the food, she blurted, "And where are the men?"

Wide-eyed with amazement, Jamie turned to Whit. Simultaneously, they both broke into loud laughter.

Rolling her eyes, Danu watched them, continuing to munch on her biscuit. At last Jamie regained some of her composure and slapped the redhead on the back, as she asked Whit, "Is she always like this?"

Whit grinned at Danu, nodding.

"Hey," Danu said calmly, as if deciding she had to defend herself, "you have to ask if you want to learn anything."

"Yer damn right," Jamie agreed, grinning at Danu. "You must be pretty smart by now, huh?"

Danu threw a quick, anxious look at Whit, and Whit cleared her throat, murmuring, "You'd be surprised." However, Jamie was turned by then, searching the crowd around them, and she missed the exchange.

"There's Granma," Jamie said. "Let's go eat with her. She'll decide what you need to know about our ways here in Seneca."

They followed Jamie through the boisterous women that formed the fringes of the crowd watching the dancers. Ahead, Whit could see a group of older women sitting on a raised platform, eating casually from plates on their laps. Most of them were leaning back on firm-looking shocks of straw, surveying the crowd before them like satisfied gentry.

Less regal accommodations, but don't they look just like the Isis Council, Whit mused.

As Whit, Danu and Jamie approached the raw plywood steps of the platform, several women in the crowd seemed to recognize Whit and moved impulsively toward her. One touched her shoulder, saying fervently, "God bless you. You saved my Becky." On Whit's other side, another grasped her hand. "Thank you. Anything we have is yours. Our Laney made it home cuzza you."

Embarrassed, Whit gestured toward Jamie. "It was *her* plan."

The two mothers openly scoffed at this, seemingly well aware of Whit's attempt to shift their attention. All the same, they each embraced Jamie with heartfelt emotion, thanking her, too. Hearing the spontaneous interaction, other women nearby made their way over, shifting forward one by one to shake hands. Bemused, Whit found grateful, slightly awestruck eyes on her. More and more women closed in, reaching out with gentle fingers, making contact with any part of Whit they could reach. Whit realized they were touching her as if she were a totem, a palpable symbol of some spirit force, or maybe just good luck.

As the press of women around them increased, Jamie took Whit's arm and pulled her toward the stairs. Whit instinctively reached behind her and grabbed Danu's hand, tugging her after them. They climbed the steps in a rush, then passed by the older women seated there to a place near Irene Rexrode.

Peering up at Whit suspiciously, the Chief of Seneca asked, "You some kind of politician or somethin'?"

"Sure," Danu piped up. "She's the—"

"Danu," Whit said quietly, the voice of command clear even to her own ears.

With a sharp click of teeth, Danu shut her mouth in midsentence.

"I'm a pilot," Whit told the Chief.

Irene Rexrode's sharp blue eyes stared hard at Danu, then moved back to Whit. "Well, you sure got a presence, Miss I'm-A-Pilot. And you work a crowd like a moonshiner with a wagon load of jugs."

"Is that what's in those jugs?" Danu asked, looking down at some women by the platform edge who were sharing an earthenware quart container. "White lightning?"

Grateful for the distraction Danu was providing, Whit broke the locked regard she'd been in with Chief Rexrode. Glancing over her shoulder at the young redhead, she wondered aloud, "White what? Where do you pick up this arcane stuff?"

Danu looked exasperated. "I read. You know—there's a ton of stuff on the comline."

Addressing her granddaughter, Irene said, "Appears we need to get us a jug up here. Maybe it'll make for a more sociable parley." Obediently, Jamie went to the edge of the stage and called across the crowd.

On some unseen signal, several women who had been lounging near the Chief suddenly stood up and moved away. Irene gestured to the open space around her. "Set a spell, why don'tcha."

Danu moved to Whit's side and raised her eyebrows, looking for direction. With a slight nod, Whit gave it. Danu settled down, cross-legged, two meters from Chief Rexrode. When Whit moved to sit next to Danu, Irene said flatly, "You by me, Major."

For a moment, Whit considered refusing her. The masked tension in the air around them fairly crackled. To Whit, and to everyone else close enough to overhear Irene, it was openly apparent that the Chief was asserting her dominance. Then Whit found Danu's wide-eyed gaze on her. Whit forced herself to take a deep breath and detach from the power play for just a moment.

There's one priority here. Getting us home in one piece, Whit told herself. *It won't do me any good to get into a pissing match with this Elder like I did with Medusa.*

A vision danced unexpectedly through her mind, as she recalled an episode a few months back.

She and Kali were alone in their private suite in the Leader's House, chatting in the early morning as they dressed, each of them readying for the full schedule before them. The bright April sunshine shone through the long window nearby, and Kali was teasing Whit her about her bristling annoyance with General Medusa.

"You don't get along because you're too much alike," Kali remarked. "You both want to be in charge, and neither of you wants to compromise."

"That is not true," Whit returned, trying not to let her voice show her indignation.

She was a bit hurt and very surprised that Kali wasn't immediately siding with her. Whose partner was she, anyway?

As if she sensed the way Whit was bristling, Kali came over and kissed her cheek, then went into the closet, searching for something.

Whit sat down on the bed, pulling on her boots, and nursing her pout.

Kali's voice floated out of the closet. "You two are like roosters strutting around the barnyard, Tomyris." And then she walked out, a red scarf pinned on the top of her hair like a comb, and bobbing her head as she imitated in quick succession Medusa's brisk, compact step, and Whit's slightly rolling swagger. She mimicked both so perfectly that the resemblance was unmistakable.

A loud laugh popped out of Whit, utterly overwhelming her bruised ego.

Kali continued to sail around the room, imitating her two roosters, and Whit laughed helplessly until tears filled her eyes. Then, Kali strolled up to her, leaned down and gave her a real kiss, rewarding her.

"There's the Leader I know," Kali had whispered, then kissed her again.

The memory made Whit smile.

Warily, Irene Rexrode asked, "What's so funny?"

Whit stepped gracefully to the Chief's side and sank down beside her. "Us." She leaned closer, and said, "I'm not planning on being here long, Chief. And I'm going to need your help to get out of Elysium." She held out her right hand, palm facing up. "Can we be allies, if not friends?"

Irene leaned forward. "You Freelanders gonna run out on us like ya did back in 2010? Just hightail it on out when the going gets tough?"

Whit straightened and withdrew her hand, her jaw tightening.

Irene raised her voice. "Leavin' us to face the Regs!"

"We have our own problems with Regs," Whit muttered.

Irene spoke right over Whit's words. "Leavin' us to the likes of a corrupt Procurator like Fowler—settin' himself up like a king and takin' everything—our crops, our livestock, even our *children*—away from us!" With an ugly laugh that had no humor in it, Irene finished. "That the kind of alliance you off'rin'? Cause if it is—we don't want it."

Whit said evenly, "Freelanders didn't run out on Elysium." She kept her eyes on the flashing blue ones beside her. "Elysians drove Americans out. It was leave or die for the Unwanteds."

Irene reared back and gave Whit an exaggerated scan. "And how are you an Unwanted? A rich whitewoman!"

Danu scrambled to her feet. "Just a damn minute!"

"Danu," Whit sighed. "Don't bother. The Regs shut down any teaching of herstory eight decades ago."

Ignoring her, Danu moved to the edge of the platform in order to stand before Irene Rexrode. "Whit's great-grandparents weren't even from this part of the continent! They lived in Seattle! They

106

ditched their identities and escaped into the Snoqualmie National Forest in 2010, hiding out with groups of people the New Order was already targeting. My people did the same—hiding up in the forest around Mount Hood. Teachers, nurses, attorneys, news reporters, anyone with any education or the backbone to stand up to the racist propaganda. There were all kinds of races, too, and bands of lesbians and gay men—all up there in the deep woods, trying to be invisible."

"Livin' like us, ya mean," Irene Rexrode commented with a dismissive sneer.

"Just like you—but we didn't stay in the woods," Danu stated.

"I don't care ta hear this," Irene said coolly.

"Why not?" Danu demanded, her face red with anger. "This is what happened to the rest of us! This is the herstory that went on while you all pretty much knuckled under for the next eighty-odd years!"

"I want to hear it, Granma," Jamie called.

Danu cast a quick gaze around at the Elders on the platform. "I think most of you can guess what happened. The Second Civil War erupted and the New Order seized control of the United States. All of a sudden the people hiding out in the woods were rebels, whether they wanted to be or not. They knew that once the reverends and procurators and tribunes got control of the West, they'd do the same thing they were already doing in the East. The Regs would search out anyone they thought dangerous, and make them just disappear, the way they'd already made so many disappear in the East.

"To save themselves and their way of life, our ancestors formed a militia. They got themselves ready, stockpiling weapons and gathering herds of horses, and training to survive. When the United States died and Elysium was born, they were still one of a bunch of ragtag bands squatting in the mountains. Then the Regs sent a missile with a hydrogen bomb into the Western Resistance army that was gathering in Las Vegas, and that big, photo-electromagnetic Border went up. In the years afterward, we were basically left outside of the Border to die.

"AGH decimated the West, and civilization collapsed. There were packs of rogue gangs, thieving from and killing anyone who managed to dodge the plague, but our ancestors managed to thrive. They built a colony about twenty miles north of the mass grave that Seattle became. Against all odds, their numbers grew. Through word of mouth people heard about a little town called Artemis, and came from all over the West to join them."

Sweeping her gaze over the older Amazon women around them, seeing them all avidly listening, Danu suddenly came to herself and stepped back.

"Don't fall off your stage, Elizabeth Cady Stanton," Whit commented mildly.

Danu glanced over her shoulder and was astonished to see that she had attracted a wider audience. The women of Seneca had gathered around the platform, and were staring at her, all intent on hearing what she was saying. For a moment, Danu swayed as she nearly over-balanced on the edge of the plywood floorboards, then with an awkward little hop, regained her place. Someone down below tossed up a jug, and surprised, Danu caught it.

"Take a pull—ya earned it, Bard!"

Laughing with the rest of the crowd, Danu brought the jug over to Jamie.

In the lively half-light of the bonfire, the women and children of Seneca were crowding around the platform, their faces eager and intent. "Tell us some more!" one shouted. "Tell us how ya'll in Freeland survived!" another chorused. Then one clear woman's voice lifted, calling, "The Regs told us they had nuked the West, that it was all gone. But then Baubo came and told us it was a lie. She told us you were alive and free!"

Whit turned on Irene Rexrode. "Baubo was here?!" she demanded.

After a moment's hesitation, Irene made a quick nod.

Astounded, Whit and Danu traded a glance, then Whit asked Irene, "She told you she was from Freeland?"

Her gaze steady, Irene replied, "Baubo kept nothing from me."

The hair on Whit's neck prickled. *What a strange way to answer the question.*

Jamie finished a pull from the jug, then leaned around Irene and told Whit, "She first came through here about fifteen years ago."

Raising her eyebrows, Jamie looked at Irene, as if for permission. Irene eyed Whit warily, then feigned boredom with a negligent shrug.

Jamie continued. "Baubo was our first witch. All the healing arts since taught to the apprentices that followed . . . well, they all came from her." The woman cast a wistful smile over to the stairs where Kate stood, looking somber. "Kate was a 'lil thing when Baubo picked her out as a talent. Even now, Baubo is revered among us, for she gave us the potion that keeps off the plague."

"She vaccinated you against AGH?" Danu asked, looking even more astonished than she had a few moments earlier.

"Yeah," Jamie answered. "And taught us how to make the potion to protect those as yet unborn." Jamie glanced again at Irene, and received another stoic shrug. "I've since found out that Baubo passed on knowledge of the potion wherever she found rebels holed up, all over the Appalachians. Now, while the Regs, the procurators, and all them fine, privileged families in them high-walled Elysian cities are afraid to have sex with anything but children, and their clans are dyin' out, we rebels are out here healthy and steadily multiplying. Our numbers are growin', year by year." Jamie narrowed her eyes. "We'll take our freedom back yet."

"Tell us about Freeland," a voice from the crowd called.

Whit looked at Irene Rexrode. "Let's make a bargain. We'll tell you all about Freeland, if you tell us why the grass and trees are so green, and the sky is so blue. Why the water is pure here. Why I haven't seen an Elysian aircraft since I flew over Shenandoah Mountain."

Irene regarded Whit for a long quiet moment, then stated, "Agreed."

Quickly, Whit gave Danu a grin and a little wave. "Go on, you're the one with the encyclopedic memory."

Still standing before the crowd at the edge of the platform, Danu reddened. She was slightly embarrassed now that her passionate anger had faded. She glanced toward the milling audience of women beneath the platform, then asked Whit, "What should I tell them?"

"Give them our Declaration of Independence," Whit answered simply.

"Oh," Danu replied. Anxiously, her eyes swept the crowd, until she noticed women hoisting small children up onto their shoulders. An expectant hush had fallen as they waited for her to speak.

And Danu realized all at once that what they were listening for was hope. Hope for a life where Regs weren't trying to steal their children for service as sex slaves. Hope for a life where there could be medical knowledge beyond what little had been gifted to them by a roving Wiccan over a decade ago. Hope for a life where they didn't have to hide their homes and crops deep in the wildwood, in the meadows of a sunken mountain hollow, in order to be left in peace.

She heard Whit, Jamie, and occasionally Irene Rexrode speaking in soft voices behind her, already trading information.

Drawing a deep breath, Danu pitched her voice to carry, as she delivered the words she had first heard while sitting in her mother's lap, many years ago.

"We hold these truths to be self-evident: Everyone on earth is born equal and born free."

The crowd murmured appreciatively.

"It is our right to worship as we wish, in a land where government and religion are forever separate; our right to read and write the books we choose, to pursue the education we desire; our right to choose the work we will do for our living and keep the profit of our labors. It is our right to hold title to and to work our own land; our right to keep our families safe and well. In Freeland, we belong to ourselves, and to our fellow Freelanders when they need us." Danu paused, making eye contact with her audience, as her mother always did at this place in the recitation. "We are the summit, the democratic ideal that mankind has been aspiring to throughout the ages. It is our duty to protect liberty and freedom in order to ensure it for those who come after us." Tears overtook Danu, as she met the shining eyes of the sixty-odd women before her. "For only in preserving our freedom is there hope for the freedom of all women and men. And only in cherishing equal justice and liberty for all, is there justice and liberty for each of us."

A long breathless silence reigned, causing Danu to lift a hand and nervously grip the beaded belt around her waist. Then a joyous yell went up, and another soon after, and then the mountain meadow was filled with the roar of cheering voices.

Surprised, Danu spun and sought Whit's reaction.

Whit lifted her head from her huddled conference with the Rexrodes, and winked.

Later that night, women began pairing off, either engaging in complex dances with a partner they eyed in that certain way, or wandering into the shadows with a well-loved spouse. Some were gambling with knuckle bones that were carved into dice. Some were daring their friends to wrestling matches.

Amused, Whit watched Danu come out of a reel line, then duck away from the affectionate hug of an overly exuberant partner. *Well, she's a great dancer. Guess the locals are appreciative.*

Glancing over at Jamie, she found the Amazon's blue eyes watching Danu, too, and was surprised to note that they were lit with a rare smile. *Why isn't she dancing with Kate?* Whit wondered. Then looking around for her, Whit couldn't find the young healer.

Eventually, Whit excused herself from Chief Rexrode's little group on the platform, saying she was tired and needed to get some more rest. She descended the stairs, caught Danu's attention and gestured. Then they both said a polite good night to the Chief and her cronies, waved to Jamie and took their leave.

111

As she walked along the dusty road in the dark, Danu yawned, then commented, "That was fun."

Whit gave a low chuckle. "I think the woman you were dancing with wanted to get to know you better—a lot better."

"Mmm," Danu mumbled, giving Whit a slight push. "Turned her down."

Whit bumped her shoulder into Danu's, chuckling.

"What did you find out?" Danu asked, serious now.

Whit took a quick look around, reassuring herself that they were alone. "I found out that Seneca has been an active community, ensconced in this hollow for the past forty-two years. They were living hand-to-mouth until Baubo found them in 2070. She gave them a primitive, but obviously highly effective variation of the AGH serum, taught them some basic medicine, some animal husbandry and crop rotation skills, and they've pretty much flourished ever since. She also helped them design a flour mill, then helped them build it over a falls downstream so a waterwheel could turn the big grindstone for them. The mill has changed their fortunes. They barter the flour to other rebel bands located throughout the Alleghenies—a pack train system set up by the clans transports their goods to one another."

"Well, it's still pre-Renaissance," Danu commented. "A merchant class emerging from the farmers and hunters. They've regressed about five hundred years."

"But they're still a functioning community, and a free one that has effectively dropped out of the society they reside in. Gutsy bunch."

Danu considered that, then nodded. "True."

Whit went to shove her hands in her pockets, and was disconcerted to find yet again that the deerskin leggings had no pockets. She folded her hands behind her back instead. "About four miles downstream there's a lumber mill, also water-powered, built from some detailed drawings Baubo gave the Sponaugle clan when their chief was up here for a full moon feast."

"What about children? This is an all woman clan, so how do they have children when I haven't seen a man yet?"

Whit smiled. "Nothing so advanced as our parthenogenesis, little sister. They have an aphrodisiac brew that they concoct and share on nights designated for fertility rites. A woman who wants to try for a child has some of the whoopie-juice, then goes off into the hills along certain designated trails in search of menfolk from neighboring clans. These clans also benefited from Baubo's 'potion' and are also AGH-free. They tell me fellas stake tents in picturesque secluded locations and hang out on pre-arranged nights, hoping for the opportunity to spread their seed."

In the moonlight, Whit saw Danu's broad smile. "Whoopie-juice?"

"Yep."

"It's like the Beltane or Midsummer rites in pre-Christian England."

"Tonight was Midsummer," Whit replied.

Excitedly, Danu informed Whit, "Did you know this part of old America was settled by the English and Scotch-Irish about four hundred years ago? They brought their customs with them, and then were isolated here by the mountains, separated from what was happening in the rest of America. Heck, even the First Civil War didn't make much of a dent here because it was too hard for either side's armies to trek over the terrain. These people were still living some of the old ways when the Second Civil War came. That's why there was a uilleann pipe, a tin whistle, and Celtic drums playing tonight. That's why some of those songs were jigs and reels, and . . ." Abruptly, she fell silent as her mind moved swiftly, jumping from one topic to another.

Used to this phenomenon with Danu, Whit waited. Danu was a Think-Tank creation. Her DNA had been tinkered with during the parthenogenetic process, basted in specialized enzymes that allowed her intellect, her memory and even her kinesthetic sense to be engineered to a super-human capacity. When Jamie had made the joke earlier about Danu being so smart from asking all those questions, Whit and Danu had both known that Danu's penchant for asking questions wasn't the half of it. Danu had a photographic memory and total recall of nearly anything she had ever read, seen, or heard.

In a wondering voice, Danu said to Whit, "That woman I was dancing with . . . she'd had a lot to drink. She kind of whispered to me that they have a powerful witch, living up in a cave above this village." Danu scanned the ridge that ran along the back of the town, then nodded her head toward the highest part of the wooded mountainside. "Up there."

Whit squinted at the place Danu indicated.

"She said every once in a while, one of them gets asked to go up there," Danu elaborated. "They are asked to 'give' themselves to the witch." Danu touched her head, tentatively scratching at the scab on her wound. "She wouldn't really explain what that meant, but I got the impression it was some kind of sexual act."

They reached the healer's cabin and stood in front of the building, neither of them ready to go inside yet.

"Jamie didn't tell me that," Whit admitted. "But she did tell me that the witch made 'a magic wall' that filters the wind and rain. The wall keeps out the industrial waste that's poisoning the rest of Elysium. That's why everything is so fertile and green, why the sky is blue." Lowering her voice, Whit confessed uneasily, "She says it's also why the Reg aircraft can't get in, and why your Peregrine went down. Nothing that flies through the magic wall can stay aloft. As the aircraft passes through this unseen wall, the wings and the fuselage are covered with some invisible flight deterrent—I'm guessing a massive ionic charge—that just compounds exponentially as the flight continues, until the craft is forced down."

"Wow," Danu breathed. "The Regs can't control this place without aircraft—it's too mountainous and remote from their power base at Andrews Air Force Base. And from what I heard tonight, the underground resistance all over Elysium is growing, because AGH is radically diminishing Reg troop strength. Seems a lot of areas of Elysian society that were supposed to be protected from the plague weren't as protected as everyone thought."

Her brows furrowed as she put the pieces together, Whit offered, "The Amazons are using classic guerrilla tactics to keep the Regs off-balance every time the Regs send a search-and-engage patrol this way. There's a ten-mile perimeter of scout outposts, and the old state highways the Regs favor are watched constantly. The Amazons have passed on their tricks to neighboring clans and they in turn have passed them on farther still. This whole country is in the midst of an insurrection that might just end the New Order." Amazed at this new knowledge, Whit ran a hand through her hair. "We may be in the most dangerous place in Elysium."

Danu faced her. "The witch seems to be the key to everything that's going on. We ought to go check out that cave while everyone in the village is either passed out, making love or still at the party."

"What if she's there?" Whit challenged. "Do we really want to meet this woman?"

Gazing at the cliff above them, Danu answered, "I think I've already met her." Seeing Whit's concern, Danu quickly added, "When they brought me in last night."

"What did she look like?" Whit asked.

"Couldn't really see her face. She wore a hood. White hair, gnarly hands. I think she was . . . old."

Relieved that Danu had just provided a description about as far removed as humanly possible from the lovely, young Arinna Sojourner, Whit felt her jaw unclench. "Okay. Let's go."

Danu led the way to a well-traveled trail that curved out the back of the village and up into the wooded hills. They were silent as they walked, climbing the dirt walkway as it steadily grew steeper. After about twenty minutes, the trees were sparser. Then the land flattened out into a broad plateau. Whit noticed a collection of painted runes on the wall-like surface of the mountainside that flanked them, but didn't know what the symbols meant. When she touched Danu's arm and pointed to them, Danu pronounced, "Strength, luck, happiness."

In a short time, they approached the wide entrance. The cave was a dark mouth in the mountainside, and the strong moonlight around them didn't seem to reach very far inside the cavern.

"This seems so familiar," Danu said, her voice odd.

"What do you mean?"

Danu seemed as if she were trying to come up with a rational answer and for some reason just couldn't. "I don't know." Impatient with herself, Danu stepped into the lead and walked toward the entrance.

"Whoa," Whit told her, catching her arm. "We'll need a light to go in there."

As if the speaking of the need caused the need to be met, Whit's eyes suddenly discerned a faint glow beyond the first bend in the tunnel ahead of them. "Well, I guess that problem just got solved."

Cautiously, she edged forward past Danu then made her way into the cave. Beyond the bend she found the source of the illumination, a torch in a sconce. Whit removed the torch, electing to carry it with them. Danu came to her side and with slow and careful steps, they moved deeper into the cave.

After a short walk, the tunnel opened up into a vast and glowing chamber. Torches were set in the walls all around them, and a smoky haze drifted up, being drawn to a natural chimney somewhere above them where the high roof emptied into the night sky. Shimmering, white-streaked stalagmites and stalactites filled the first portion of the cavern, obscuring a clear view of the rest of the chamber. Then they came into an open area. Half the space was filled with a wide black pool of eerily still water. Whit squinted, but couldn't see into the dark where the pool backed up into the farthest visible reaches of the cave.

Intrigued now, Whit turned to what appeared to be a living quarters off to the right, and moved that way. She touched disbelieving fingers to the long antique table that gleamed with polish. An arrangement of matching chairs surrounded the table. It struck Whit that the furniture could have been borrowed from some exquisitely appointed local manor. A series of two-meter-high bookshelves flanked the walls in the farthest part of that section. Whit walked over and read the titles, finding all manner of old printed paper volumes, from herbology to medicine to mechanical engineering. She examined the little cot nearby, the cook fire, the large chest with the padlock that threaded the latch. All of the items were clean and well-cared for, all of them looking as if they were in current use.

She turned to look for Danu and found her across the chamber in the shadows. As Whit walked closer, she saw that Danu was staring at a pair of chains that dangled from two separate pulleys mounted in the lower ceiling of the section. Leather cuffs dangled from the ends of the chains. There was a small metal pan sitting over a little stove-like arrangement, and the strong smell of incense. Farther away, a large stone slab fit into a niche in a corner. It was obviously a place where some kind of ritual played out on various occasions.

Whit touched one of the cuffs and caused the chain to swing. It seemed to break Danu out of her trance, for she started, then blushed until she was crimson.

"Looks like no one's home," Whit said.

"Looks like," Danu echoed, her eyes drifting to the darkness that hung over one side of the pool in front of them.

Whit shot a scrutinizing gaze that way, saw nothing, then contemplated Danu. "You look tired, my friend. Let's go. Besides, something tells me Chief Rexrode would take great exception to us snooping around up here."

With a nod, Danu took a last look around, then followed Whit as she led the way out of the chamber. They were in the tunnel, close enough to the large mouth of the cave for the moonlight to guide them when the torch sputtered a few times and then went out completely.

Whit dropped it to the side of the cave entrance, remarking, "I want to meet this witch."

Chapter 6

"Hey," a voice close by said. "You're snoring."

Kali started awake. She blinked groggily several times before she realized that she was lying on her back staring up into a gray dawn. She moved her head and found Tor standing by her side, shoulder-length dark hair lifting in the breeze. With a smirk, the woman sat beside her in the flattened field grass, munching on something.

"Found some blueberries," Tor announced. She inclined her head toward the far side of the meadow. "Foraged around during the perimeter check." Her fingers swept into the mess kit pail in her lap, and more berries disappeared into her mouth.

Feeling extremely slow-witted, Kali looked at the high grass a few feet away, blocking her view of the direction Tor had indicated. She sleepily noted the amber glow in the fog. Cold, damp air caressed her face, the only exposed part of her, and Kali shivered reflexively. She snuggled deeper into her insulated sleep sack. A cacophony of birdsong emerged from the deep wood that stood a distance away, surrounding their camp site.

"Mmph," Kali mumbled, feeling helpless against a great weight of exhaustion.

Yesterday's adventure had taxed her, and she really felt it now. *If Whit were here*, Kali thought, *she'd be getting mad at me for pushing things.* She smiled slightly at that, and then the reason why she was here, asleep in a field on the crest of a mountain, came rushing to the front of her mind. *Get up*, she silently exhorted herself. *Find her.*

Kali pulled open the velcro edge of the sack, wriggled free and clambered to her feet.

"No rush," Tor said, her dark eyes compassionate.

Am I that easy to read? Kali gave a tired, grateful smile, then dipped a hand into Tor's pail and snagged some berries for herself.

Within twenty minutes they had eaten, stowed their gear, and mounted the motorcycle again. They crossed the meadow, brushing through the wet grass, before plunging downward into the forest again. Hundreds of fine-needled ferns lay before them, their slender forms bending under the night's dampness. Tor carefully steered the bike down the slope and they dropped lower into the thick valley mist. Moisture gathered in tiny beads on their helmets, faces, and clothing. They passed thousands of delicate spider webs, each strand glistening with watery diamonds. Any glimpse of the land beyond the trees was lost in the drift of the low clouds still clinging to the hills. The cycle bounced over slippery rocks and crumbled leaf matter, finally rolling out of the wood and into the lowest part of the valley. Kali thought she heard water rushing somewhere on the other side of the wooded lane, but couldn't see the stream. In the almost poetic perfection of a rosy dawn fog, they once more took up their journey along the broken macadam of what was left of Route 33.

Leaning against Tor's back, Kali gazed over her friend's shoulder, realizing she was beginning to feel invigorated. *Maybe today is the day we'll find them.*

She reached inside and called up the Sight, then unfurled the awareness like a lazy cat extending a paw after a ball of yarn. In her mind's eye, a ghostly picture formed. Indicating the kilometers between her and the vision, the colors were not strong. She was testing the limit of her Sight, she knew, and if she didn't stop within the next few seconds she would suffer a skull-splitting headache for hours. But she recognized the well-made, handsome form below her, lying asleep in a rough log cabin in a green mountain hollow. A burst of joy rushed through Kali.

It will be so good to see and hold you again, Love. I'm coming. You must know by now that I'm coming.

Whit abruptly sat up in bed, gasping.

Anxiously, she cast her gaze around the dimly lit cabin. She heard birds—a clatterous racket of birds. Instantly she recognized the cabin and knew she was in the healer's quarters, in Seneca. On the other side of the room, she could just make out Danu's still form in the darkness, as the young woman slept peacefully on her cot.

Whit frowned, going over the dream, thinking of how real it had seemed.

She had seen Kali, riding behind Tor on a Freelandian dirt bike, the two of them cruising down a pocked strip of what was once a paved road, looking like a pair of eight-year-olds pretending to be intrepid explorers. Disconcerted, Whit thought hard on what she had seen, recalling the green-leaf deciduous forest that flanked the road on either side and the steep slopes of a narrow valley.

"She can't be here," Whit whispered, feeling a wave of alarm.

She had never been psychic. Outside of some basically sound instincts for self-preservation when she was flying an aircraft or engaged in hand-to-hand combat, she knew she was just a warrior grunt with a tongue glib enough to get her elected Leader of a colony. Somehow, though, she was certain that what she had dreamed was real. She also knew that the dark, oppressive feeling that accompanied the vision could not be good.

"Danu!" she called. "Get up!"

120

Used to the sudden awakenings of boot camp and flight school during the past winter, Danu surged out of the bed. She saw Whit pulling on the deerskin leggings and tunic from the night before, and Danu reached for her own set, hastily dressing. "What's happened?" Danu ventured, her voice rough with sleep.

"The worst thing possible!" Whit muttered cryptically.

A few minutes later, Whit and Danu were running down the dirt path that served as Seneca's main street, looking for Irene Rexrode's cabin in the golden fog of dawn. A scattering of odd cottages and homes lined the road, but they easily found it, largely because the Chief, Jamie and a band of Amazons were congregating in front of the two-story log house. The women were carrying rifles and crossbows and were busily stowing packets of food and ammunition in the slouch bags that draped across their shoulders.

As Whit and Danu slowed to a walk, it was apparent that Jamie was receiving instructions from her grandmother. Jamie followed the gaze of several Amazons and turned toward them.

Annoyed, Irene pushed by Jamie, eyeing Whit fiercely. "Scout just brought word that there's a company of Regs about ten miles east of here. 'Pears they're searchin' fer someone. Wonder who."

Whit found herself feeling chagrined. How could she ask these people for another favor when she was already causing them nothing but trouble?

Irene nodded. "Yeah. We all know who." She pulled a pipe and a leather pouch from a pocket, filled the pipe bowl with crumbled brown tobacco, and stuck the pipe in the side of her mouth. "Well, the clans ain't gonna stand fer them Regs runnin' loose in our hills. We're all massin' two ridges over." She peered up into Whit's face. "You up fer a fight?"

Whit hesitated, unwilling to get drawn into a distraction.

Before she could speak, however, she overheard the scout at Jamie's side, eagerly continuing her report. "And hey, I saw the dad-blamedest thing. I saw a coupla women a-ridin' a motorcycle—and the engine didn't make a sound—how 'bout that?"

Whit felt as if someone had punched her in the stomach. "Where?" she demanded.

"They was followin' Old Route 33, headin' into what's left of Elkins, purty as ya please, lookin' fer all the world like theys out o' one of them old liberry books . . ."

Exhaling sharply, Whit asked, "Was one of them blonde, long hair—really pretty?"

"Yeah—a yeller ponytail was blowin' out from under her helmet. The other was one of them Asians." The scout cocked her head at Whit, looking genuinely puzzled. "I thought all them Asians was gone. The way the Regs and the Reverends tell it, all the non-whites was killed off in the cleansing a'fore the Great Rift."

"Oh, shit," Danu muttered, her eyes wide.

Whit told Irene, "The blonde is my partner, Kali. The other woman, Tor, is of Japanese heritage, and is Danu's . . ." Whit glanced at Danu, uncertain.

Danu cleared her throat, and asserted, "Future partner."

"They come to fetch you home," Jamie surmised.

Whit muttered, "Seems so, yeah."

"If they're travelin' Old Route 33," Irene said, "they're in harm's way. They're gonna cross paths with the Regs."

Swallowing hard, Whit stared into flint-like eyes. Then she grasped Irene's forearm. "Help me."

Her face unreadable, Irene held her gaze. Then, with a sigh, Irene slid a sideways look at Jamie.

A grin flashed. "Cavalry charge oughta do it."

"I won't lose good horses to grenade launchers and automatic weapons fire," Irene returned hotly. "We're savin' them horses for the Big Fight that's comin'."

Jamie returned quietly, "Granma, we'll flank them. With speed and surprise, we could send 'em runnin', like Old Stonewall did at Chancellorsville. We could sweep in, catch the Regs off-guard, get the women, then swing north and cut back through the shallows. No trail."

Irene grimaced unhappily, then aimed a steady gaze at Whit. "If we want ya'll to help us, we gotta help you—that it?"

Whit watched Irene. "I'll help you as much as I can, either way. But I have to get to Kali."

With a disinterested shrug, which did not disguise the understanding in her eyes, Irene turned to Jamie. "Go on—take a troop of thirty," she grumbled. "But I don't want one dead horse, Jamie Lynn, or I'll be takin' over that still ya got set up on the high hill."

With a huge grin, Jamie agreed. "We'll make ya proud, Granma." She turned to the rest and shouted, "Spread the word! Horse troop is goin' out!"

Some women ran off through the village, shouting, "Horse troop is headin' out!"

Jamie grabbed Whit and Danu by the shoulders. "C'mon, Freelanders!"

Whit and Danu joined the rest of the band, running up to and then clambering over a four-rail wood fence, then racing across the pasture behind Irene's cabin. Whit eyed the long, low building by the edge of the forest, wondering where they were going. As they neared the building, many of the Amazons slowed, giving long, calling whistles.

Horses that had been farther out in the field, dallying in the shade of the tree line, turned and came cantering toward them. In the low building, other equine profiles appeared in the open upper halves of stall doors; many began to nicker or bob their heads in greeting.

The band hurried into the building, into a large, cedar-planked room devoted to tack. In an organized rush, women grabbed the hand-tooled saddles and bridles and carried them outside. Whit picked up a saddle and examined the construction of leather and softened hemp, recognizing the basic design from her days as a cadet warrior when she'd been required to study nineteenth century U.S. Cavalry gear.

"How good are ya on a horse?" Jamie asked, coming up beside her.

"Good," Whit answered, not embellishing.

The confidence Whit felt seemed to reach Jamie, for the West Virginian smirked and returned, "You're good at a lot of stuff, aren'tcha?"

Anxious to get going, Whit shrugged and started toward the door. As they went, Jamie quickly draped a waterskin and a cloth bag over Whit's torso in a criss-cross of shoulder straps.

"And ya might be needin' this at some point," Jamie said. She pulled a small, leather shape from her slouch bag. Startled, Whit recognized her pilot emergency kit. Jamie stepped closer and shoved the kit into the slouch bag resting against Whit's side. Smiling mischievously, Jamie drew out the bundle of parachute line Whit had salvaged from the tree where Danu had landed, stowing it in Whit's slouch bag as well. "Good rope, that," she commented. "We'll get ya some rations before we ride out."

Then Jamie was steering her to a big bay horse Florey led up for her. Florey held the bridle while Whit set the small saddle on the blanket.

Whit was cinching the girth, when Florey interrupted her, commenting, "This 'un's got a bad habit."

Stepping closer to the bay, Florey smacked her flattened palm against the underside of the horse's belly. Air expelled from the animal in an outraged cough. The bay's head whipped around, and a foot stomped as the gelding eyeballed her tormenter accusingly. Florey cinched the girth to the proper tightness, telling the horse, "Ya won't be dumpin' no one on their ass today, Beauregard."

Suppressing a laugh, Whit thanked Florey, then swung up on the horse and settled herself. She'd learned how to ride as a warrior cadet, seventeen years ago. Though a few of the warrior academies in other city-colonies had dropped the requirement, horsemanship was still part of the curriculum at Artemis War College and Whit had loved the horse-based classes.

She leaned over and quickly adjusted the rope stirrups to her leg length, then spent a few minutes crooning sweet things to the horse, getting him used to her being at the other end of the reins. Finally, she took a deep breath and cleared her mind. She felt a smooth steadiness descending upon her, the prelude to battle.

A young girl came by, handing up a small, cloth sack. Whit opened the drawstring and peered inside, surprised to find a little net bag of strawberries, a chunk of jerky and some young string beans. Impressed with the healthy and portable meal, she dropped the ration sack in her slouch bag.

The rest of the Amazons were mounting up, keeping a tight rein on their horses as the animals picked up the edgy excitement of their riders. Whit moved Beauregard through the crowd, to where Danu sat astride a little brown mare. The young redhead was grim-faced, checking her laser pistol and then tucking it into her belt. She met Whit's gaze with a nervous glance, then looked away.

"You okay?" Whit asked quietly.

Danu gave a short nod. She wouldn't meet Whit's eyes, instead focusing on Jamie as she mounted a gray horse and grabbed an M-28 that someone handed up to her. The tawny-haired Colonel slid the rifle into a long, slim buckskin sleeve attached to her saddle's pommel and resting on her mount's withers. Seconds later, Jamie caught a flashing length of steel out of the air as another youngster ran by. Taking a closer look, Whit realized the girl was carrying old-fashioned sabers; the long blades were nestled in tarnished and battered scabbards with neat leather belts attached. The girl was tossing a saber up to each mounted woman she passed.

Jamie pulled her horse around, then unsheathed her saber, brandishing in a flashing arc as she called, "Recognize these old standbys, Whitaker? My Great-Great-Granny stole 'em from the War Between the States Museum over in Fredericksburg when the Great Rift was jes startin'. Ain't no sech thing as a relic these days!"

In response, the other women drew their sabers and swung them over their heads, yodeling and yipping. Whit felt a chill run down her back. These good, simple women were behaving the way warriors readying to shed blood had behaved since time immemorial.

The girl dashed past, throwing a saber to Whit, then to Danu, and Whit saw Danu's freckled face go startlingly white.

Realizing that this would be Danu's first ground battle, Whit felt a sudden burst of compassion for her. Dog-fighting in a jet was one thing, but it was merely a sterile, detached execution of tactics to take down another aircraft. Shooting at a man in hailing distance on Gaea's green earth was something else altogether. You saw the effect of the weapon you'd fired. You saw the man crumple and drop, or fly off to the side in that strange surrealistic way that instantly suggested a mortal wound. To compound matters, these preparations seemed to indicate that a cavalry charge with drawn sabers was likely.

Whit swallowed unhappily. Attacking a man with a saber was primal bloodletting. It was up close and personal; you saw every detail of your opponent: their height, physique, the expression on their face, the color of their eyes. You saw the slicing violence, the blood, the spilled intestines.

The stump of an arm.

A large rock took up residence in Whit's throat, choking her. Whit coughed, then said to Danu, "I want you to stay by me today. Understand?"

Danu finally looked at her, relieved gratitude in her eyes, then nodded again.

Ahead of them, Jamie put her saber away and ordered, "Two-by-two column on the Over-Ridge trail. After we leave the trail, stay close together and ride quiet. We're goin' over Spruce Mountain, weavin' through the stream beds of the high hills after Spruce, then goin' over Cheat Mountain. We'll form up in a line of attack in the woods southwest of Elkins."

Jamie looked down the line and pointed to Whit and Danu. "Hon'rable guests, I'd 'preciate it if you'd ride in the center of the troop."

With a wave of one arm, Jamie signaled for them to move out. She rode at the head of the group as they trotted onto the dirt path that led up into the tree-covered ridge.

Whit and Danu maneuvered their horses into the middle of the parade and they all rode into the bright, morning sunshine.

A cluster of villagers lined the trail, their faces anxious, waving goodbye. Children raced alongside the horses, calling wishes for good luck. Gradually, the band left the well-wishers behind and the trail became quiet but for the soft clop of horse hooves.

Both Danu and Whit rode in an uneasy silence. Whit found herself trying not to think about the fact that the person she loved most in the world was somewhere out there, cruising along on a motorcycle, with no viable defense against the roughly five hundred Elysian Regs searching the woods.

Set against a backdrop of emerald mountains, Elkins turned out to be another crumbling shell of a town, another little community whose brush with the plague was still written indelibly upon it.

Tor slowed the bike as she threaded a path around the potholes, heading up the hill and into the main street.

Rusted hulks of cars were amassed haphazardly in front of a moldering police station. Kali knew those cars had probably been parked there at the beginning of the disaster, during a frantic planning session; nine decades later the cars were still there. She realized it was a lingering proof of how quickly the plague had paralyzed the East.

A short ways down the main street, they passed the empty medical clinic, and were astounded by the dozens of disintegrating skeletons piled in the side yard. Tufted rags, the remnants of their clothes, were still clinging to odd bits of bone and fluttering like gruesome little flags. The skeletons were waiting for burial details that had sickened and died themselves before the grisly task of collecting and burning the bodies could begin.

The entire residential section of Elkins was a series of collapsed houses. Most of the homes had orange vinyl signs that warned QUARANTINE in big black letters, the signs still nailed to a wall by the front door. Kali knew there were skeletons there, too, inside and out of sight and never to be buried.

It all spoke of two things: the overwhelming ferocity of the AGH virus and help that never came.

AGH is still motile in Elysium, Kali thought wonderingly. *What's happened to the descendants of the people who once lived here? We've traveled nearly a hundred kilometers now, and we haven't seen a soul. Surely some of these poor people survived.*

Tor kept the bike moving and neither of them said a word, though Kali felt Tor shudder once, when they passed a child-sized skeleton lying by the road out of town.

Soon they were about a kilometer or two beyond the town. To the right, the morning sun had finally cleared the long forested ridge that was the southeast horizon. Kali squinted. The road ahead went through a long dark tunnel formed by tall and ancient trees. Leafy branches arched over the rough remnants of pavement and stony soil, the tree limbs extending high above like the beams of the Isis Cedar House. Tor slowed the cycle and dropped a foot down, using it to plant as she muscled a tight turn. Soon they were weaving smoothly around a series of sinkholes that seemed to emerge out of the deep shade when they were but a few meters away.

"You're good at this," Kali told Tor.

Tor turned her head a bit, while still managing to look forward. "Used to do road rallies as a kid."

"So you were a biker babe?"

Tor laughed at the joke. "Yeah. You girls up in Artemis, Isis and Boudica were big into the horse stuff. Down in Morgan we were crazy for motorcycles. Guess it makes sense, since that's how our forebears defended themselves against the gangs that came pouring out of L.A. during the Great Rift. Our great-great-grandmothers lived like nomadic tribes up in the San Gabriel Mountains and used ethanol-powered dirt bikes to stay out of reach of the bandits. There's a lot of tradition involved with learning to distill your own fuel and build and maintain your own ride."

Something ahead caught Kali's eye as she looked over Tor's shoulder. Then she saw it again: an odd glint of light among the sunlit trees on the other side of this shaded section of roadway.

"Tor, pull over," Kali said.

Immediately, Tor braked and headed for the side of the road. "What is it?"

Kali concentrated, letting her sixth sense sweep outward in an all-encompassing probe of the area roughly two hundred meters around them. Her Sight narrowed to a quick beam, landing on the sunlight that was reflecting from the barrel of an M-28 as a man marched close to the road. Her scope broadened and with a gasp of shock Kali realized that the woods around them were filled with men. Then the true horror hit her. They weren't just men. They were Regs and all of them heavily armed. She even caught the thoughts of several commanders who were idly thinking about the women they were looking for and what they would do with their prizes once they caught them.

This is a slave hunt.

"Tor, there's a huge group of Regs up ahead," Kali whispered to Tor. "We have to get off the road. Now."

"Which way should we go?"

As if a mapped route of least resistance unfurled in her head, Kali instinctively knew the answer. She pointed to the right. "Through there, straight up the ridge."

Decisively, Tor aimed the bike for a gap in the trees where the rhododendron bushes were low. The bike accelerated, bouncing across rough ground. They both instinctively ducked their heads as the cycle plunged past the outward splay of leaves and branches. There were several loud snaps as the small limbs gave way, then they were past the big bushes and churning past less hardy sister scrub. Kali glanced at the knee-high rhododendrons they were crashing through, thanking Gaea that not much could grow beneath the canopy of maples, oaks, and tulip trees here.

Gradually, the land began sloping upward. Tor leaned forward over the handlebars and Kali leaned with her, keeping contact with

Tor's back. They traveled uphill for several minutes, and past the trees to her left, Kali could see a winding trail threading down from the large ridge they were climbing.

And then, as if someone had dropped a bell jar over her, Kali suddenly felt her psychic senses blocked. Instinctively, she pushed, trying to get past whatever was obstructing her. When a mere push didn't work, she forced a rush of energy out in a half-angry, half-panicked reaction, and with a strange internal sputter, she felt the power fail.

The bike came up over an exposed ledge of slate, went airborne for about three seconds, and came down still on the ledge. There was a trickling stream of water, probably from a nearby spring, beneath the back tire, and the bike abruptly skidded sideways. Inhaling anxiously, Kali tightened her arms around Tor's waist. Tor leaned with the bike and gunned the engine. The bike righted, and they shot off the ledge.

They raced higher as the decibel squelch on the cycle kept the engine noise to a low hum. Kali was beginning to think they were going to make it. They broke into another copse of rhododendrons and Tor slowed the bike, trying to spare the impact damage to the machine. They crashed through branches, pushed past a large pile of leaf mulch and came to what was obviously a trail. Tor dropped a foot into the calf-high grass, balancing them as she stopped the bike.

Tor turned around in her seat. "Where to?" she asked.

Kali stared at her. Tor was breathing fast, and a sheen of sweat had broken out on her face, betraying the work she was doing. The dark eyes grew concerned. "Kali?"

"I—I don't know," Kali admitted. "My mage thing . . . it's gone, somehow," she confessed in a quiet rush. "I don't know what happened. I tried to push whatever's blocking me away and any power I had left just . . . fizzled out." She drew a shaky breath and finished. "I can't sense anything, Tor."

"Something blocked you?"

Kali nodded, unable to describe the stifled closed-in feeling that overcame her.

"Does it feel like the hormonal stuff you've been dealing with, or did it feel like what happened to you up at Hart's Pass?"

Amazed, Kali felt her mouth drop open. "Damn, it felt just like Hart's Pass." She shot a quick look around her, checking the innocuous forest scene. "But afterward, when I tried to overcome it, the Sight just punked out on me, like one of those typical hormonal episodes."

"Could be another mage blocked you first," Tor offered, making her own visual check of the area.

Kali felt a wave of panic. *Another mage?*

Tor nudged her with an elbow, interrupting her little breakdown. "Hey, take it easy. Let's focus on our immediate problem: getting out of here."

"What do you want to do?" Kali asked quietly.

"Too late to stay home, I guess," Tor answered, and Kali promptly thumped her on the back with a fist. "Ow!" Tor protested, laughing. "Quit that!"

"*You* quit it," Kali half-laughed. "C'mon! We're in trouble here!"

"Okay, okay. Just trying to lighten the mood. Don't know about you, but it helps me to think." Tor looked down the trail, where the land rose in the sweeping incline of a steep uphill climb. "Why don't we just keep heading in the same direction. East. That's where we want to go. That's where Danu and Whit are."

Kali took several deep breaths, trying to center. She reached deep within, tentatively trying to coax back to life the fine vibration she usually felt running just under the surface of her skin. She wanted so badly to feel that low, sensuous song. *Nothing. Jeez. Can I be any more inept at this?*

Patiently, Tor was watching her. "No dice, huh?"

Kali muttered, "I hate this stupid wizard crap."

"Okay. East it is, then. On this trail," Tor proposed.

Looking down the shady dirt path, Kali nodded. "Okay."

Tor gunned the motor and they rolled forward, gathering speed. In no time, they had traveled about a kilometer, and then the road began climbing ever higher. They came to a series of winding curves, and Kali shifted with each lean of the cycle. They were coming around a wide bend to the right when Kali caught sight of them.

Green-jacketed men. Row upon row of Regs, all with rifles at the ready, forming in lines across the trail in front of them. Roaring Regs were charging out of the trees and shrubs alongside them, flanking both sides of the trail.

Tor turned her head back toward Kali, and barked, "Hold on!"

She braked hard, planted a foot, and then wheeled the cycle in a tight turn. Then Kali saw for the first time the masses of Regs gathering behind them. Hundreds of rifles lowered, pointing at them with deadly intent. Inanely, Kali wondered if missing a shot from this close a range was statistically possible.

Tor kept turning the bike in a tight circle. Kali knew Tor was gunning the engine because the frame was vibrating with power. She clutched Tor's waist tighter, her eyes widening with terror.

From somewhere in back of them, a male voice yelled, "Take them!"

The Regs stepped toward them with a uniform precision and Tor released the brake. The bike leapt forward and Kali felt air between her and the leather seat. In a surprise move, Tor jerked the handlebars, and the bike hooked suddenly to the left. They were in a ninety-degree turn, and within seconds they were running directly into the lines of Elysian paramilitary, knocking aside the stunned men or smashing over crumpling bodies. Several large hands landed on Kali, trying to pull her off, but she molded herself to Tor and the bike speed only increased.

There were shots now, long, loud, uninterrupted bursts from automatic rifles. Men were screaming, a spray of blood was spattering Kali and Tor, and great chunks of some wet, unidentified matter smacked Kali's left arm.

132

They're firing into their own ranks, Kali realized with a sick shock.

Tor kept going, plowing the bike through the mass of Regulators, intentionally or not using the Elysians closer to them as shields. And then they were through the mob and into an open space.

Two Regs stood by an old Hum-vee, waving pistols and shouting. Ahead, a Reg jumped out of a canvas-topped one-ton truck and ran at them. Kali saw the bursts of fire from the rifle he held at waist level. Over Tor's shoulder, Kali glimpsed green grass and a distance of fifteen meters between them and the wood. They were traveling so fast the gap was disappearing in the blink of an eye. Even through the helmet, she heard a bullet whine as it passed by her head. Then Tor was slammed back against her and a pain as if from a hot poker lanced straight through Kali's right shoulder. Everything seemed to go into slow motion. Tor sagged heavily sideways, and the bike tilted, falling to the right.

They smashed into the grass and dirt, kicking up a shower of earth. Pain flared in Kali's knee, and her helmet banged, once hard, then again more softly. An agony of sensation blossomed in her head and across her side. Then it seemed as if they were sliding a long way before stopping.

Kali found herself staring stupidly at the trunks of the enormous trees that stood a meter from where she lay. *Almost made it.*

The fire in her shoulder flamed again, and Kali heard herself whimper. She thought she heard cheering, but a thick fog seemed to be rolling in around her, making everything quiet and unreal. Then there were rough hands on her, pulling her away from the warm body she lay entangled with, separating her from what she knew was her only protection in this place.

As her left hand grasped for Tor's chest, she felt the slick wetness there. "Tor," she whispered, trying to turn her, to see what had happened.

Two large Regs pulled Kali to her feet. She swayed, nearly collapsing from the blast of pain, but their viselike grips on her upper arms held her. She watched them grab Tor and roll her onto her back. There was blood—so much blood—on the grass, on Tor's chest, oozing across her jacket in a bright red flow. A river of life was escaping from holes punched in her right chest. For a brief moment, Kali struggled to get free and go to her, but she could not exert much force, and shocked, she looked down and found herself bleeding, too.

The young Reg beside Tor carefully undid the strap and took off Tor's helmet. Kali saw the sleek black hair spill out, and the Reg tenderly cradled Tor's head. Then the Reg turned toward the man with the shiny stars on his shoulder epaulets.

"Sir. I think this is an Unwanted!"

Over-sized black boots clumped through the grass as the general and his staff of five hurried closer. Sounding shocked and appalled, one of the general's aides pronounced, "It can't be! They've been scoured from the earth!"

The general leaned down and checked Tor's face carefully, as if expecting a disguise, then moved away shaking his head in disbelief.

At that moment, Tor opened her eyes and looked up at the young Reg holding her head. Slowly, she cast her gaze about, found Kali, and seemed to sigh. "Sorry," Tor rasped.

"Oh, Tor," Kali answered, tears filling her eyes.

Desperately, she tried again to break free of the grips of the men who held her. A swirl of black dots rose up before her, and she willed herself to stay conscious. As the dizziness cleared, she stared at Tor, stricken. Despair and fear had reduced everything to a keen, raw, moment-to-moment awareness.

The general and his staff were a short distance away from them. In a quiet voice the general was speaking into a large, handheld two-way radio.

"S'okay," Tor told Kali, as if trying to soothe her. "I knew what I was getting into." She coughed, then solemnly stated, "This is the death I wanted. In battle . . . fighting for my friends."

Around her, several Regs looked reflective, as if empathizing with the young warrior lying in the grass. Those men looked puzzled and dropped their gazes as if they were trying to understand what they were feeling. Others shot fearful glances at their commanding officer.

Half-smiling, Tor told Kali, "This was my chance . . . coming here . . . with you. My chance to be a warrior again."

"You aren't going to die! I won't let you!" Kali uttered. She looked at the men on either side of her, who were staring at Tor with incredulous eyes. "Let go of me! Let me help her!" she pleaded.

The general marched back over and stood directly above Tor, peering down at her, like an avid scientist inspecting an insect specimen he had thought extinct. "You *are* an Oriental," he pronounced, but his voice said it in a manner that suggested that this was something that could not be.

Tor smirked. "Eighth generation . . . Japanese-American." She was speaking with difficulty now, taking shallow gasps. "And my forebears . . . were all more American . . . than you, bub." The utterance cost her, and she grimaced in pain.

The general's lip lifted on one side, in a disdainful snarl. He turned to a hulking Reg on his left. "Finish her."

"Goddess, no!" Kali screamed. Distraught, she reached for the psychic power that had been such a sure and fluid thing just a few months ago, only to find nothing, not even a trace of the glowing warmth that had once been as vital and dependable as her eyes or ears.

The boy-Reg holding Tor's head seemed to reluctantly ease her down into the grass. He stood, then hesitated for a long moment, just looking at her. He was pale and thin, and looked as if he had seen scenes like the one unfolding too many times.

"Stand clear, soldier!" the general snapped.

The boy jumped a little, then stepped aside.

Thoroughly agitated, the general shouted at the big Reg. "Do it!"

Expressionless, the big Reg lumbered forward. He aimed his rifle at Tor and delivered a short but effective blast.

A second raw scream curdled in Kali's throat. Her breathing ragged, she stared at the torn and bloodied form of her friend.

The general's eyes lighted on Kali, and with an interested grin, he strode closer. "Take the helmet off," he ordered the Reg to her right.

The helmet was removed. As the general appreciatively ran his hand over her blonde hair, Kali sucked together any moisture she could find in her dry mouth. The general smiled.

Kali spat in his face with all her might.

He stumbled back, astounded. Furious, he sputtered, "Why you . . . !"

Quickly he came at her, grabbing her wounded shoulder and delivering a steadily increasing pressure. "Is this where it hurts?" he demanded in a smooth but lethal tone.

The pain skyrocketed, and against her will, Kali began losing consciousness. She felt her chin sink to her chest. The men were literally holding her up now. Her eyes closed, and reality slid from her.

She felt a thumb caressing her lips.

"What a prize. Yes, I think Procurator Fowler will reward me well for this one," the general remarked. A hand rode across her abdomen. "By the Lord's blessing, she's pregnant, too."

A young voice piped up, "Who are they, sir? Are they Freeland warriors?"

"They are only women, whatever else they may be," the general stated. "As women, they are born to serve men, thus saith scripture. The Unwanted was worth nothing . . . but this one . . . this one will bring us a good reward."

The general began giving orders. Kali heard them say that she would be transported back to Buckhannon in the truck, with a detachment of twenty troopers. The rest of the regiment would go on searching for those "dirty Amazon bitches."

Briefly, Kali's heart quailed at the thought of these brutal men going after anyone else. Then she felt herself lifted, and she was awash in pain. The acrid scent of male perspiration seemed to surround her. A black wave enfolded Kali like an ice-cold sea, and she lost it all.

⚘

Whit looked around at the huge trees they were passing through. She frowned, uneasy with how indistinguishable the countryside was; each new place looked amazingly like the place they had just left behind them. The same lush green forests and dark shaded streams, the same grassy glades and steep hillsides. Much as she wanted to strike out on her own and find Kali, she knew she would never be able to find her own way.

They had been riding now for an hour, at least. The morning sun was visible through an occasional break in the leafy overgrowth. The landscape continued to look much as it had in the hills around Seneca. Turning to Danu, Whit realized the young woman looked as tense and unhappy as Whit felt.

"I've been thinking about what that scout reported, about seeing two women riding a motorcycle . . ." Whit began.

Almost as if she'd been waiting for Whit to broach the topic, Danu interrupted, "It didn't sound like they had a warrior escort. What the hell was the Isis Council thinking—sending Kali and Tor into Elysium alone?"

Ruminating on the stubborn woman she had partnered with for nearly two years now, Whit cleared her throat. "Maybe they're here in an unofficial capacity."

A line appeared between Danu's brows, displaying her confusion.

"As in . . . without permission," Whit clarified.

Danu's eyes flared with comprehension, then anger leapt into her blue eyes. "That damn Tor! Warrior Command is gonna bust her to private before she even gets off medical leave!"

Feeling anxious, Whit continued. "And neither Tor or Kali is exactly in great shape. Tor's got a heart condition and Kali's entering the fourth month of a pregnancy."

"So, what's the plan?" Danu asked.

Frustrated, Whit gave a small, tight shake of her head. "Don't know. We'll either find them before the Regs do, or we won't." She exhaled heavily. "This is getting so out of control."

Suddenly one of Jamie's scouts came into view, riding down the steep bank on their left, then splashing across a stream and moving toward Jamie at the head of the troop. Jamie raised her arm and all the riders reined in, bringing the party to a stop.

Jamie listened to her woman's quiet report, then raised her rifle above her head. She pumped it three times and used it to point toward the heights. The Amazons around her swung their horses about and urged them up the side of the mountain. As Whit and Danu followed along, Whit knew in her gut that they were going into action.

Chapter 7

On the other side of the North American continent, in the Isis Cedar House, Lilith paced the tile floor in the area behind the Deputy Leader's chair. She eyed the small monitors embedded in the circular pine table, angrily noting that the crystal screens still shone purple. Located before each of the Councilwomen, the screen used color to declare the status of the decision on the floor. Purple indicated that the decision before the assembly was still under deliberation.

Nearby, Lilith could hear one Councilwoman describing the beautiful lines on the thirty-meter fishing boat she was building. Another group a little farther away was discussing some new wheat seed that the geneticists were experimenting with in Artemis. Still another voice was wondering how an inter-colony baseball game had gone.

The hall was filled with the noise of hundreds of women speaking at once and the occasional burst of smothered laughter that, in Lilith's experience, often accompanied idle gossip.

It's been over twenty-four hours since Kali and Tor left! Her spine stiffening with fury, Lilith swept her gaze over the women milling about the hall. *Why aren't they in their seats? Why aren't they voting on a plan and getting the rescue teams airborne?*

While many of the Councilwomen around her looked earnest, tired, and slightly disheveled, for every one of those figures there were two others who seemed to have lost awareness of why they were there and instead were discussing meaningless nonsense.

"Whit would have cursed someone out by now," Lilith muttered. "Kali, on the other hand, just went off to do it herself. And I'll be damned if I don't feel like doing the same thing!"

Determined to get a vote on the mission within the next hour, she stalked over to the Deputy Leader's chair and dropped into it. She snatched up the Leader's wooden gavel and delivered a series of sharp raps to the small square platform. At first, only a few women turned, but when Lilith began banging the gavel on the platform so hard that the little platform finally skittered off the table, she soon had the attention of every woman in the hall. Silence descended save for the quiet whispering of fabric as women hurried back to their places.

Lilith glared at the assembled Councilwomen. "What in Gaea's name is taking so long?! We're here for one reason—to come up with a plan! Why haven't we done it?!" After fuming for a moment, Lilith glared across the table at Anne Cameron, the woman who had volunteered to head the mission committee. "Well? Report."

Cameron stood somewhat laconically, but betrayed her uneasiness with an expectant glance at her fellow politicians. The others all looked away, wordlessly expressing their unwillingness to serve as backup when the Deputy Leader was in a temper. Cameron glowered at them resentfully and fluffed the back of her silvered brown hair a bit, gathering herself before facing Lilith and replying.

"We have agreed on sending two Cormorants," Cameron began, "and two separate search and rescue details, numbering one hundred and fifty warriors each. We have also selected Captain Razia as the leader of the detail assigned to go after Leader Whitaker and Lieutenant Sullivan."

The other Council members supplied a murmur of self-congratulation.

Encouraged, and obviously feeling bolder, Cameron folded her arms across her chest. "We have not, however, been able to come to a consensus about who should lead the party sent to collect Kali Tyler and Lieutenant Yakami." The woman gave Lilith an openly challenging look. "As you are aware, Deputy Leader, we will need someone not only of rank, but who has already established a strong, personal rapport with Kali, if we are to secure her without authorizing an outright arrest." Eyeing Lilith, Cameron finished, "No one wants the job."

Lilith gritted her teeth and gripped the arms of her chair, wanting nothing more than to leap up, march across the chamber and slap Councilwoman Cameron. Then, all at once, there was a steadying hand on her shoulder. She turned and found Styx, slightly out of breath, standing beside her.

Raising her voice in order to be heard by everyone present, including the gallery, Styx announced, "Just finished a call with Cimbri Braun, Leader of our sister colony Artemis." Everyone in the chamber leaned forward. "Leader Braun has granted an extended loan of her Deputy Leader, Nakotah Berry, to Isis. As you all know, Captain Berry is warrior reserve and an old friend of both Kali and Whit." Styx sent a hard gaze at Cameron as she concluded, "Captain Berry has been requested by Warrior Command in Boudica to lead the group of warriors sent to find Kali Tyler and Lieutenant Yakami. Captain Berry has agreed." Gazing across the chamber at the women around the table, Styx asked, "Dilemma solved?"

Councilwoman Cameron hesitated, but the other women all answered with a hearty "Yes!" that rumbled across the hall.

"Then cast your ballots," Lilith ordered.

Within the next few minutes, the votes were entered and the

council screens all turned green. Lilith checked the tally on her monitor, then declared, "The proposal on the table is passed and the motion for the mission to proceed is carried."

Lilith turned and faced Captain Razia, who moved from the shadows by the big oaken doors where she had been waiting patiently for hours. "Captain, we are green for go. Ready the two Cormorants for take-off from Isis Airfield at 1600 hours."

A relieved cheer went up, a cheer that grew as everyone present suddenly understood that at last there was action. Within a few moments their collective voices thundered through the Cedar House.

Lilith slipped an arm around Styx's waist, pulling her closer. "However you pulled this off, I can't thank you enough!"

Styx just chuckled. "I'd go myself, but the young pups here have already denied me—and made me feel like I'm the most ancient of Elders as they did it!"

Lilith hugged her tighter. "Oh, I could never spare you, Styx. Not now." She blinked the tears back. "Gaea, not now."

"We'll have them all home soon, Lil," Styx promised, willing it with all her might. "What else could go wrong?"

Only the soft, shuffling sound of rustling mulch accompanied the mounted Amazons as they crested the height of the wooded mountain. Jamie waved them to a quick stop.

Below them, a verdant green carpet of treetops covered hills that rolled into the distance. In the haze of the hot afternoon sunlight, the gentle mountains farther away were more blue than green. A stream flashed in the lowland before them, on the far side of a long meadow that sloped steeply upward.

On Jamie's quick signal, the deerskin-clad troop, as one, dismounted. Some began restlessly walking their horses in circles, while others took the opportunity to check their weapons or steal long sips from waterskins.

"Whitaker," a hushed voice called.

Whit turned to her right and saw Florey waving her closer. After making a nod in that direction to Danu, Whit nudged her bay. The two Freeland warriors steered their horses over to her.

"Colonel wants to see ya," Florey stated.

Nodding, Whit touched Beauregard's flank with the thick heels of her moccasins, and trotted to Jamie Rexrode's side. Danu obligingly reined in and waited a distance away.

Pointing to the land below, Jamie remarked, "The Weyford clansmen is off to the left, prob'ly a hun'nert or so on foot, mostly armed with shotguns and hunting rifles." She moved her hand to the right. "The McCalls and the Sponaugles are moving down from the heights over there. Prob'ly another hun'nert on foot, with crossbows and some repeatin' Winchesters."

Perplexed, unable to see a thing before her except trees, Whit asked, "How do you know that?"

With a slight grin, Jamie divulged, "Bird calls. Regs pay no heed to the simple joys of nature, don'tcha know. Hear that?" A particularly long series of warbles came from the distance to their right. "Code. Sponaugles are in position. They say there's near four hun'nert Regs movin' easterly, comin' right at us." Another set of whistles. "No artillery, no mortars, no tank support. Only Regs with automatic weapons."

Only, Whit thought.

She knew the horror a single M-28 could wreak in the space of a few minutes. She had seen it several times while she was an undercover operative stationed in Elysium two years ago. She remembered one occasion when a baker in the street market had protested the casual looting of his bread cart; the Reg filling his pockets with rolls had reacted with a casual spray of gunfire, leaving thirteen wounded and six dead. The baker had paid for his complaint with his life.

Cupping a hand to her mouth, Jamie sent the cry of a hawk into the early afternoon wind.

143

"See that meadow right below us? Here's the plan," Jamie said, then described in brief sentences and swift hand motions the head-on assault she was going to use to drive through the Reg lines. "By the time we blow all the way through them, they'll be runnin' to the sides—seekin' cover in the woods, and rushin' straight into the ambush waitin' there for 'em," she finished.

Thoughtfully, Whit gazed at the terrain and had to admit it seemed like a good plan. It was hard for a foot soldier to stand on open ground and face charging horse troops, especially when the sabers were brandished, hacking and slicing. Taking aim at a fast-moving target, even with an automatic weapon, was the last thing a fighter unaccustomed to a cavalry charge was likely to think of in the first minutes of battle. And leaving the other rebels in the shelter of the trees with their old single-shot rifles and crossbows seemed wise. They would take down many Regs before the Regs understood they were fleeing directly into an ambush.

"Once we make it through to the far side of their lines, we'll dismount and lay down covering fire, pushing the rest of them snakes into the trees for the clansmen. Then you and yer Lieutenant Sullivan can search the area west of this ridge fer yer Freelander friends."

"Sounds good," Whit agreed, then asked, "How do you know so much about battle tactics, Jamie?"

Flushing, looking almost guilty, Jamie opened her mouth, then stopped and glanced nervously around. "The Witch puts dreams in my head," she whispered. "Granma made a deal with her a long time back. We give her what she wants, and she . . . well, she uses her craft to get us what we want." Giving a slight shudder, Jamie stared hard at the ground. "But she is pee-culiar, I gotta tell ya, and it gives me the willers goin' there for help."

Feeling a dark fascination, Whit asked, "Is this the witch in the cave above Seneca?"

Like a small child, Jamie was wide-eyed. "Yeah. She used to come visit us two or three times a year, but since December, she's come to stay full time."

"What did you say her name was again?" Whit prompted nonchalantly.

"Didn't," Jamie muttered. "It's forbidden to speak it . . . or speak *of* her." Flicking her pale blue gaze at Whit, she confessed, "If she finds out I been out here blabbin' to ya, she'll punish me."

Some internal instinct told Whit to keep pressing for information, that this was important. "And how does she do that?"

Jamie set her jaw, and for a moment Whit thought she wasn't going to answer. Then, softly, Jamie spoke. "She hurts Kate."

Whit's gray eyes locked onto Jamie's blue ones and held.

"You . . . like Kate." Whit stated.

Her smile was brief, but Whit saw it flicker across Jamie's face, then disappear in a melancholy frown. "I wanted to jump the broomstick with her . . . but, the Witch . . . well, the Witch has claimed her."

Whit remembered Kate standing just outside the door to the healer's cabin when Danu had been screaming and convulsing in the midst of some dream. An uneasy fear made Whit turn in the saddle and scrutinize Danu. The young redhead was slowly and methodically swinging her saber in careful figure eights, as if trying to become familiar with the weight of the weapon.

Unexpectedly, Jamie began speaking in an earnest tone. "I been noticin' that yer pretty damn resourceful, Major Whitaker. So, I'm hopin' you can think of somethin' here. My Granma invited home the devil 'bout five years ago. She was tryin' to save Seneca and the rest of the villages us Allegheny clans have made from Procurator Fowler and the thousands of Regs that came and set up their fortress in Buckhannon. But I'm gonna be the clan chief when Granma passes and I cain't let what's been goin' on in that holler keep takin' place."

"What's been going on?" Whit asked. *This is the key to everything.*

A long series of trills filled the air. Below them, the first rows of Regs came marching out of the forest. In measured steps they began striding into the tall grass and black-eyed susans that stood so still and quiet in the summer heat.

Her eyes on the Regs, Jamie gave a long sigh and straightened her shoulders. "Guess that's a discussion fer another day."

"Hey," Whit said softly. When Jamie looked over at her again, Whit solemnly promised, "Once I find Kali, I'll do whatever I can to help you."

Jamie gave a small smile and nodded her acceptance of that.

The Amazons on either side of them were mounting up again.

Whit watched the detached and hardened air of command slip back over Jamie, as the woman turned and surveyed her troops. The glinting blonde strands in her light-brown hair caught a shaft of the sunlight filtering through the trees.

What an interesting woman, Whit thought. *I'm growing to really like her.*

She hadn't expected to find a friend in the midst of this logistical disaster.

Looking down the mountain, she saw Regs continuing to march into the meadow, until long lines of men were moving toward them. Finally, the rear line of the Reg company was entirely clear of the trees. Green-jacketed men were exposed in the big field, heading purposefully uphill, straight toward the Amazons hidden just inside the tree line.

There's hundreds of them down there!

For a moment, Whit felt her body tense in reaction. Then she looked closer. The Regs were leaning into the climb to higher ground, their heads down, one foot plodding after the other. Their clothing was darkened by perspiration stains, and M-28s were slung carelessly over their shoulders. Their body language shouted fatigue and inattention.

Looking at the jaunty green caps the men were wearing, Whit thought, *Mother's Blood, they're not even wearing helmets! Overconfident jackasses!*

Jamie cupped a hand to her mouth once more, and the hawk cry echoed through the trees. Immediately afterward, her hand went to the scabbard hanging from the belt at her waist. All in one motion, she smoothly drew her saber and lifted it over her head.

A hiss of sound followed as all of the Amazons, including Whit and Danu, did the same thing.

Whit motioned to Danu to move her horse up next to Whit's and as the girl came closer, Whit whispered, "Remember, stay near me. Keep your head and shoulders low and use the horse's neck for cover. If your mount is shot out from under you, hunker down behind the carcass and use it as a brace to aim and fire your laser pistol."

Swallowing hard, Danu stared at the men below her. "Yes, ma'am."

Jamie swept her saber down and kicked the buckskin. With a terribly beautiful elegance, the horses all sprang forward.

Except for the muffled snapping of grass stalks and the thud of hooves into soft earth, there was little noise. Wind rushed past Whit's face, rich with the sweet smell of June and horse sweat. They were twenty meters clear of the forest and about fifty meters from the Regs before the men in the front lines lifted their heads.

Banshee screams rose around Whit as the Amazons declared war in a language more primitive than Whit had ever known. On the faces of the Regs, Whit saw stark disbelief and then absolute gaping fear. Too late, the Regs fumbled for their rifles. Then the cavalry was riding the men down.

A Reg close by raised his M-28, aiming at Jamie, and like an angel of death, Florey chopped him until he dropped. Another Reg grabbed Danu's stirrup, then grasped her sword arm and tried to pull her off her horse. Whit's blow nearly took the man's head off. The horror Whit felt was shoved into a back corner of her brain, as she fought to keep Danu and the Amazons around her alive. Blades were flashing like lightning in the bright afternoon sun. Blood flew in showering arcs, or poured from ghastly wounds. Men toppled. The Regs in the front four lines of the company never got off a shot.

Then the battle plan disintegrated. Instead of plowing straight through the field of men, as Jamie had ordered, the Amazons began driving their horses from one victim to the next, swinging the sabers with a relentless, deliberate vengeance.

"You killed my brother!" one woman was shrieking.

Others were yelling in the wordless tongue of rage.

A few M-28 bursts were heard, but those who dared to stand and fire were quickly targeted. Huge beasts swooped by those Regs, with fierce opponents aboard, unleashing razored-edge blows with deadly efficiency. Women with age-old scores to settle were settling them now and as if they sensed the blood lust, there was a low, gathering wail of panic from the men. Like sheep beset by ravenous wolves, the Regs turned from the Amazons, stumbling, falling, some even dropping their weapons, and running from the field.

Whit could scarcely believe her eyes.

Desperate for shelter, the majority of the Regs were racing into the trees on either side of the meadow.

Jamie screamed, "Hold your positions!" at her troopers, trying to restore order.

Wild eyed with battle fever, blood-spattered and eager, the Amazon cavalry barely managed to rein in their mounts.

The Regs went crashing into the brush at the forest's edge on either side of the meadow, and then the forest erupted with gunfire. Whit saw whole groups of green jackets drop only a few paces into the shady depths. The men who turned and tried to get back into the field were dropped by arrows from the crossbow snipers perched in trees above them. Some of the Regs raised their arms, trying to surrender, but the clansmen, with their own list of grievances and years of suffering under these men, were obviously of no mind to take prisoners. Whit watched, her gut twisting, as the Regs were mowed down like wheat before a grisly and merciless reaper. The Regs were being repaid in kind for every act of viciousness they had visited upon these West Virginians.

Within twenty minutes it was over. A company of roughly five hundred Regulators lay dead or wounded in the field, or at the forest's edge. The Amazons, their mounts prancing restlessly in the meadow, raised their sabers and began shrieking a wild, chilling victory yell that sent shivers down Whit's spine. Then all Amazons except Jamie were slipping down from their horses. The big animals shifted about, stomping and snorting, reacting to the scent of blood; some nervously trotted farther away before coming to a stand as they had been trained to do.

Moving like stealthy shadows, the clans came out of the woods.

Together, grim-faced, the Amazons and clansmen began looting the fallen bodies. Whit watched them grabbing field packs and dumping them, rummaging through the contents for what they considered valuable and discarding the rest. Amazons and clansmen were shouldering M-28's, shoving revolvers in belts, stowing ammunition in pockets or in deerskin pouches. The clansmen were even pulling knee-high black boots from ghoulishly limp legs.

Hearing a gasp, Whit looked over at Danu. The redhead had her face turned away from the scene. Her shoulders were rigid and the hand grasping a bloody sword was white-knuckled.

On the other side of Danu, Jamie had also heard the gasp. She gazed into the young Freelander's face with a weary compassion.

"Yeah, it's awful, I know." Jamie exhaled deeply. "But this has been a long time comin'." Her eyes moved to the bodies nearby. "Seems like the mean ones just think yer always gonna take gettin' kicked, gettin' raped. Always gonna take havin' them come and steal most of the crops at the end of a long hard summer. We starved while they feasted." Jamie looked out over the decimated army, the bright green jackets easily visible in the sage-green grass of the meadow. "Seems like they cain't stop doin' sech meanness until someone *makes 'em* stop." Her face immeasurably sad, she said, "We got outta their way. We went up in the hills, built little hide-outs in the hollers. We just wanted to be left alone." Shaking her head, she asked, "Why cain't they do that?"

Then fixing her gaze back on Danu, she said, "I know you think we're damn near beasts to do what we done today. But remember . . . the Procurator in charge of these Regs sent a patrol of them out a few days back with orders to steal our children for their sex trade. Because we stopped them, that same man has sent this army here to exterminate us."

Whit spoke up. "Your grandmother seemed to think the Regs were looking for us."

Giving a wry, humorless grin, Jamie replied, "Oh, they are. Somehow the Regs know it was you in one of them jets. But this lot waren't searchin' for ya'll."

Whit offered, "I don't understand."

"That stuff about this company of Regs searchin' fer ya was jes Granma bein' cantankerous. She knows the Regs are swarmin' all over the hills where your jets went down, forty miles or so east of Seneca, just west of Shenandoah Mountain. We got scouts up in deer blinds out there, watchin' them. They cain't find our trail. Course, that's cuz we didn't ride over there. Horse prints can be tracked, see, but moccasined feet are a might too hard fer them fool Regs ta foller."

"Why were you so far from Seneca that day?" Whit asked.

"We'd gone over that-away lookin' fer runaway serfs. Every early summer they start appearin', stragglin' in from Virginia and Maryland, followin' old Route 33 through the gaps in the mountains." Jamie shifted in her saddle, then fished a scrap of cloth from a small pouch on her beaded belt and wiped the blood and gore from her saber. "Some of the runaways got plague so bad the poor souls don't last long. Others we try the cure on. Sometimes it works and sometimes not. Either way, we need numbers to fight the Big Fight that's comin'." Nodding toward the field, she murmured, "This may have been the start of that."

Jamie's solemn gaze once more rested on Danu. "The Regs who died here weren't forced to be on Procurator Fowler's payroll. They weren't forced to be at his murderous beck and call. They did Fowler's evil work cuz it suited 'em. They coulda been reg'lar citizens like the rest of us, hustlin' fer the next meal, tryin' to make a place in the world fer themselves an' their kids, without bringin' pure hell to their countrymen and women. They didn't have to be paid thugs, dispensin' pain and death at the whim of the rich, or the politicians, or the Reverends."

She touched her moccasins to the horse's side, moving the gray forward. Over her shoulder, she said, "These Regs got what they came fer. They found a pack o' rebels and had themselves a reckonin'. Too bad it didn't go the way they thought it would." Jamie spat to emphasize her point, then finished quietly, "Damn 'em to hell, I say."

Her face so pale her freckles stood out like flecks of dirt, Danu never said a word. Instead, she sent a confused glance at Whit.

Unable to think of anything to say that would set right for Danu the massacre they had both just witnessed, Whit slid down from her horse. She grasped some tall grass and tore it free, then used it to wipe clean her bloodied saber. Tossing the grass aside, she slid the saber back into its ancient scabbard and remounted. After a moment, Danu did the same thing.

"Let's search the other side of the woods," Whit proposed. "See if we can find the road the scout told Chief Rexrode about. Maybe we can find some sign of Kali and Tor."

Danu nodded. Whit called her intentions to Jamie, then she and Danu nudged their horses into a trot. Whit reined Beauregard toward the downward side of the hill and Danu followed on her brown mare. In moments, they were traveling a deer trail through the old maples and sycamores. Hearing hoof beats, Whit turned and found four of the Amazons and Florey, joining them under the forest canopy.

"Colonel thought ya might need some help trackin'," Florey offered.

Whit thanked them and the Amazons spread out, each rider about seven meters apart. They walked their horses, searching the crumbled leaf debris beneath the fat trees, winding around the clumps of lush ferns and blueberry bushes. The small group of seven came to a stream and splashed through the shallows, then climbed through the trees of the next ridge.

After about two kilometers, they suddenly came to a break in the tree cover. Whit noticed the broken sections of macadam ahead. Even with the trees growing from the middle of the more disintegrated parts, she could tell it was an old roadway. After coming to the gravelly edge, Whit stopped and looked each way, peering into the hazy distance.

"Which direction is . . . what was the name of that town where the scout saw our friends?"

"Elkins," Florey supplied. With a wave to the left, she stated, "That-a-way."

They trotted over the grassy ground on the side of the uneven road bed. After traveling about a half a kilometer, the Amazons in the front of the party came to an abrupt halt. Whit squinted past them and saw something large dangling from a tree limb.

"Tor!" Danu screamed.

They all began to move toward the still form, but with her heels drumming on the sides of her mare, Danu shot by them, straight up to the tree. She pulled her horse to a skidding stop, then grasped the knees and booted feet as she came even with them. Unable to look away, she stared past the noose around her neck, into the face of the woman she loved. Slowly, she reached up to the oozing, concave red holes that were the remnants of Tor's chest, and felt the gore smear across her hand.

"Oh, sweet Gaea, no," Danu whispered. "Oh no, no, no."

Stunned, Whit came to her side, as two Amazons clambered into the tree to cut the rope.

Whit grasped Danu's forearm, knowing there was no comfort for what Danu was enduring, no words that would soothe her agony.

Then all at once, it hit her. *Where's Kali?*

Breathless, she moved her horse farther down the trail. Noting the track of motorcycle tires in the tall grass to the left, she began methodically searching that area. She spent the next five minutes steering the horse in careful sweeps through the grass. She didn't find the bike, or the weapons, or the packs she knew Tor and Kali would have been carrying. She did find the place covered with shell casings. She also found a blood soaked patch of earth, and knew with a sinking heart that this was where Tor had died. Nearby, she found the slight track of blood that led to a place where the grass was impressed; a four wheeled vehicle had been parked there.

They've captured her, Whit thought, her throat so tight she could scarcely breathe. *And she's hurt.*

She stared numbly at the tracks, recognizing them. In Bethesda two years ago, she had seen vehicles that left such tracks. Synthetic rubber had disappeared from Elysium when the last pre-Great Rift tires had rotted and fallen apart. Now ethanol fueled their gas engines and the wheels of their transports bore flattened, steel rims. Whit eyed the tracks that circled through the grass and then led back onto the trail.

Florey rode up beside her. "I think yer friend is in shock," she stated, glancing back at the scene beneath the tree.

Swiveling in the saddle, Whit looked behind her. Danu was kneeling on the ground with Tor in her arms. Through the thick forest quiet, she could hear Danu weeping. A more forlorn sound Whit had never heard.

Her heart felt squeezed and for a moment, tears made seeing impossible.

Purposefully turning away, Whit made herself focus on the wheel tracks. "Where did that truck go?"

Florey gazed at Whit, obviously aware of the swiftly increasing tension in Whit's demeanor. "Buckhannon. That's where their fort is. 'Bout ten miles northwest o' here."

Whit shook her head. "I don't get it. They found two armed Freeland warriors, obviously here on a mission. Why would they capture Kali and take her off and just outright execute Tor?"

"Yer friend Tor is an Unwanted."

Slammed by the simple insanity of that rationale, Whit couldn't speak for a minute. In the grip of a blinding rage, she snarled, "Fucking racist pigs!"

"Yeah, that they are," Florey agreed, then asked, "Is this Kali white? Easy on the eyes?"

Whit clenched her jaw so hard she felt the muscles jumping.

Nodding, Florey said, "They took her for Procurator Fowler. Clean women are gettin' a mite scarce these days."

Eyes narrowing, Whit faced her. "Clean women?"

"We hear Bethesda was gradually overwhelmed with plague. All the city girls had it. The Regs moved a big portion of their operations out here to get a fresh crop fer the Breeding Pens. But the eastern clans spied all them military convoys comin' through the gap from old Harrisonburg and the alarm went up. Us hill people lit out. They ain't got many women in Buckhannon. And most of the ones that are there are already diseased. The high and mighty Reverends and Regs tell ever'body they ain't infected, but we hear that them that got left behind in Bethesda are dyin' of it, so that jes don't make sense."

A fierce determination moved through Whit. *I've gotta get Kali.*

Moving her horse through the grass, Florey remarked, "I'm guessin' a small party split off from the company here and maybe headed back to Buckhannon with the loot they took off'n yer friends. And with yer girl." There was a slight pause. "She's bleedin', ya know."

"I know." Whit took her laser pistol out and checked the settings. Her hand shook a little as she gripped the stock. "Got something I have to do, Florey." She slipped the weapon back into its holster. "Tell Colonel Rexrode I'll owe her for the loan of the horse."

"What?"

With a slight, but firm kick, Whit urged her mount forward.

"Hey—hold up!"

Whit set Beauregard into a steady, ground-eating canter. Florey shouted after her once, then twice. Whit ignored her and started riding faster.

Whit kept her eyes on the crumbling road as the surface changed to a dusty trail. Anyone could follow the track of the Reg truck. In some places, the steel wheel rims had actually gouged ruts into the ground. She drove the horse harder, trying not to think. She couldn't let herself consider what fate Kali might have met.

As her mind shut down, fear tasted like cotton in her mouth.

She told herself she'd figure out a plan once she got closer to Buckhannon. All she knew right now was that she wanted to kill the first Reg she met with her bare hands.

Chapter 8

Kali opened her eyes, not sure where she was or what had happened. The small, dimly lit space she was inhabiting was rocking slightly, from one side to the other. The motion hurt her. A hot stabbing sensation was radiating from a place just below her collar bone.

She smelled something oddly familiar, then recognized the stale and musty scent of stored canvas. It reminded her of her days as a warrior cadet and the bivouac tents they used when they were out on maneuvers. Feeling dazed, she realized that she was propped upright against something soft. With great effort, she turned her head.

A boy was kneeling next to her. Frowning, he was concentrating on the bandage he was placing just below her right shoulder. He was not old enough to shave, but he was wearing the uniform of an Elysian Regulator.

Kali looked down at herself. Her anorak was gone, and the top seam of her shirt had been sliced open and peeled back. The remnants of the shirt were heavily stained.

Blood.

Mildly surprised, she realized the bandage was covering a wound. *How the heck . . . ?*

With the impact of a physical blow, it all came back. The unexpected rendezvous with hell on the ridge trail. A series of images flashed in her brain, like photographs on a chip display, crystal clear slices of memory presenting themselves for review.

Regs, so many Regs, everywhere, all around them. Glimpsing from the corner of her eye that last man running toward them, the M-28 in his hand. That last man between them and the woods, and the safety that surely waited there. The burst of fire. The cycle falling. Then Tor lying in the high grass, drenched in a slick, wine red flow, the understanding of what was about to happen to her evident in the stunned, sad gaze she gave to Kali.

A sob wrenched free and suddenly Kali was shattered.

The boy quickly finished securing the bandage. "Oh, please, don't cry. I'm being as careful as I can not to hurt you." He rocked back on his boot heels and surveyed her face with compassionate dark eyes. "I just got the bleeding stopped. You have to stay calm."

"Oh, Tor, I'm sorry," Kali wept brokenly. "So s-sorry. It's all my fault."

The boy moved closer, awkwardly touching her upper arm. He let her cry for a bit, looking worried, then firmly he began telling her that she had to stop, that she had to think of the baby.

She moved her hands to protectively cup her abdomen. *The baby, oh Goddess, the baby.* "Is everything . . . ?"

The boy blushed. "So far, yes. I did a check while you were unconscious." He held up an old-fashioned stethoscope, then stowed it in a green backpack by his side. "Still in a good position—riding high. Healthy heart rate."

Weakened and gasping for breath, Kali sank deeper into the softness at her back. The boy used a fresh cloth to wipe off her face and gently coaxed her to blow her nose. Then he handed her a bottle of clear liquid.

"Spring water," he said. "You bled a lot and need to replace fluids."

Wearily, Kali complied with the admonition, drinking until the dryness in her mouth abated a bit. She handed the empty water bottle back and felt the tears welling up again.

"It wasn't your fault," he said quietly. "Your friend was dying. The first wound was irreparable."

"I could have saved her," Kali protested. "I did once before."

The boy sorrowfully shook his head. "My father would never have allowed it. Besides, no one could have saved her. There was too much damage."

Kali whispered, "Y-your f-father?"

"General Macowmber." The boy shrugged unhappily. "My father had five sons from three different women. Of them all, sons and mothers, I'm the only one left. So even though I'm no fighter, he keeps me by him now. Don't know why." He slumped a bit. "I'm a big disappointment. Maybe he just wants to keep the family name alive for at least one more generation."

"He lost four sons and three wives? What happened?"

"One was a wife, the others were . . ." He stopped, glancing at her guiltily.

"Breeding Pen women," Kali guessed.

"Yeah. My mother caught pneumonia. I never knew the other two women. I heard they came down with plague. "His eyes took on a wistful, internal gaze. "Measles and diphtheria got their two little boys." He shrugged. "My eldest brother, Charles, died last year in a brothel, brawling over a woman who hated him. My second eldest brother, George, spoke out against the Reverends once too often, I guess. Maybe he thought being Father's son would protect him. Anyway, he disappeared one Sunday night after church. He's been missing for six months and the authorities aren't much interested in checking into it."

158

Kali watched him. "You were the one who held my friend."

He nodded, looking incredibly sad. The boy was about seventeen and in a sweet way, very handsome.

"That was . . . a good and decent thing to do. Thank you."

Blushing, the boy looked away.

Perplexed, Kali kept her gaze on him. "Your father doesn't know you're gay."

The boy started, then turned sideways and darted a fearful glance toward the back of the shadowed space.

Following his eyes, Kali saw the gap in the rear where the canvas top was gathered, reminiscent of the rounded covering of Conestoga wagons. Beyond the gap, she saw the deep green leaves of the trees they were passing. It hit her that she was in the back of a truck, being transported somewhere. *Where?*

Satisfied no one had overheard, the boy used a hushed voice to clarify, "The correct word in Elysium is 'deviant.' And if Father knew, I'd be shot."

He didn't say, *Just like your friend was*, but the phrase hung in the air, so tangible that he may as well have said it.

Feeling stricken, Kali swallowed and said nothing.

"How'd you know?" the boy asked, looking fearful and anxious. "Don't I act normal? Am I . . . not acting right?"

Kali couldn't help her wry smile. "Family knows family, I guess."

He looked at her intently, searching her eyes. "Family?"

"It's an old saying . . . from the twentieth century." She gazed into the distance, feeling baffled by the boy's obvious distress over who he was. "What is 'normal'? What is 'acting right'?" She shook her head a little, and commented under her breath to herself, "Funny, how the use of language can say so much about a place."

"Sometimes 'normal' is whatever you have to be in order to be alive the next day," the boy said quietly.

Sighing deeply, accepting that, Kali nodded. She was suddenly overwhelmed with fatigue. Examining the young face before her, wondering at the life he had led, she felt a wave of empathy. "You're right. Don't worry. You're acting right. I'm . . . sort of a seer."

"A what?"

"Like a magician. I know things without knowing how sometimes."

He watched her with an almost disbelieving wonder. "Really?"

"I'm not very good. Can't make it work half the time . . . especially when I really need it to work." Her throat tightened and she said bitterly, "Can't save my friends."

"Well, they'll burn you for a witch if any of *them* have the slightest inkling you can do magic. Don't tell anyone else," the small Reg cautioned.

Kali felt her eyes drifting closed. She managed one last question. "What's your name?"

"Miles," he replied.

"Nice to meet you, Miles," Kali returned. She heard her words slur at the end but didn't really care.

"Who are you?" he asked.

Remembering Tor, she whispered, "Kali Tyler, Wizard of Isis." Tears ran free and coasted over her pale cheeks.

She heard him repeat, "Isis," in an awestruck voice, then whisper, "There's a story . . . No one is supposed to repeat it—the Reverends sentence anyone they can catch to public whippings—but the story keeps spreading—even among the Regs. Everyone knows the Regs got into Freeland twelve years ago, then attacked and destroyed a place called Isis. They burned it to the ground. The Chicago Procurators were so proud of it that the Reverends made proclamations in church and newsboards were posted in the marketplaces on big signs. Then about three or four months after the big victory, the Tribune who had led the attack was assassinated—no one knows for sure how."

Kali scrunched her eyes tighter, fighting the flashback. It pushed through with the impudent strength of truth.

She was half-dressed, standing over the body of a naked man, in the lush, red upholstered apartment of a sound-proofed pleasure room, deep in a Breeding Pen just outside of Chicago. She was gripping a ceremonial short sword tightly in her damp hand and yelling incoherently. The whiskey bottle that had been on the table beside the bed was lying on the scarlet rug, spilling its chestnut-colored contents and beside it, intermixing, was the blood that was surging from the Tribune. He was dying of wounds she had given him mere moments before.

She grimaced, still having no clear idea of how she'd ever managed to get out the locked room, or past all the Reg guards posted in and around what was essentially an immense bordello. Somehow, she'd escaped from the penitentiary and wandered into the half-demolished suburbs of what had once been northern Illinois.

Her next memory was far less jarring.

She was sitting in the sunshine by a lonely dirt road, surrounded by empty rolling plains and winter-brown grass. Baubo was sitting beside her, talking in kindly tones to her, as if she were a feral kitten. There was a piece of jerky in her extended hand. Strands of Baubo's white hair had escaped the bun she wore and were dancing around her face in a swirl of cold wind. Kali was so hungry she ached with it.

For the millionth time, she wondered how Baubo had ever found her.

Beside Kali, the young Reg was still talking. ". . . then about a year ago the rumors began. They say that . . . a powerful magician has brought Isis back."

At last, Kali opened her eyes. She found him gazing at her with such raw, earnest hope that Kali felt pierced.

"Are you that magician?" he asked.

Awash in self-recriminations and despair, she was ready to deny it, and then another memory intruded.

She was standing beside her tall, broad-shouldered partner in a high meadow above Isis, gazing at the sight of the city-colony spread out below them. They'd hiked into the mountain foothills for a romantic picnic in the late summer afternoon. The cider, fresh bread and cheese were consumed and they were on their way home. As they came over the crest of the hill,

wading through the flame-red indian paintbrush and the deep blue del-
phiniums, they found a breathtaking sight. Beneath a luminous blue-green
horizon, the houselights of Isis covered the valley like a carpet of stars. They
stopped and joined hands, both of them overcome.

"You made this," Whit said, her voice hushed with fervent wonder.
Then she turned and gazed at her as Kali had shaken her head no. "Yes,"
Whit insisted. "I never could have faced it alone . . . faced all that I'd lost
here. No, you did this. You made us all believe in . . . who and what we are
. . . again. You made us believe in the destiny of this place."

Then Whit dropped the knapsack she was carrying and enfolded Kali,
drawing her into an embrace and a long, passionate kiss that reached
within Kali and laid her open. On one level, Kali knew that, as ever, Whit
was expressing her deepest emotions through actions rather than words. Yet,
on another level Kali knew that Whit was consciously making a memory,
something new to take out and examine when she thought of Isis. An image
that simply obliterated the forlorn devastation that the burned original
colony had created.

When they parted, Kali was lightheaded, and Whit laughed softly as she
rested steadying hands on Kali's side and shoulder.

They walked home through the waving meadow grass, holding hands.
Kali was filled with a reverence for what they were together, for everything
around them.

She shook her head slightly. The next day, Whit had been elected
the Leader of Isis. And from there forward the intensity of their
bond had been deepened by their acknowledged commitment to the
city-colony where they made their home.

"Are you that magician?" the boy repeated.

If Isis were the living proof . . . "Sometimes," she whispered.

The boy frowned, as if dissatisfied with the qualification. Like any
black-and-white thinker, when presented with gray, he simply chose
an extremity. After a moment, he leaned back, satisfied. "Well,
you're a legend here."

Kali gave a quiet snort, and let her heavy lids descend for good.

The truck continued to bounce unevenly as it went toward the western sun, taking her farther and farther away from Whit.

From here on, nothing good was going to happen to her. She knew it with a bone-deep certainty that had nothing to do with her now thoroughly dormant psychic gifts. A shudder ran through her, jarring the wound, and as if a branding iron had pierced her flesh, pain engulfed her. Slowly, the gray inner fog closed in again. She was dizzy and cold. She felt a dense sleep descend, and exhaustion eased the grief and terror away from her.

As the truck approached the massive eastern gate of Buckhannon, Miles Macowmber ducked down, lifted a canvas side a bit and peeked outside. He watched as the head Reg gave the password. Slowly, the steel doors swung open. The truck rolled into the city and they were soon enclosed within the six-foot-thick and fifty-foot-high rock and concrete walls.

Murmuring excitedly, the raggedly-clothed crowd in the street parted to let the truck pass by. Some of them warily eyed the fifty Regs quick-marching on either side of the truck, while others craned their necks to get a glimpse of the freight within the heavily guarded, canvas-topped vehicle. A contingent of the Procurator's special guards jogged through the crowd from the opposite direction, surrounding the truck and the field Regs in a bristling display of top security. Then the truck was escorted through the streets to the sprawling complex of buildings that sat on the highest hill in town.

Letting the canvas drop back down, Miles moved back to his patient's side. Feeling melancholy, he cradled his medic kit against his side and leaned against a tent sack, watching Kali sleeping. His eyes moved over the curve of her cheek and the shining wisps of hair that were drifting free of the bright, yellow braid.

Bewildered, he realized he felt inexplicably protective of this beautiful young woman. He knew he was delivering her to a monster, and his conscience gnawed at him like a mouse at a grain silo door. He wished he could think of some way to set her free, then realized any part he played in her escape would be quickly detected and would more than likely result in his own death. Lowering his head, he cursed himself for being a coward.

Nakotah irritably used two fingers to pull her collar away from her neck, brushing the small silver eagle there and wondering about the promotion. *They didn't have to make me a colonel, for cryin' out loud. Hell, they'll probably bust me to private as soon as I get back, if I do this the way I'm planning.*

The afternoon sun was hot on the Isis Airfield tarmac. Sweat trickled down the side of Nakotah's planed face as she stood there, watching the troops fall in for inspection. She was a tall, big-boned figure, and she wore her long coal-black hair in two neatly fashioned braids. Black eyes glittered like flint, and smooth skin gave her the appearance of a girl in late adolescence rather than a woman in her late twenties.

Two camouflaged green Cormorants were parked in the background, both of them being loaded with material. In addition to the basic necessities of food, water, and medical supplies, Nakotah could see scores of dirt bikes, ten electro-trucks and six light laser cannons maneuvered aboard through the rear bay entrance.

"Colonel Berry, ma'am!" a sergeant barked near her right ear. "Rescue Mission Companies One and Two ready for review, ma'am!"

Nakotah gave the sergeant a sideways glance. "Stow that heavy-on-the-ma'am crap, Sergeant Vaid."

A slight smirk came to the enlisted woman's face. "Can't fault an old foot soldier for bein' proud to have a mustang leadin' us, can ya . . . ma'am?"

Uncomfortable under the beaming smiles of the warriors close enough to hear that remark, Nakotah swung her gaze over them and the warriors lost their grins and all came to attention. Satisfied, she put her hands behind her back and began a slow stroll before the lines, coolly examining each face under the guise of doing a uniform inspection. Amazed that she was where she was and doing what she was, Nakotah allowed the press of memories to steal over her.

She had never attended officer training, like Whit or Loy. After cadet training, the rest of her class had followed the accepted career path, going to one of the many city-colony flight schools, or Gunnery College, or the Warrior Command Institute. But the Fall of Isis had coincided with Nakotah's first year out of cadet school and that had changed her life.

She was fourteen when her friend, Kali Tyler, had disappeared into a maelstrom of napalm and madness while posted on guard duty before the Isis Cedar House. The news of the merciless Reg sneak attack had stunned Freeland in 2083. Then came the reports of the thousands of bodies found in the huge meadow that surrounded the Cedar House, most of them shot point blank, execution style, with automatic weapons. Worse, hundreds of women had been burned at the stake. In less than a few hours one summer afternoon, Nakotah had lost her large and boisterous family, her home, and every warrior she had once served with at the Isis barracks. Then the Reg heli-jets had slipped back over the Border before their deeds were discovered.

Posted to Boudica in northern Oregon a week before the sneak attack, Nakotah had been out of town. She'd heard the news while taking her Gunnery College qualification exam. Midway through the test, someone had broken the exam lockdown and had run in shouting. The wallscreen had been activated and Nakotah found that the comline was broadcasting the carnage in high-definition color. Horrified, Nakotah had put her computer slate and stylus down, and fled. She'd found herself alone in a corner of a nearby chapel garden where she cried until her guts rebelled. The camera footage from Isis was burned indelibly in the recesses of her mind, like a photographic image burned onto an old tintype.

Time passed. She'd never gone back to try to re-qualify for Gunnery College. Instead, she began running. For a full year she volunteered as a driver in the night military supply convoys that ran between Artemis and Boudica. Then gradually, because it was a place so strongly associated with the end of her former world, it became too difficult to go to Boudica at all. Somehow, she wasn't really sure why, she'd requested stationing in Artemis and had immersed herself in the life of a warrior private. She'd volunteered for and done all the dirty details, working fourteen-hour days just to be able to sleep at night. She finally ended up on a fortifications building detail, and a tough sergeant had noticed that she was uncommonly good at math. The next thing she knew, she wasn't carrying a shovel any longer. She was doing the design computations on the project and carrying a rangefinder to accurately plot the laser cannon trajectories.

The years had slipped by and Kali's body was never discovered. Over time, idle minds had turned to fantastic gossip in order to fill in the missing pieces about what had happened to the ill-fated city-colony. It had surprised and infuriated Nakotah when she heard that people were beginning to whisper that Kali might have been a traitor, might have been the one who had used Maat's DNA code to open the Northern Bordergate and let the Reg heli-jets into Freeland. Promoted to sergeant by then, Nakotah had hotly defended her friend, telling anyone she heard slandering Kali what she thought of them in spectacular military profanity.

By then, she'd designed and led the construction of armament emplacements in Artemis, Boudica, and Morgan. That year, 2093, when Nakotah was promoted to lieutenant, she found her promotion made some people uneasy. After all, she *was* a mustang. She had worked her way up through the enlisted ranks, bucking the usual path of school and more school, and then serving on the staff of some politically skilled mentor. Whit had Lilith to guide her. Loy worked for the Leader of Boudica. For Nakotah, only her own workaholic tendencies and her uncanny ability with the big guns had generated the slow and grudging recognition from Warrior Command.

And then, in the most surprising event of Nakotah's life, Kali

Tyler had come out of Elysium on the arm of Nakotah's friend, Tomyris Whitaker. In quick order, Nakotah's determinedly unattached lifestyle had been overthrown. While engaging in a casual flirtation with Kali, she'd somehow ended up spending time with and then dating a heartbreaker named Cimbri Braun. To their respective shock, they'd fallen in love with each other. After a few months of game playing and, courtesy of Whit and Kali, a few harrowing experiences, Nakotah and Cimbri were handfasted. A few months later, when Cimbri was elected Leader of Artemis, Nakotah was elected Deputy Leader.

It was nearly a year now that Nakotah had been executing complex plans, organizing teams and translating public policy into concrete results for the citizens of her city-colony. It was the sort of work she'd been doing for years, only now it was done with a much higher profile, in a much more public arena. And now once again, her life was changing.

She had come a long way from the grunt in the trenches. She was respected as a formidable leader. And so they had given her a job to do.

This morning, she had been tapped by Warrior Command and asked to re-up for active duty. Her orders were to lead these warriors and take whatever means were necessary to secure four missing personnel. It was a huge insertion of troops into Elysium that might well be interpreted by their leaders as an act of war. The mission might cost every one of them their lives. Looking out over the women lined up at attention before her, she knew they knew the risk involved in their shared endeavor.

And still, they were here, every one of them volunteers.

They were aware that she was one of them, that she'd once been the lowest of low—dirty and sweat-soaked and humping a fifty-pound pack. They were aware that she wouldn't waste their lives and skills, throwing them into a series of ill-conceived assaults for the glory of the flag. She would use them with precision. Some, the faithful Sergeant Vaid among them, were predicting that Colonel

Berry would employ the fierce talent of her troops with an artistry not seen since Robert E. Lee. Right now, the faces before her shone with trust as well as pride.

Nakotah wondered if their faith in her would survive the first battle. *Nothing like seeing your friends blown to bits to bring the epiphany: War is never a good choice. There is no glory in unleashing the beast within yourself and purposefully taking another life.*

She came to the end of the line of warriors, pivoted and walked back to her original position. Squinting against the bright sun, she looked up at the cloth standard curling and unfurling lazily in the summer breeze. A leaping gray dolphin was set against a green circle, on a deep purple field. The Freeland colors waved against a breathtaking blue sky. It made her heart beat faster just to look at it.

Frowning, she remembered that Elysium had initiated this conflict. Nearly twelve years ago, the Regs had napalmed Isis and burned the survivors at the stake. Last May, only thirty days ago, while the Border was failing, the Regs had used an opening in the photo-electromagnetic screen to slip through and drop a small thermonuclear bomb on Lang. And a few days back, the F-24s had taken another run at Isis. As far as Nakotah was concerned, it was time to take the fight to Elysium. War was never a good choice. But sometimes it was the only choice.

And so, it begins, she thought.

Her eyes shifted, once more traveling over the roughly three hundred warriors standing ramrod straight. The usual light gray uniforms had been exchanged for green camouflage clothing. The boots were polished, the laser rifles, sidearms and packs were all squarely in place. They were ready for action.

We're gonna go through West Virginia like a mama grizzly coming for her cubs. We're gonna find our friends and bring 'em home.

She drew a deep breath and blew it out.

And Gaea help anyone who gets in our way.

~∽~

Kali was dragged up the wide staircase, across the polished wooden floor of the hallway, and then through the oaken doors. Two Regs were on each side of her, grasping her by her upper arms, moving forward at a brisk pace. Lightheaded and frightened, Kali concentrated on keeping her feet moving. Surrounding them was a group of twenty or so guards, all of them dressed in black and shouldering automatic rifles. The men were stomping heavily with each step. In the back of her mind, Kali dazedly realized that some sort of militaristic show was being put on, and she was the center of it.

Once they'd marched down the long hall, they were stopped by a group of four guards before another huge door. A series of passwords were shouted back and forth, then the door was pulled open for them. The soldiers moved inside, dragging her with them.

Even though she was paralyzed with fear, she couldn't help taking long looks at the vast space around her. It was an ornate creation, with plaster designs on the ceilings and colorful tapestries depicting Biblical events on the walls. There were no windows and the interior was lit by smoky torches that seemed to vent from slats in the solid rock walls. The Procurator's palace had all the trappings of a medieval fortress. A faint haze hung over a crowd of people, many of them looking well-fed and wearing colorful exquisitely made fabrics that declared their wealth. Sleek, ankle-length black robes identified the four Reverends present. Beyond them all, at the end of the chamber on a raised carpeted platform, sat a man in a large chair with red cushions. Wide steps were constructed along the length of the platform, and a thick red carpet covered the floor for about ten meters out.

No one stood on the carpet. And before the carpet, there was a three-meter-by-three-meter space where the wooden floor seemed permanently stained with some unidentified darkness.

The guards accompanying the Regs in their loud march through the chamber stomped to an abrupt stop at the carpet's edge. The two Regs on either side of her hauled Kali forward, all the way up to the edge of the stairs. There they stopped and waited.

Breathing hard, Kali called upon her last reserves and made herself stand straight. She looked up at the man lazing in the chair, one leg tossed over the arm of it and his back curled in a deep slouch. Kali noticed the gold jacket and the many ribbons on his chest. *A Procurator*, she realized.

The last time she'd seen someone this highly ranked . . .

Her fear backed off as she remembered again the cruel thin man she had once faced alone in the captivity of a Chicago pleasure chamber. Clutching that memory to her like a weapon, she raised her chin and met the Procurator's hard stare. It could have been her mother Maat's voice whispering in her ear. *Show him what a Freelander is made of.*

"So. It's true," the Procurator hissed. "Freeland warriors are on the loose all over Elysium." He lifted his gaze to the crowd. "We are being invaded."

Amused by the absurdity of the charge, Kali nearly laughed. In a wave of reckless flippancy, she stated. "That's right, Procurator. Surrender or die."

There was a low, collective gasp from the people behind her.

Clearly unused to his prisoners talking back to him, the Procurator shot to his feet and descended the stairs in a rush. "Outrageous! What insolence!" he shouted, then came within inches of her face. "This one needs a lesson in how a female behaves with her betters!"

A massive hulk of a man gripping a coiled whip came from one side, while a black-robed Reverend swept in from the other side. The hulk stood patiently, his eyes staring straight ahead at nothing in particular, while the Reverend insinuated himself between Kali and the Procurator.

"Let us remember that she is pregnant," the Reverend stated soothingly.

"Not with my get!" the Procurator shouted.

"Still—it could be a boy—a gift from the Almighty Savior to take the place of—"

170

"That last wench was carrying a girl!" The Procurator swung around on the Reverend, spittle flying from his mouth in his rage. "You told me the Lord would cause her to deliver me a boy!"

"The Almighty works in—"

"Bullshit!" The Procurator moved around the Reverend and said to Kali, "You'll live as long as you bear me sons, Freeland slut. And if that's not a son you have in you now, you and the babe will meet the same fate the last whore and child did."

"You killed a woman . . . you killed a child . . . ?" Kali was breathing fast as she was flooded with her own rage. "Because the child wasn't the gender you wanted?!" Overcome with disbelief, she turned to the Reverend.

He made a small grimace and averted his eyes.

After the sickening horror of Tor's casual execution at the hands of such men, Kali could bear no more. Energy rushed through her and with a growl, Kali shook off the grip of the two Regs who held her. "You don't deserve children!"

An amber glow centered on the space around them, like a small spotlight. The two Regs gave small shrieks and let go of her arms, staring at their hands as they shrank back.

"What are you doing?!" the Procurator shrieked at them. "Seize her!" To the big man with the whip, the Procurator said, "Chain her up and give her ten lashes!"

The Reverend raised his voice. "You're going to kill the child!"

"All right!" The Procurator amended, "Give her five!"

The big man reached for Kali, and she danced out of his reach, "Touch me and it will be the last woman you'll touch!"

The light around her intensified, becoming a golden-green hue, and Kali squinted. *Where's the skylight that's letting all this in? I didn't see one . . .*

The big man succeeded in grabbing her braid, and pulled her to him. He shifted his hand to her wrist and then screamed. As he bent over and dropped to his knees, the Reverend whirled on Kali.

"What manner of demon is this?"

"I want her chained and whipped!" the Procurator yelled, oblivious to what was unfolding except that his will was not being immediately fulfilled. "Get up!" he yelled at his man, then grabbed the whip when the man didn't immediately stand.

The crowd behind them was making a noise that seemed to Kali to be halfway between a roar and a frightened wail. Kali glanced back at them and thought, *Maybe I ought to capitalize on that fear.*

Red-faced, the Procurator drew an arm back, preparing to wield the leather whip on her himself.

Infuriated, Kali shouted, "You dickless wonder! I curse you!" She swung unsteadily around and faced the crowd. "I curse you all! You don't deserve the gift of being sexual. You don't deserve the gift of having a child." She threw up her arms.

"Stop her!" the Reverend yelled, even as he took four steps away from her.

"I curse you to"—her mind sought for and found the worse curse any male could conceive—"to impotence!"

A collection of gasps echoed throughout the chamber.

"I curse you to infertility!"

Another series of gasps, and someone began screaming. A man called out, "Oh God save us, she's a witch!"

Kali lifted her voice and flung all her loathing and hatred at them. "From this day forward you will have no manhood!"

Pandemonium broke out as the Procurator's audience panicked and began running for the large door at the end of the hall.

She never saw the Reg behind her, moving in closer with the club. She only felt the pain explode at the back of her head.

Chapter 9

From her spot on a limb, high in a huge oak tree, Whit checked the one road leading into Buckhannon. Squinting against the late slant of sun, she held aside a few of the leafy branches that hid her, watching two small horse-drawn carts rumble along the crumbling remnants of a macadam road. She was amazed that after eight hours of telltale silence, another company of Regs had not been sent to see what had become of the first expedition group. Grimly, she contemplated the fact that hundreds of Regs were still no doubt lying in that meadow and no one in Buckhannon seemed to know or care.

She wondered if Danu was all right, then shied away from the stark memory of Tor hanging from a tree limb over the road. *Oh Gaea, help her. Help us all.*

Leaning against the tree trunk, she rubbed her neck, trying to ease the headache that had stolen over her late in the day. She already knew what she wanted to know about Buckhannon's perimeter defenses and had made her plan. Now she was just waiting for the sun to set.

There were ten guards posted at the main gate, twenty posted on the seventeen-meter-high walls. There were also eight separate roving groups of four guards that were on a constant circular patrol of the grassy cleared area that encircled of the walls. It was this last group that she found the most intriguing. The men were not paying much attention to the dark woods approximately a quarter of a kilometer from the wall. Instead, they were talking among themselves and plodding along disinterestedly throughout much of the walk, then straightening up and marching showily when they came within range of being observed by the main gate guards.

She had chosen this tree at the edge of the forest because it provided a good view of all the areas she wanted to see and because its location was among a clump of older trees that extended into the cleared area. In the next hour, she would be climbing lower. When full darkness came, she anticipated a short dash to the edge of the wall.

An hour earlier, as she approached Buckhannon on a narrow deer path, she had dismounted and freed Beauregard, sending the big bay horse trotting off in the general direction of Seneca. She had knelt down in the quiet forest and pulled the emergency kit and bundle of parachute line from her slouch bag. In the kit she had found what she knew was there. The canteen with its built-in water filtration unit. A flare gun with ten flares, a box of waterproof matches, some MREs and a small mirror for signaling. There were also basic first aid items, including bandages, some antiseptic wipes, and several anesthetic and antibiotic osmosis syringes. But the object she wanted was the collapsed, lightweight grappling hook and its attached pre-knotted, climbing rope.

The hook was included in the kit so that a pilot who had parachuted and ended up caught in a tree had a means of escape. Isis was surrounded by kilometers of fir forests, and anyone forced to eject from their aircraft needed a tool to descend from what would be the most likely landing place. The equipment was designed so that it was light, could be easily stowed, and was simple to use in an emergency. A pilot could fasten an anchor on a tree limb, cut herself free of the chute lines, and shinny down the rope.

When opened and secured in the umbrella position, the prongs of the hook would be wide enough to catch on Buckhannon's wall and would allow Whit to climb it.

Earlier, she had studied the wall, looking for the area that was most vulnerable. Then she had noticed the long section where a series of massive buildings inside the city backed up to the wall, their structures actually linked to the concrete and rock construction. Whit's eyes had narrowed as she focused on the flag flying over those buildings. The stars and bars on a navy blue background. The Elysian flag. Which meant they were government buildings.

Now she had a plan, the means, and a target. All she had to do was wait.

Never was much good at that, she thought. Kali had always tweaked her about it.

Memory came stealing over her, like the sweet scent of fermenting berries from the huckleberry bushes below the oak. Kali was called Amelia then. It was a name Baubo had given her, a shield to carry against memories of death and destruction that were so wrenching and painful, Kali had bracketed them away in her mind, in a psychological amnesia that took years to penetrate. But Whit never thought of her as Amelia when she remembered them then. In those days, neither of them knew who Kali was. Neither of them knew about the powers she had at her fingertips. In reality, they had just met.

They were huddled together in the dim light the fire provided, in the domed hut on the Freeland side of the Northern Bordergate. They had escaped Elysium only a week before, and Kali was still recovering from the sword slice she had taken across her right upper shoulder as they'd fought off some Regs.

Kali was lying on a pallet, snuggled under blankets, still looking slightly

175

feverish and endearingly sleepy. Whit was nearby in the close quarters, struggling with the casing on a comline computer, trying to open the unit to do a diagnostic on it. For some reason Whit couldn't fathom, the unit wasn't working. Without it, Whit knew she couldn't send a voice or written message to anyone in Freeland. She needed the comline in order to contact her superiors in Artemis, and ask for a ride out of this remote location on the other side of both the Toxic Zone, and the Wilderness.

After ten minutes of struggling with the tight screws, the Phillips-head screwdriver slipping in her hand, Whit was still unable to get the casing screws to loosen. Because she couldn't accomplish that first step, she was being prevented from getting the computer open and examining the internal works. Frustrated, Whit muttered curses and shouted them, finally shoving the unit away from her with a hard push. She threw the screwdriver down with a particularly colorful expletive. Glaring at Kali, daring the Elysian peasant to say anything, Whit had jumped out of her chair near the little communication desk and stomped out of the hut.

She wandered unhappily in the cool summer night, wondering how she was ever going to get home, how she was ever going to be able to take care of the badly injured woman she had brought illegally across the Border with her. After a long while, she returned to the cache hut, feeling embarrassed about her show of temper.

She entered to find Kali sitting at the desk, her face pale but her expression determined, using her good arm to remove the metal box that served as the computer case. The screws and Phillips-head were beside her on the desk. Whit hurried in, taking the case from the young woman and staring at her, confounded.

"You're not supposed to be up," Whit snapped, then immediately realized how churlish and ungrateful that sounded.

Kali looked up at her, surprised by the tone. "It just seemed . . . so important to you. I thought I'd give it a try."

Feeling a great load of confusing emotion, Whit flashed, "You're important to me, not some stupid machine!"

Blond eyebrows lifting, Kali gave her a wide-eyed stare.

"Now go lie down!" Whit ordered.

176

Whit hustled to put the case on the floor, and caught her when Kali swayed as she stood. She helped her to the pallet, settled her, and covered her with the blanket, then sat a moment stroking Kali's hair back from her face. Kali lay there quietly, watching Whit from beneath lowered lids.

"You don't have much patience, do you?" Kali commented softly.

Whit stiffened. "Sure I do. The damn screws in that thing are worthless, badly cast pieces of . . ." Frowning, Whit demanded, "How did you get those screws to release?"

"Well, they were tight, but I just stuck with it." Kali's warm, soft brown eyes slowly blinked with exhaustion. "I just kept trying to turn the screwdriver and then the screws were turning themselves." Consternation crossed her face, and she whispered, "Sometimes, when I really want something to happen . . . it just does."

Whit remarked, "That can't be." She realized that Kali seemed to be on the edge of sleep, and she had no actual reason to keep stroking the woman's soft, yellow-gold hair. Reluctantly, she drew her hand back. "It doesn't make sense."

"Oh, like throwing down the screwdriver did," Kali mumbled.

Whit sat there, eyes narrowed, trying to think of a perfectly reasonable explanation for her behavior that did not also involve a childishly biting retort. By the time she did, Kali was breathing deeply, her mouth slightly open in an obvious surrender to slumber. Feeling enchanted and at the same time oddly disturbed, Whit watched her, contemplating the appealing face and the surging emotions she felt around this stranger.

Later, she worked on the comline computer for hours and never did figure out what was wrong with it, or get it to work. Finally, she gave up, grabbed a blanket, and lay down beside the lovely young Elysian.

It wouldn't be until months later that she discovered Kali was as much a Freelander as she was. It would be a long while before she found out that Kali was the daughter of the infamous Maat, who had supposedly let the Elysians into Freeland to annihilate the first city-colony of Isis, a lie put to rest once Kali found the real villain. A long while before she found out that Kali, by her mother's hand, was a genetically engineered mage, capable of causing extraordinary things to happen through sheer concentration or extreme emotion.

And what a ride it's been since then.

A little grin made the corner of Whit's mouth crook up before the terror gripped her. *I can't lose her. I can't.* She touched the gray-brown bark of the oak she rested against, praying to the Goddess with a desperate urgency, praying as she never had before. *Goddess, please, please protect her. Please help me find her.*

After a bit, she drew a series of calming breaths and willed herself to reclaim her serene resilience. Gradually, she settled back into the support of the tree trunk. By now she knew it grew very dark in the heart of West Virginia once the sun set. And the moon wouldn't be up until after midnight.

Kali heard someone moan. For a moment, she tried to push through the thick, almost palpably viscous layers separating her from consciousness, then somehow lost the will to do it, and simply floated between wakefulness and sleep.

Gradually, she became aware that her head hurt so badly the pain would have brought her to her knees if she was standing. *Good thing I'm lying down.* She knew this because she could feel a chill, flat, hard surface all along her left side.

"She's waking up," a male voice close by announced.

"Make her take the spell off!" another slightly hysterical male shrieked, the volume making Kali wince.

"This is a delicate matter. We must pray for our Lord and Savior's guidance and handle this with—"

"Listen to me, you self-castrated queer in a black frock! That female will take her curse off me or you will burn beside her in the square tomorrow!"

There was a brief, electric silence, then the gentle, firm male voice began again. "Sire, I do not think it is in your best interest to kill this woman, let alone burn her for a witch. The people are . . .

very upset." Another pause. "This summer's crops have not yet begun to give a yield and since the last harvest was meager, there is little food. The Regulators are barely supplied. The common people are starving. Since we left Bethesda and retreated to Buckhannon, we have perhaps been a little too far removed from the government convoy routes and so we have not been delivered our share of bimonthly munitions. Without food, the population is . . . turning against us. Whatever skills this woman has can surely be put to our use. We need resources to continue to stay in power . . ."

A cold voice lashed him. "I know! Do you think I don't read the reports? If every other stronghold in Elysium wasn't doing as badly, I'd have been shot and replaced long ago! I can't do anything about it! If the serfs weren't so lazy and didn't hoard the crops they raise, there'd be enough for everyone. Damn serfs! I should just kill them all!"

The figure that had been standing above her shifted away, toward the angry man. "Sire, we've discussed this before. You can't continue to kill serfs. It robs us of our labor force. We need them, especially since the plague is taking so many just now. Sometimes a few examples are all that's needed. A flogging in church for food theft. A shirker in a tiny cage, suspended above the crowd in the marketplace. Laming a captured runaway. Small penances."

The angry man was pacing. "Not in *her* case. I want her burned!" She heard him abruptly move closer to her. "Tonight I was going to have a good dinner and that special wine, and then have *her*, but I can't even feel anything there—it might as well be paralyzed!" He seemed to be struggling to keep from crying. He whispered to the other man, "What if it *is* paralyzed? What if it's going to stay like this forever?" His voice broke on the last few words. "I'm ruined."

"You must pray for forgiveness, Procurator Fowler, for surely God has brought this to pass. You have done something to offend the heavenly Father, and so you are being punished in the most heinous of ways."

The angry man choked, crying, "Pray for me, Reverend Sharkey."

"Meet me in the chapel, sire. We will appeal to God's divine mercy and try to make amends." The Reverend moved closer to Kali. "Let me spend a few minutes alone with this sinful harlot, to see if I can bring about her repentance."

Kali heard the other man walk hurriedly from the room.

Several minutes crawled by as Kali lay still, resolving that as long as she could she would try to hide the fact that she was fully conscious.

Then, a soft voice caressed her ear. "So, little demon, now you will choose. Either you serve me, or you die like Saint Joan in the flames. It will be an awful death."

The ruse over, Kali blinked open her eyes and rolled over. The Reverend was kneeling on one knee beside her. "What do you want?" *Let's cut to the chase, hypocrite.* Moving with care, frowning against the headache, she sat up and looked around.

No longer in the throne room, they were now in a large, richly appointed chamber. The floor was smooth slate flagstone and nearby thick royal blue rugs lay beneath plush furniture. A hearth fire was crackling softly, and a large window gave a view of a wall and a rooftop.

The Reverend surveyed her. "You shriveled every man in the throne room a short time ago."

I did? I thought I'd just give them a good scare . . .

"Remove that fearsome and unholy curse, and agree to do my bidding." He placed a hand on her hair, stroking her like a dog. "With special contritions, you can be granted absolution. You will be my handmaiden and I will keep you safe from . . . that ignorant boor."

Kali refused to meet his hard gaze, but she felt it on her, demanding compliance.

"The Procurator has become . . . difficult to manage." The Reverend sighed. "With the populace near open rebellion and the Regulator ranks being steadily depleted by plague, my superiors will consider it appropriate when I . . . take action and usurp the Procurator's role within this community."

Gracefully, he leaned over and kissed her cheek, causing Kali to go very still. She was filled with foreboding.

"I am a learned man, a patient man." He moved his mouth across her ear in an openly sexual caress and Kali flinched away, making him laugh. "A man with appetites. And you have caught my fancy, girl. I want you and I'll have you. You are too fair and gifted to be wasted in a few savage encounters with the Procurator."

"I can't do what you think I can," she said. "It was . . . the power of suggestion, not a spell."

The Reverend shook his head. "Oh, but you *did* shrivel us." He reached down, smoothed his hand across the robe, and began to stroke himself suggestively.

Disgusted, Kali turned away.

He stopped, caught the shoulder closest to her wound, making Kali wince and writhe.

"Much as I'd like to teach you your rightful place right now, on this very floor, there is no strength in my rod. You have stolen my righteous power."

A nervous laugh escaped Kali at that analogy. *What a crazy way to say he can't get it up!*

In a soft, reasonable tone, the Reverend finished, "You will remove the curse you cast and recant your witchery. You will submit to me. You will use your . . . demon craft . . . only as I direct, in my cause." He let go of her shoulder, folding his arms. "Or you will die."

Kali knew only one answer. "No."

"You realize, of course, that you are sentencing your child to death."

Better to get it over with than condemn us both to years of a living death. "No."

Furious, he backhanded her, splitting her lip and knocking Kali against a chair. He jumped to his feet and she huddled into a ball as his boot struck her back. Instinctively responding to the danger to the baby, she grasped her own startled anger and lashed a yellow rope of mage fire across the space he inhabited. A scream alerted her

181

that her impulsive reaction had more substance than she guessed. She raised her head and saw him clutching his arm, then saw the red slice across it and the burned black sleeve.

"Witch!" he roared. The patronizing smugness was gone. Sheer terror had transformed his face.

Wide-eyed, he scurried away from her, racing to the thick wooden door. Throwing it open, he called, "Guards!" The same two burly Regs who had marched her before the Procurator clumped into the chamber. "Take her to the stake in the market square. Chain her and ready the pyre for a great fire."

The Regs glanced at each other, a rigid look of fear in their eyes.

"Do it!" the Reverend yelled. "Or I'll make you wish you had!"

Visibly gulping, the two Regs came slowly toward her in sideways steps, as if approaching a trapped bobcat.

Weary and dizzy with pain, Kali got her feet under her and stood. "C'mon. I won't hurt you."

One on each side, the men took her upper arms. The muscles in her right shoulder were stretched as they began to move and pain overcame every other perception. She felt herself stumbling as the Regs gave her a brisk escort from the room.

The Procurator followed them to the door. "The next time I see you, witch, you will crave my mercy." He paused in the threshold, watching them go.

She was only ten steps into the hall when she passed out. The Regs draped her arms over their shoulders and carried her through the Procurator's stronghold and then down into the square just outside the structure.

She was awake again when Miles Macowmber arrived with his green backpack and a serious expression. Kali was sitting forlornly on an overturned wooden box, her wrists encased in a pair of shackles. The two Regs who were her escorts stood dourly off to the side, looking as if they wanted nothing more than to get away from her.

Miles was gentle and caring as he tended her wounds. He murmured apologies for his countrymen as he worked, saying he wished he could do something to help her. Kali's eyes were on the twenty or so Regs nearby who were busily building a four-meter-high platform in the center of the vast cobblestone square. The platform was relatively small and was being constructed around a blackened and broad wooden column that seemed to be a permanent fixture. There were blackened rings fastened at various heights. When Miles was done administering to her, he handed her a bottle of water and asked her to drink as much as she could. While Kali tipped the bottle to her lips, Miles went and fetched his own box, then sat down beside her in a show of moral support.

She had no illusions about his role in this. He was obviously conflicted, but, bottom line, he was wearing an enemy uniform. She knew that Miles was basically a nice, sensitive boy who was uselessly battling his sexual orientation in a land where homicidal bigotry was encouraged, rather than condemned. The jaded part of her suspected that Miles was beside her because Reverend Sharkey and Procurator Fowler wanted to be sure that she was awake and lucid for the next morning's festivities. The end result of Miles's ministrations would be that she had enough fight left to provide a good show.

A truck rolled up with a load of long slender logs. Voices murmuring quietly as they talked among themselves, the Regs offloaded the logs, placing them beneath the platform in a carefully built construction.

Within her, Kali felt her daughter whirling madly, a tiny tadpole protesting the events unfolding with a bout of frantic activity. Kali's eyes filled, and a tear rolled down her face as she bent over, her arms reaching across her middle, hugging herself.

At least Whit isn't here, she thought, trying to find some consolation in the bloody mess her rescue effort had become. *At least I'll be made properly accountable for Tor's loss.*

A ghostly voice came to her. *Hey . . . what a load of shit.*

Kali turned, looking for her, for the owner of a voice she knew so well. "Tor?!" she called.

Miles sat up from his defeated posture by her side, watching her expectantly. The Regs busily building the pyre turned and looked at them.

"What is it?" Miles asked.

Kali shook her head, not knowing how to explain the feeling of hope that had accompanied that voice.

Don't give up, the faint voice whispered. *It's not over, yet.*

"Did you hear that?" she asked Miles in a low voice.

"Hear what?"

Tense and uncertain, Kali gently bit her lip, unable to answer. She doubted her abilities; she was half-convinced that exhaustion and loss of blood were playing havoc with her mind.

Then, from out of nowhere, a great swell of feeling rolled over Kali, engulfing her, completely enfolding her in the warmth of a presence unlike any other in her life. *Whit. She's here. She's somewhere very, very close.*

Kali lifted her head, searching above her. "Oh, Gaea. Please help us."

On her right, Miles sat patiently, his expression worried.

I have to trust someone, Kali thought. After a moment, she asked, "Do you really want to help me, Miles, or are you just . . . trying to ease your conscience?"

Hand over hand, Whit pulled herself up the knotted rope. The night outside the wall was a black void. A collection of torches lit the wall above, placed at uneven intervals that seemed more a haphazard show than an actual deterrent. Whit hesitated at the top edge of the wall, suspended in the night, listening for Reg patrols and hearing only what sounded like a hammer banging in the distance. She stretched an arm over the top, then cast quick glances in either direction. When she was satisfied the immediate area was clear, she scrambled over the flat surface and dropped down to the walkway on the other side. She was in a darkened space, but to reduce the risk of being seen, she moved into a corner next to the wall of a building.

She loosened the grappling hook as she passed its landing place, collapsed the hooks and recoiled her climbing rope.

Now to scout around.

She shoved the hook and the rope back into her slouch bag, then crouched down, taking stealthy steps along the walkway. Just as she came to the corner of the huge government building that was blocking her view into the city, she heard voices. There was a rain spout fastened to the wall, connecting with the gutters that were attached to the edge of the roof. Without a second thought, Whit shimmied up the rain spout, hoisted herself onto the slate shingled roof and crawled halfway up the slightly angled incline. Trying to keep her breathing and movements quiet, she froze in the darkness and listened to the two men below her.

"Sire, calm yourself. This threatening to whip someone every other minute is causing your counselors to think something is terribly wrong. You'll create a panic if you are not more careful." It was a smooth, rational voice. A voice accustomed to appeasing a superior. "Now why did you insist on coming all the way out here to talk?"

"We can't be overheard here," a querulous man replied brusquely. "I've assigned the watch to the gate, in expectation of an attack."

"An attack? Why? What have you heard?"

"There's a witch here!" The deeper voice was slightly hysterical. "It's a sign! We're doomed!"

"Sire, she is not a strong witch. We have her under our control. Her arrival is not a sign of doom, but rather of great good fortune. We will blame the crop failures of the last few years and the recent difficulties with the serfs and the plague on her, and then tell the peasants her death will bring a great cleansing. Once she is burned, the spell she cast on us this evening will surely fall away."

The second man sounded harsh and bitter. "You fool, this isn't just about *her*! The base at Andrews isn't answering our radio calls, or anyone else's for that matter. Up and down the eastern seaboard, not one stronghold has been able to raise them for two days now. The other strongholds say no flights are coming out of Maryland."

There was a thick, troubled silence, then the first man said, "Could it be that the other strongholds are encountering what we have been dealing with—the way the heli-jets all seem to crash once they fly into the Alleghenies?"

"No, it's more than that." Another tense silence. "There are reports of refugees fleeing Maryland. Reports of a mushroom cloud."

"Oh . . . dear God."

"And now, there's some sort of escalating rebellion. In Massachusetts and Vermont, the barracks were assaulted and the Regs overwhelmed. Procurators were strung up like common criminals. The Pennsylvania and Carolina Procurators have both locked the gates to their strongholds. They're expecting an attack."

"From whom?"

"From the populace—you blind ass! They *hate* us—they have always hated us!" There was a sound as if someone was being struck repeatedly. "How can you be so stupid?!"

"How dare you? I am a man of God!" the other protested.

"Shuddup!!" the angry one hissed. "You'll take whatever I give you!"

The sound of tussling went on for several minutes, then one man broke free and footsteps sounded as he ran away. The other followed, cursing to himself about "damned castrating priests."

In the silence that descended, Whit heard the hammers banging busily, not too far in the distance. It was as if something were under construction on the other side of the roof she rested upon.

Andrews isn't answering their radio calls. And there are refugees talking about . . . a mushroom cloud?

Swallowing hard, Whit had a brief flash of memory: the Elysian F-24 she had dueled with over the Shenandoah River Valley, black smoke billowing from its wing as it broke off the engagement and banked toward the southeast horizon. With his retreat, Whit had taken her own opportunity to prioritize, choosing to search for Danu

186

instead of fighting to the death over enemy territory. *It was the F-24 I thought had a nuke*, she realized. *He took it home with him.*

Instead of feeling righteous vengeance, instead of thinking of all the maimed and burned-to-dust Freelanders, first in Isis, then in Lang, she felt only a cold hole in the pit of her stomach. Not only Regs, but thousands of innocent, oppressed Marylanders had died two days back. Because a stupid pilot, afraid to improvise, afraid to admit to his superiors in a quick radio call that he had not dropped his payload where they told him to, had dragged his wounded jet back to his home base, and probably crashed while attempting a landing.

The people of Elysium didn't deserve that kind of death. No one did.

It came to her then, that she had finally met the real people of Elysium.

They were not the corrupted, self-serving, and ignorant individuals she had known in Bethesda during her undercover work there two years ago. Bethesda was a city dominated by the Regs, the Reverends, and the Procurator, in that order. For the people of Bethesda had made despicable bargains long ago to preserve their lives and livelihood; there was no vileness, no low act they were not capable of doing with both cunning and glee.

But there were others, people who chose to live outside of the Procurators' strongholds. People who had resisted the New Order from the start, and who still resisted it, more than eight decades later. People like Jamie and Irene Rexrode, Florey, and the rest of the Seneca Amazons. People like the men of the mountain clans; men who were brave enough to go into battle against automatic weapons, clutching only their ingenuity and their ancient, single-shot rifles. People like the serfs who ran away, and infiltrated the West Virginian forests, risking the unknown countryside and death by exposure in order to get out from under the cruel thumb of their rulers.

Gazing up at the starry sky above her, Whit examined the fact that she no longer hated Elysians. In fact, she wanted to help them. After all, it was their Gaea-given right to be free.

Aware suddenly that the hammers had ceased pounding, Whit wondered what was so important that it had to be built this late at night. Carefully, she began climbing up the roof again. She needed to see the layout of the city from a high vantage point before deciding how she was going to proceed. She'd just take a good look and then develop the end of her plan.

There are insurrections breaking out, Whit thought, still processing what she had heard. *This whole country could be on the verge of revolution . . .*

She came to the edge of the roof and peered over. Her eyes found the large gathering of Regs in the square below, scanning the small plywood stage and the large dark pole that rose from it. The Regs were scurrying about, placing logs carefully beneath and around the stage, as if building the works for a big camp fire. *What the hell is that?*

Then, in the bright torchlight that lit the area, she saw a slim young man dressed like a Regulator. He was standing, talking to someone who was sitting down, but Whit couldn't quite see the seated person. Then the young man moved to the side, giving Whit a clear view. Her eyes took in a slender, yellow-haired figure, sitting on an overturned box. There were chains on her wrists, and she looked tired and disheveled.

Kali. The shock hit Whit so hard that she gasped aloud. *Oh, sweet Athena, no.*

Danu strained her eyes against the night as the Amazons dismounted and tied their well-trained mounts to the slight branches of the trees. She could tell by the broad squatty outline of trees against the lighter starlit sky that they were at the far edges of an apple orchard that bordered the southern side of Buckhannon. She remembered the map Jamie had shown her and knew that they were perhaps two hundred meters from the main gate.

Emboldened by their victory over the Reg company they'd battled earlier that afternoon, the Amazons and clansmen were about to embark on a raid of Buckhannon itself. Exhausted and distraught, Danu was operating on automatic pilot now.

Earlier in the afternoon, she had found herself on a horse, with Florey in the lead. They were traveling back to the main group of Amazons and the clansmen, who were still congregating and sorting loot in that awful field of death.

Tor's body was on Florey's horse, draped over the saddle and covered with a homespun gray blanket, looking for all the world like a sack of dry goods, except for the bloody hand hanging down, swinging with the slow stride of the horse. Once she stopped crying, Danu felt herself sliding into an emotionless space. Her throat felt raw and her skull blazed with a headache, and gradually, a bleak gloom seemed to pierce every cell in her body. No amount of tears could assuage her pain; she stopped crying and pulled everything in tight.

Florey described to Jamie how Whit had asked where the Regs would have taken Kali, and then had galloped off "like all she had to do was ride in there and demand her lady." Jamie sat quietly on her gray horse, thinking hard. Then she raised her head, and called to her troops, "How 'bout we take this fight to Ol' Fowler himself, ya'll?" The cheer that came back was deafening.

The Amazons gave her the option to return to Seneca with the few youngest who were ordered to take Tor back to the village and inform Chief Rexrode and "the Witch" about the day's events and the latest plan. They seemed to take it in stride, though, when Danu answered that she intended to be in on the action in Buckhannon. Maybe it was because they knew she was Whit's friend, or maybe it was because they knew that she wanted a chance at the ones who had killed Tor. In either case, there were no attempts to dissuade her, send her home, or ascertain her mental health, which her Warrior comrades would have done if they had been there instead. The Amazons merely gave her one of their newly captured M-28s when she asked for one, and then made sure she knew how to use it. She had no idea which method of allowing her to work through her monumental grief was the more humane.

As they moved through the apple orchard in the utter ebony night, she could see the dimly visible phosphorous blotches on the backs of the buckskin shirts all around her. The phosphorous, Jamie had told her, was from the depths of the old caves near Seneca. Once night had fallen, Jamie had asked Florey to open a pottery jug and paint a stripe on everyone's back. They would be able to know who was who if they came across a Reg perimeter patrol, or ended up being chased through the woods after the raid.

She knew the clansmen were spread out on the east and north sides of Buckhannon, coming in through the deep woods as quietly as the Amazons with the same bloodthirsty intent.

Ahead, through the trees, she could see small flaming torches on the crest of something looming in the dark. Tiny figures were visible, parading in front of a huge panel with a dull and dark surface, suggesting that it was a door made of iron. *It's a walled city*, Danu guessed. *And the wall has to be more than fifteen meters high. We don't have enough firepower to take down that door or breach the walls. How the hell are we going to get over a wall that big?*

A whippoorwill sang nearby, and the Amazons came to a stop. Danu turned her head, listening. Amid snapping twigs and a quiet rush of movement through grass, there was a constant, low-pitched humming noise drifting from the open field off to their left. Puzzled, Danu thought she recognized the sound, but then thought, *No, can't be. The only thing that could sound like that are hundreds of motorcycle troopers out on night maneuvers.*

Jamie gave a quiet hawk whistle and all the Amazons turned, bringing up their M-28s and hustling to crouch behind individual apple trees. Another whistle and the Amazons began moving from tree to tree, steadily closer to the edge of the field.

"Colonel Rexrode, wait!" Danu hissed.

She was squinting, trying to find the double stripe of phosphorous that was meant to distinguish the commanding officer from the rest of the Amazons. Unable to find Jamie and suddenly terrified about what she suspected was going to happen, Danu decided to take a chance. She shouldered her weapon and ran straight out into the field.

Knees lifting, legs striding quickly, she called back over her shoulder, "They're Freelanders—don't shoot!"

Facing forward, running faster, she began calling in a clear, carrying voice, "Warriors, stand down! Warriors, stand down! Allies on the field!"

Within minutes she was dodging the motorcycles hurtling by her. Almost immediately, someone grabbed her around the waist and took her to the ground. A sharp edge was against her neck and a lean, hard body was holding her down.

A few feet away, a hushed voice said, "How do they know our code?"

"Shut up," the body on top of Danu rasped. A hand felt between Danu's legs, then moved up her chest, lingering on her breast. "It's a woman," her captor reported to another figure who dashed up, one of several looming up against the stars. "Get an officer."

In the dim starlight, Danu saw that they were wearing night vision goggles, which explained why they were having such ease seeing her. "I'm Lieutenant Danu Sullivan," she began, but a hand closed over her mouth, silencing her.

A few minutes later, the officer was there, and Danu was pulled roughly to her feet. "She says she's Lieutenant Sullivan, but she stinks like an Elysian," the woman who held her announced.

All at once, Danu had had enough. "Get that fucking blade off my throat."

Incautiously, the woman pressed the knife harder. Danu felt the edge cut her, then felt the steady trickle of warmth pour down her shirt. Growling, Danu grabbed the woman's arm, twisting and snap-

191

ping it up behind the woman's back, making her cry out, and then drop the knife. Danu shoved her away from her.

The dark figures around her all had their weapons drawn, their postures wary and tense in the faint starshine from above.

Quietly she said, "I'm Lieutenant Danu Sullivan, born in Boudica, now making my home in Isis." Danu drew a breath. "But I've also been serving with the Amazons of Seneca these past few days, so I guess you could call me an Elysian, if you wanted to. I'd be proud of it. And so would Whit."

The officer said, "Anyone here know Sullivan well enough to vouch for her?"

"Yes ma'am," several different voices answered readily. The women moved closer.

"Kneel down, all of you. We gotta keep the light low."

Danu went to a knee, and several others knelt beside her. Everyone around them slipped off their night vision gear. A small flashlight was turned on and the light aimed toward the ground so that the small illumination escaping sideways caught Danu's face.

"It's her," one voice confirmed. "Yeah, it's Sullivan," another supplied. "Hey, good to see ya, kid!" a veteran offered, grabbing her shoulder and squeezing. "How'd ya find us?"

Feeling a bit ragged, realizing that she could have easily been killed by her own forces, Danu felt a wild laugh burble up unexpectedly.

None of the warriors joined in; instead, they all stared at her, as if she were crazy.

Quelling her laughter, Danu said, "You're damn noisy."

The officer retorted stiffly, "These are decibel squelch engines. Can't get any quieter machines."

Shaking her head, Danu offered, "Try yer feet."

"There better be a ma'am at the end when you're talking to me, second Lieutenant. I'll forgive you in this dark for not being able to see my insignia. I'm a first Lieutenant."

Danu snorted.

Once, only days ago, she would have cared deeply about the correctness of rank and the courteous observances of civility. She was that kind of person. Details mattered. But the experiences of the past few days had changed her. None of the old political devices seemed to matter anymore. Now, there was only one thing on her mind. She had to help Whit get Kali out of Buckhannon. Then she could crawl off to some corner and figure out a way to deal with the fearsome agony wailing in some walled-off section of her soul. Tor was dead. And nothing was ever going to be the same.

Her voice soft, Danu addressed the first Lieutenant. "I brought some friends. One of them outranks you."

"What?" the first Lieutenant asked. "Who . . . ?"

"Resistance fighters. Send word to your C.O. that we have close to two hundred allies on the field, all of them very familiar with the target you're moving against." With a calm certainty, Danu suggested, "We have time to meet and consider some strategy."

The first Lieutenant turned to a warrior beside her. "You heard her. Go."

The warrior jogged over to her motorcycle, flipped up the kickstand, and took off in a quiet hum and a soft shushing whisper of grass.

Eyeing Danu, the first Lieutenant asked, "The cycles are too loud, huh?"

"The group I'm running with have sensitive ears. They were setting up to ambush you when I figured out what was going on . . ." Danu fell silent.

". . . and ran out into the midst of us, calling a 'stop operations' code that's no longer in use as of yesterday." The first Lieutenant went quiet, then shifted closer. "You're lucky you're not dead."

Danu repeated, "Lucky," and laughed bitterly.

"Have you seen Kali Tyler, or Tor Yakami?" someone close behind her asked.

Danu struggled to answer, gulping against the hard lump that grew in her throat. "They were caught by a company of Regs."

A round of gasps came from the darkness around her.

"I've seen Tor. She's dead."

More gasps. A small, "Oh, no . . ." in particular made Danu's heart twist.

Danu took a shallow breath, trying to hold on to her numbness. "Kali was taken prisoner and we think she's been given to the Procurator in Buckhannon."

Another swell of unhappy murmurs.

The first Lieutenant reached out and touched Danu's arm, expressing sympathy. With a detached comprehension, Danu remembered that her relationship with Tor was common knowledge in Isis. A stretch of uncomfortable silence passed. Then the demands of the moment made themselves felt. Developing a coordinated plan of attack encompassing the Warriors, the Amazons, and the clansmen took precedence over everything.

The first Lieutenant cleared her throat. "Can you get your friends to come out to talk? Colonel Berry is probably gonna move up into the woods back that way and set up a command quarters, go over cartography maps and the like with the squad leaders."

"Give me a minute," Danu stated.

She moved away through the grass. She wasn't far from them when she heard someone remark, "Well, she's stranger than ever." No one countered the observation.

Oh, Tor! Danu called, her inner voice a wail of loss. *You made me normal. How in Hecate's name am I ever gonna be able to make it without you?*

She began to run, stumbling through the grass, until suddenly the Amazons were moving out from behind the trees and surrounding her. Jamie moved to her side, touching her neck and feeling the trickle of blood.

"We watched and listened," she said shortly. "You saved their lives, but they sure didn't thank you none fer it. They just don't seem to treat you right, youngun. They certainly don't respect you like they oughta. I'm thinkin' they's a bunch o' damn fools."

Stunned by the sudden, unsolicited affirmation from such an unlikely source, Danu's mouth dropped open. Then, lamely, she tried to explain. "I'm . . . uhm . . . I'm different from them—and they all know it. It's always been like that. It doesn't . . . bother me much . . . anymore." Danu shrugged, trying to appear unaffected.

Arms reached out and went around her, drawing her slowly closer until Jamie was fully embracing her and using one hand to guide Danu's head to her shoulder. It was a comforting hug that seemed to reach down into Danu and soothe the raw nerves and adrenaline she was running on now. Tears flooded Danu's eyes.

"Hang on. Yer doin' fine."

Danu nodded.

After a moment, they separated. Danu observed several tough Amazon braves wiping their eyes.

"Now, I'll go parley with their muckey-mucks, but I want you by my side, 'kay Freelander?" Jamie placed her hand on Danu's shoulder.

"Me? I'm a two-bit Lieutenant. You don't need me. Take Florey with you. She's like a seasoned master sergeant."

"No. Yer my . . . attache . . . ain't that what they called it in ol' Longstreet's corps?"

Danu nodded, remembering reading about the foreign soldiers who had traveled to Gettysburg and back with the Confederate army.

"Yeah. I want yer advice and counsel, my Freelander friend." Jamie began to move forward, toward the ranks of motorcycle warriors who were dismounted and waiting across the field. "I know a valuable officer when I meet one, unlike some other durn fools."

Feeling unexpectedly succored and flattered, Danu fell in step beside her. The hug had felt like a long, cool drink when she was parched to near collapse. She could hang on now. She glanced shyly over at Jamie; the sorrow she felt was still almost unbearable, but she had been reminded that she was not alone. And it amazed her how much that helped.

Behind the two women, the Amazons arranged themselves into a loose formation.

They crossed the field silently, jogging together like a pack of wolves.

Chapter 10

Feeling cold and damp from the night air, Whit carefully stretched one by one her stiff and aching limbs. Her position on the roof was not precarious, because it was not that steep an incline, but the slate shingles were coated with dew, and slick. The last thing she needed to do was slip and fall off the roof or make a clatter trying to prevent it. She had kept a vigilant watch all night, and she was tired now. Her eyes burned and she rubbed them, feeling hungry and irritable and so worried about Kali that her mind was running in circles.

One thing was certain. She knew the deeds that lay before her on this day might be the most important of her life.

The sky was turning lighter. Dawn was coming with the indefatigable precision of fate. The day was beginning, and Kali's execution was set to play out in front of her.

Think of something! she told herself. *There's got to be a way to get her out of there!*

Yet every plan she weighed came out the same: Kali being torn apart by automatic weapons fire before Whit even got her out of the square.

We need a distraction, and the bigger it is, the better.

Down below, once the construction of the pyre was complete, the truck had been sent away. A group of thirty Regs had encircled Kali, obviously standing guard. Whether it was a guard to keep others away or to keep Kali captive, Whit was unable to guess. However, there were far more men there than were at the main gate, and she noticed that none of the brawny men would turn their backs on the defeated-looking blonde at their center.

Oh, what have you been up to, love, to scare the big, bad Regs like that?

Much earlier, the young Reg who had been a constant presence by Kali's side had sent for a blanket and a basket of food. Whit had watched as Kali had eaten only a little, then at the boy's gentle urging, had laid down wearily out on the cobblestones, huddling beneath the blanket. The boy Reg had sat on his crate, staying by Kali's side for hours.

Under the brightening sky, the boy stood and went over to one of the largest Regs. The boy took the Reg aside, speaking with him and gesturing to the government building below Whit. As if to emphasize a point, the boy shook his head "no" as he pointed at Kali's sleeping form. Continuing his instruction, the boy pointed at the Reg, then made a motion with that same index finger, dragging it slowly across his own throat. It was the universal miming of death.

The big Reg nodded grimly and returned to his place in the circle. The boy returned to Kali, leaned down and adjusted the blanket, then grabbed up his knapsack and began to walk toward the building beneath Whit. He passed out of sight, into the shadows.

Whit inched down the incline of the roof, processing what she had seen. Her eyes were wide with understanding. *That kid just warned off the officer in charge of that detail. If anything happens to Kali while the kid is gone, the Reg will die. The kid's gotta be backed by someone with power for that to mean anything because he'd never be able to take out one of those brutes.*

Wondering what she was going to do, feeling the harsh edge of panic slipping up on her, twisting her gut, Whit lay back on the slate shingles and stared up at the sky. Fine threads of fog were drifting from the forest, ghosts of vapor wandering over the walls of Buckhannon. With the increasing breeze, the fog seemed to come swirling into the city, dancing eerily as it gathered and slid from the rooftops to the ground. Beyond the fog, the sky was changing. What had been bright diamonds in a dome of black ink was now a lesser pageant of stars glinting from a royal blue glow. Shifting her gaze to the southeast, Whit noted the thunderheads on the horizon. Dimly lit clumps of cirrocumulus clouds nestled there, dark and gray underneath and fluffy white on the crests.

Think, she exhorted. *Who the hell cares if a thunderstorm is coming?*

The sky was growing lighter. She lay there, almost despairing, shifting puzzle pieces around in her mind. With a gradual, inexorable certainty, the shapes and outlines of the structure she rested upon were becoming visible. Whit realized that she was going to have to get off the roof soon, or risk being seen from the battlement walkway as it ran along other sections of the wall in the distance. She was casting a gaze about, trying to decide her next move, when she heard a short, but definite, "Psst!"

It sounded close, so Whit willed herself to stillness and waited. "Pssst!" The noise came again, more insistent this time. Not sure what was going on, Whit pulled her knife from the sheath on her belt.

A quiet voice floated up to Whit from the walkway below the roof edge. "She says to tell you that she knows you're here."

Every fiber in Whit's body vibrated.

"And—oh yeah—the password is 'Bean Sprout.' She said to tell ya that—sorry."

Bean Sprout. Lilith's nickname for her when she was a little girl, before Lilith and Maat had divorced, before the horror of the Fall of Isis, before

Kali had been stolen by a marauding Reg Tribune and forced to murder him in order to take her freedom back.

"Come down. I've sworn an oath to help you."

Moments crawled by while Whit debated whether to move or not. Then she realized that she really had no choice. If whoever was below planned on entrapment, Whit was not going delay the arrest long by huddling on the wet and slippery slate shingles.

Decisively, she scrambled to the edge of the gutter. She took a quick glance over the edge and saw the boy Reg she had seen in the square with Kali.

He looked up at her, his apprehensive eyes tracing her buckskin attire and then the knife she grasped in her hand. Whit saw him swallow twice in quick succession, but he didn't draw the pistol from the holster on his hip, and he didn't turn tail. Wondering what was underway, but satisfied that the boy was on an errand from Kali, Whit decided it was worth taking a chance. She returned her knife to its sheath, then grasped the gutter and the drainpipe and swung a leg over the edge. Within seconds she clambered neatly down the drainpipe and landed beside the boy. He backed away, wary.

Whit realized that she must look quite the wildwoman, with her dirty hands and probably a dirty face, too. All the riding, fighting, and tree and wall climbing had no doubt left their mark on her. She knew her shoulder length, dark hair was windblown and snarled. And then there was the Amazon clothing, all skins and beaded belts.

"Whose side are you on?" Whit asked, her voice low.

The boy looked surprised and glanced each way, checking the battlements walkway to be sure no one was coming.

"Why are you doing this?" Whit pressed. She had to know before she went anywhere with him. *Either I can trust him or I can't.*

The boy's dark brown eyes were on her with the cautious attention one gives a fierce dog. At her second question, they wavered, dropping a bit. "They want to kill her." He shook his head, resigned to what was probably commonplace in Elysium, but still mildly indignant. "She hasn't done anything . . . except get caught while she

199

was passing through." He grew a little angry. "It's not right. Like just about everything else they do . . . It's just not right."

"Why her?" Whit asked, feeling a surge of jealousy. He was a good looking youngster, and she suspected he wanted Kali for himself. "You've seen years of this shit, I'm thinking. Why does it matter that it's *her* they want to kill?"

In a classic adolescent reaction, he was first sullen, then embarrassed. "How should I know?" He made a quick grimace. "It just does." He checked the walkway again. "What's with the Socratic discourse? We gonna do this, or not?"

Hmph. How does he know about Socrates in a land where the first order of business in 2010 was burning most of the books? All at once satisfied, and not really clear why, Whit held her hand out and slowly stepped closer to him. "Tomyris Whitaker."

The boy immediately responded. "Miles Macowmber." They shook hands with a firm warmth.

Quickly, the boy opened his backpack and reached inside, pulling out some tightly folded black clothing and a pair of black boots. "Hope these fit," he said as he set the articles in front of Whit.

Whit stared dumbly down at the heap of cloth and the footwear. *What on Gaea's sweet earth is that?*

"Go ahead," the boy urged. "Go back in the corner there and change." Appearing very prim and courteous, he turned his back. "Bring me back the stuff you have on and I'll stuff it in my healer's bag. Then we can get down there. She has a plan."

Feeling fractious, Whit picked up the black garments and the boots, heading back into the recesses where the wall curved by the government building. "This building I was up on . . . it seems to be the biggest place it town. What is it?"

"The Procurator's palace."

"Figures," Whit muttered. "I picked the best place to hide . . ."

"Hurry. Most of the guards that usually patrol the walls have been watching Kali all night, so the rest of the watch has been taking advantage. I haven't seen anyone patrolling for hours. I'm guessing they've got some poor woman somewhere . . ."

He didn't have to finish the statement. On one of her computer repair jobs in Bethesda, three years ago, she had gone into a neighborhood where a gang rape had occurred roughly a month earlier. Whit had never forgotten that sunny October afternoon.

Not one Elysian merchant would meet her eye, and the women, whether by choice or the edict of the male family members, remained behind locked doors. The thirteen-year-old rape victim had survived, largely through the tender care of her mother. However, the stain of what had been done to her, and the community's unwilling but instinctive guilt that they had not saved her from it, had made her a pariah. Though still looking bruised and fragile, the pretty girl was sitting on her doorstep in the warm sunshine as Whit strode down the street, looking for the tax collector's house. The girl's eyes were haunted when they flicked up at Whit and then away. Whit saw the way everyone pointedly ignored her. Later that afternoon, after her work next door was completed, Whit had gone out of her way to make a human connection she thought was needed like water in the desert. She sat down beside the sad girl, sharing the doorstep unasked. The girl shrank back, startled. Trying to appear harmless, Whit had shared with the girl the meal she had earned at the tax collector's house. Whit talked about the fine weather they were having, and looked into the girl's eyes as she spoke, saying without words, "I see you. You're going to be okay." When she left, a few hours later, she felt better about the girl's chances of true survival.

It was a year later that she heard that the neighborhood elders had let the girl regain her health, and then sent her to the Bethesda Breeding Pen for what was locally held to be a fit use for a despoiled virgin. Whit had cried herself to sleep with grief and rage the night she had heard it. The Regs preferred girls to grown women. Everyone knew a girl didn't live long in a Pen. She got too much attention. Later, when Whit surreptitiously checked into her fate, she'd learned the girl had died in early December the year before, less than a month after her incarceration had begun.

Trying to push her renewed anger aside, Whit hoped the boy was wrong about what the Reg watch was up to, but sent a fervent silent prayer to Gaea for whoever had distracted them long enough to keep them from this part of the wall. In the chilly dawn air, she made quick work of shucking off the deerskin moccasins, leggings and tunic, then picked up the long black garment the boy had given her. As Whit held it up and slipped an arm into a sleeve, she recognized the clothing of a New Order Reverend.

"Shit," Whit commented, feeling her skin crawl at the thought of donning the robe. *Probably more evil has been done in this outfit than I want to know about.*

"Yeah, I know," the boy empathized quietly, with a matching shudder. "But it was your friend's idea. And the Reverend was out of his quarters, just like she said he would be."

Fastening up the buttons on the front, she realized the robe was a good fit, giving her just enough room in the shoulders and chest that her relatively small breasts would be hidden. She reached for the black boots, saying, "Fill me in on the plan."

The boy began fidgeting. "She says no matter what happens, stay at the back of the crowd. After a while something will happen that you'll know as a sign. That's when you move up close to the platform and wait."

Flabbergasted, Whit stopped trying to yank on the boot. "What the hell kind of plan is that?"

Shrugging, the boy turned his head, not daring to actually look back over his shoulder, but letting her see his profile. "She says . . . trust her."

Frustrated, Whit put the boot down on the concrete and shoved her bare foot into it. "And what will we be waiting for?"

"Don't know."

"Oh, this is great!" Whit muttered to herself. "Just great!"

She got the other boot on and then straightened the robe with nervous hands. "Okay, check me out," she told the boy. He turned and took her in with wide dark eyes as Whit caught her hair in one hand and said, "What do I do with this?"

The boy reached into his backpack and with a tug pulled out a floppy-brimmed straw hat that had been crammed in the bottom. The woven blades were raggedly edged and definitely the worse for wear. "Borrowed this from a peg on the wall in the kitchen on my way up here. Shouldn't be any lice, 'cause the palace servants gotta wash with lye soap once a week."

Whit glowered at him, took the hat, and said another prayer. *Please let there be no bugs in this!* "What's my cover story? There can't be many Reverends here. I'm a stranger. How do I keep from being noticed and then questioned by the Regs?"

The boy picked up her discarded Amazon deerskins, folding them neatly and placing them in his backpack. He put the moccasins on top, then fastened the closing catch. "There's four Reverends here right now. One, Reverend Sharkey, is the city confessor. The other three were still studying and hadn't made full entry into the ministry. Your build is enough like Decker to pass for him if you keep your head down."

Whit moved to the edge of the palace wall and peered around it, gazing down into the square. A small crowd was gathering on the cobblestones. Some of them had small pushcarts and carried a meager selection of bread or produce, or the feathered carcasses of a few abysmally scrawny chickens. Others looked like people who had been going about an early morning errand, for they were carrying sacks or had preoccupied expressions. All of them were moving toward the platform at the center of the square, morbidly curious about what was happening. Even from this height, eighteen or so meters above them, she could see the fascinated speculation in their eyes.

Entertainment by execution, Whit thought, feeling disgusted.

Taking a deep breath, she turned away from them. "Won't this Decker be out there?" Whit asked. "Won't the other apprentice Reverends be out there, too?"

"No. They left last evening, just after sundown. They'd been in the throne room when the withering occurred. The youngest one, my friend Karl, told me that they were going to Pittsburgh, to report it to the High Reverend there." He gazed down at his boots, stating, "I think they were just scared and were running away. Reverend Sharkey doesn't know they're gone."

"What's a 'withering'?" Whit asked, unable to follow.

"I wasn't there, but the rumor is all over the city. They say Kali got mad at Procurator Fowler and cursed him, then cursed all the men there." He swallowed, and explained, "She made their privates get small and useless."

Stunned, Whit blinked at him. "Really?"

"Well, I haven't seen actual proof, but . . . everyone who was there is really upset."

I'll bet.

"We better get down there. The trial will be starting any time now."

"Wait," Whit said. The boy complied, checking the walkway on the wall again. "Give me an idea what's about to happen."

Miles took a few breaths, then wiped angrily at the tears in his eyes. "The church bell down the road will start ringing, tolling the death knell, and then all the other church bells will join in, too. That'll bring out anyone who hasn't heard what's going on. They . . . like a big crowd for these things.

"Procurator Fowler, General Macowmber and Reverend Sharkey will come out on the palace balcony that over looks the square. The Procurator's counselors will call for witnesses. Some guys from the Coalman's Bar, who have been bribed, will give testimony. No one survives a trial here, innocent or guilty. Then they'll take your friend to the platform and lash her to the rings on that big post. Last night they threw a lot of ethanol on the logs below the platform, so everything's ready for action. The Reverend will come down and say a sermon full of fire and brimstone and end it by throwing a lit torch on the wood. It will take about an hour from start to finish and the smell won't leave this town for a month."

Whit stared at him, aghast at the detailed description. "You've seen this happen before."

"Yes," he whispered, his shoulders slumping.

The possibility that she was going to see the person she loved most in the world burned alive descended on Whit like an avalanche. A swift, racing wall of white slammed into her. For a moment, she thought she might faint. Willing herself to maintain a grip on self-control, she struggled to breathe.

Her voice was strangled when she asked, "This General Macowmber—he any relation to you?"

"I'm his son."

She turned and looked at him. He stoically met her eyes as the silence stretched out.

Feeling a surge of affection and respect for him, she touched his shoulder. "Well bless you, Miles, for surviving growing up here, under such a father, and still knowing how to be a good man."

He gazed at her, struck dumb by the praise. Slowly, he straightened to his full height. "Thank you."

Whit said, "You're welcome." She returned her attention to the square below them. "Guess we better get down there."

The boy led the way. At the door in the back of the building, he turned and warned, "After the trial is over and the verdict is read, Reverend Sharkey will come down the palace steps to begin his sermon. Stay away from him, because he'll want you to assist him with the all the props—like holding his Bible and lighting the torch. Just keep in the back of the crowd until he's really going and then move close to the platform. He likes being the center of attention and will probably have forgotten about you by then."

Whit nodded and glanced up. It was fully light now, and big white thunderheads passed overhead in a slow but steady parade. Farther away in the southeast, more clouds were visible, all of them a deep purple and gray.

She threw one last look back at the wall, and then wondered why she didn't hear the loud morning symphony of bird song. It seemed ominously odd.

Mother's Blood, focus! You're freaking out about everything, she told herself.

With determined calm, she let the concern go. She didn't know this land well enough to know what was odd and what was usual. Maybe the forest outside Buckhannon was just a place the birds didn't favor.

Still, it's strange.

Miles used an old-fashioned metal key to open the door to the palace, then waved her by him. Whit moved inside, and Miles bent down to place a small length of wood in the gap between the door and the jamb so that the door only looked as if it were shut.

"So you can get out if you have to backtrack this way," he explained.

Miles shouldered his backpack and began walking quickly down the darkened hallway, with Whit following. *Gaea grant me the strength and faith to trust in Kali's plan—which I know nothing about and have no confidence in because it's not my own . . . Anyway, help me to honor my wife, by honoring whatever she's got in mind.* Whit strode deeper into the hallway, hurrying to come even with Miles. *But, Gaea, give me the sense to know when to pitch it the hell over.*

Satisfied, she lengthened her stride. In a reflexive act, she sought the reassurance of the weapons she carried before going onto the field of battle. She touched the lump under the fabric at her waist, which was her knife, still in its sheath on the Amazon beaded belt at her waist. Then she slipped her hand into the right pocket in the robe, where the laser pistol rested. *Now, I just have to get through listening to them damning Kali to Hell for an hour without pulling this out and giving them all a taste of Freelander brimstone.*

❧

She heard the bells ringing and pushed herself up, only half awake. As she moved, the hot pain in her shoulder was shocking, making her whimper and hunch over, cradling her right arm. She remembered her circumstances again, and felt the bite of fear. Then she remembered the ecstatic rush she had felt just before exhaustion claimed her.

Whit. Is she here? Kali asked herself, reaching with her sense, trying to latch onto that singular life force. She reached and found nothing.

And then she saw the two Regs coming for her. She pushed aside her blanket and scrambled unsteadily to her feet. One caught her under the arm while the other checked the cuffs on her wrists and the chain that ran between them, making sure she was still shackled. Without a word, they began pulling her along, toward the wooden platform a short distance away.

It was then that she saw the crowd beyond the ring of armed Regs. A sea of faces, hundreds of them, and more moving in from the rear, streams of humanity pouring from the side streets. They were peasants, dressed as she had once been dressed when she roamed with Baubo in Elysium: homespun butternut made into loose trousers and shirts, dresses that fell below mid-calf. Most of them were without shoes. In the windows of the buildings all around the square, she saw the wealthy. Their hair was neatly done in complicated arrangements, men and women alike, and their clothes were well-tailored and colorful.

The Regs marched her to the plywood stairs and supported her as she stumbled on the first step. When they reached the top, they turned, facing the crowd and the large building that was the Procurator's palace. Her eyes were drawn to the three men standing on the palace balcony. One was dressed in the green uniform of a Regulator General, another was in the gold uniform of a Procurator, and the last was dressed in the black robe of a Reverend.

Oh, Hecate, I wish I could muster up a big energy blast and toss it up there at them. She felt a wry grin overcome her at the thought, imagining the smug, superior men scurrying off the balcony and back into the palace, terrified and trying to take cover. Then she sagged helplessly, into the grips of the Reg on either side of her, nearly unable to stand on her own. *I don't know how much l can take of whatever they've got planned for me before I pass out. All I can do is hope that flash of foreknowledge is right and hope that Whit can get to me when all hell breaks loose.*

The morning sun was blocked as thick, dark clouds passed over. The peasants below all lifted their faces, a bit disturbed by their appearance. More than a few were looking from the clouds to her with increasing trepidation.

They probably think I'm calling in the elements, Kali realized. She suppressed a laugh and willed herself to stand straight, so she could at least act the part of a fearsome witch.

The Procurator signaled a row of pompous looking, richly dressed men sitting on wooden chairs arranged to form a front row near the platform. The seven men all stood as one and moved forward, mounting the steps and joining her on her plywood stage. In the rather close quarters, one particularly rotund man pulled out a piece of parchment and began reading a list of offenses that Kali had supposedly committed. Since the crimes ranged from "wearing her hair in a witch's braid," to "dancing in the moonlight with Satan," Kali soon ceased listening and let her mind drift. The clouds overhead grew thicker and darker and the peasants below Kali shifted anxiously beneath them. The breeze began to gust, rattling the paper in the nobleman's hands.

There was a particularly tall Reverend moving along the back edge of the crowd and Kali found herself desperately hoping that it was Whit. The figure, however, was wearing a wide-brimmed straw hat, pulled down low over the face. Kali couldn't see that face well enough to confirm her hope.

A strong swell of wind raced through the square, tearing the nobleman's parchment from his grasp and swirling it up in the air. The crowd made a murmuring noise of startled wariness, watching

208

the paper sail high up and then lift over the wall. Kali, however, was watching the tall Reverend in the rear battling with his hat, trying to keep it on that bowed head.

"Witnesses!" the nobleman demanded, his voice breaking a little.

Two men came forward, both of them bleary-eyed and one of them prodded by a Reg. Each in his turn mumbled something, Kali couldn't hear what. When they finished, whatever they had stated was enough for the nobleman to declare, "The evidence supports the State's case."

Obviously impatient with the ceremonial aspects of the proceedings, the Procurator yelled down to the seven noblemen, "Find her guilty and get on with it!"

The round nobleman immediately turned to Kali. In a voice loud enough to carry over the crowd noise, he asked, "Are you a witch?"

She debated the wisdom of answering. After all, what good would it do? This trial was a sham and anyone who knew a real trial already knew that. *Ah, what the heck.* Raising her own voice, Kali answered, "I am the Wizard of Isis."

Some in the crowd cried out in alarm, while others moved back, away from the platform.

"I was born a mage, and I have used my power to defend the weak, to serve Freeland, and to avenge the innocents. If that makes me guilty, then guilty I am."

Casting nervous glances at her, the noblemen gathered close together, talking quietly among themselves. Kali knew it was more pretense that actual deliberation of a verdict.

"You withered us!" a rich man yelled from a window close to the platform. "You dared assault the men of this town!"

"Your manhood has made Elysium a hellish place," Kali yelled back.

The crowd grew silent, obviously intent on hearing what she said. In the back of her mind Kali realized that these oppressed villagers had rarely seen anyone standing up to a nobleman, let alone debating with him.

She told the crowd, "Every good thing in America was sacrificed to the concept that a man needed to be elevated above a woman. Your New Order politicians and the Reverends said it was a tenet of Christianity and used your holy book as a weapon to suppress women and destroy the Unwanteds. And did your society grow stronger, or better, as they promised?"

"No!" several anonymous voices rang out deep in the sea of peasants before her.

Feeling as if she had one chance to reach these people, she shouted, "Look what has happened to you. Whole races are gone from this land. Your cities are choked with contagion. Your pollution has fouled the air and the land—except in this place—and you came running here in the hope that you could escape yourselves, when in your hearts you knew the truth. You've become an ugly, ignorant, mean-spirited people, and you will ruin this place, too.

"Your men no longer know how to be men without raping and killing. Your women are either locked away, flanked by bodyguards, or at the mercy of whatever man decides he wants her. A long time ago, your ancestors exchanged freedom for promises of safety, and you're doing it still. You stopped being Americans.

"But it doesn't have to be like this! You are the descendants of a free people! The dream they made is your dream—if you decide to dream it, too!"

Leaning his hands on the balcony railing, looking nearly apoplectic, the Procurator yelled, "Shut that woman up!"

Truly angry, she turned toward the Procurator. "If you do not have respect for women, perhaps it's time you became one, and learned what it is to live in terror of Elysian men."

Below her, the trial audience all began talking at once.

Banging his hands on the railing, the Procurator screamed, "You fools! Shut her up!"

Obediently, the Regs on either side of Kali shook her hard, and the bullet wound sent an agony of pain through her. In the haze that followed, she saw the portly nobleman advance on her, pointing at her with a dramatic flourish as he yelled, "We find you to be a witch and sentence you to death by fire. May God send you to the fiery pit and damn your soul for eternity."

The Regs who held her moved, and she felt the tops of her trekking boots scraping across the plywood boards as she was dragged to the huge black column in the center of the platform. One Reg produced a new chain and looped it through her shackles, then threaded the chain through a ring high above her head. With a savage snap, he pulled the chain taut, and Kali's arms were yanked above her head. Gritting her teeth against the pain, she leaned her back helplessly against the charred wood and soot of the column.

"Let's see ya get out of this, wizard," the Reg taunted.

The other Reg laughed and ran a hand over her breast. "You're damned good to look at, for all that mouth. I'd of liked to have had you, goldilocks. I'd of taught you what a woman is for." He moved away, still laughing.

Kali looked out at the crowd and saw them pressing closer to the platform again. Some of them were crying, men and women both. Some of them were shifting about, confused and worried. Others had that eager glint in their eye, and Kali knew they were high on bloodlust. She searched with a sense of quiet despair and couldn't find the tall Reverend anywhere.

The crowd all looked to the side, and Kali saw the Reverend she'd met in the throne room descending the broad steps of the palace, moving inexorably closer. From the pious look on his thin, ascetic face, she guessed he would be the one who would kill her.

The wind sprang up, again, swirling through the square and taking a few hats from heads. Shutters on the buildings nearby creaked eerily, then as the wind increased, banged against the brick walls. Kali lifted her eyes. Above her, storm clouds were folding in on themselves, as air pressure sucked the bottoms up into the centers. The clouds were roiling, and dangerous looking.

She was suddenly buffeted by the wind and the Reverend had to lean forward as he walked across the square. Once more the crowd noise grew. People were pointing at the sky and cowering lower, as if not knowing what to expect.

The Reverend mounted the platform stairs, then moved to the center of the structure to stand beside Kali. Turning to the crowd, he shouted to them, but as close as she was, Kali could only hear snatches of words. The crowd obviously couldn't hear at all. Kali saw some people glance fearfully at the sky, then turn and purposefully head away from the platform, obviously leaving. To her surprise, she heard a chant going up from one side of the crowd. Unclear what it was at first, she at last distinguished, "Free her! Free her!" From closer to the platform, another group began shouting, "Burn her! Burn her!" On an angry slashing motion from the Reverend, Regs began moving into the crowd, beating anyone who dared disrupt the Reverend's sermon. In the bedlam that followed, the Reverend shouted and gestured, smacking the back of his fingers against his other palm for emphasis, and the wind took the words away before they reached his audience.

At last in a fury, he swung around on Kali and shrieked, "You're doing this!"

She wasn't. She had long since given up trying to use her power, but since it would do no good to deny it, Kali merely looked at him.

"Well, I'll have the last laugh, Freeland whore! I'll watch you and your child burn alive!"

He struck her then, across the face, so hard that she lost a few moments.

When she finally managed to open her eyes and lift her head, she saw him down on the ground. A Reg walked up to him with a lighted torch, and the Reverend grabbed it with an enthusiasm that betrayed him. Anyone watching him now could see that this was no man of God. The ones nearest to him moved back, afraid and disturbed. Around them, the rest of the assembly was roaring in anticipation. In the rear of the crowd, the Regs continued to assault anyone who dared to dissent and protest quickly diminished.

Kali tried to summon her strength, tried to put the Reverend's torch out by sheer act of will. ÏFrantic when the flame burned on, unaffected, she turned her attention to trying to pull the rain from the clouds above them. A sob broke from her as nothing worked. The only moisture falling was the rain of tears streaming from her cheeks. *Oh, Gaea, I'm sorry, Lilith. I'm sorry, Tor. Oh, Whit . . . oh, Whit.*

It occurred to her that her partner might never recover from this.

The wind suddenly died, and the still, humid air was crackling with portent.

Waving the torch over his head, the Reverend was parading in front of the crowd, reveling in their attention. She closed her eyes, afraid to watch him any longer, afraid to see him turn and throw the torch onto the fuel-soaked logs below the platform. She found herself praying that it would be over quickly.

A voice in her ear said, *C'mon, wizard. You're the first one waiting to be burned at this stake who really is what they say she is.* Kali's eyes snapped open, and disbelieving, she looked to her left. There beside her in the dimming morning light was Tor. She was misty and wavering, but she was the same beloved companion, with the same wry look in her eyes.

"Oh, Goddess," Kali whispered.

Not quite that high a ranking, but thanks for the vote of confidence, Tor returned, laughing a little. *Listen to me. You have a lot of backup here. You just don't know it yet.* In a glimmering move of light and color, Tor stroked the same cheek that the Reverend had struck.

Kali felt a swell of magic rushing through her, infusing her cells from that spot just above her jaw. A hum of warm, tingling sensation stole through her neck, compounding and glowing as it reached her chest, then racing on and filling her arms and legs. A strange energy was zinging under the surface of her skin, from her cheek to her fingertips and toes. With an unsettling precognition, she knew that this magic wasn't hers at all. It was wilder and far more powerful, and it was bursting to get out and set irrevocable events into action.

Watching her, Tor instructed, *Get yourself free, and then get off the platform. Hell on earth is gonna drop in on these people in the next few minutes.*

"Tor, I . . . I got you killed. I should never have asked you to come."

You gave me the chance to be your friend. One of many. And I thank you for it. Besides, I would have come anyway, you know that. Now don't mess this up. You're supposed to be around for a long time yet. A lot of people will need you in the years ahead . . .

And then, Tor faded until she was simply gone.

Amazed at what had just happened, wondering if she were hallucinating, Kali looked out over the half-crazed crowd screaming below her. A short distance from the city, a blinding fork of lightning erupted from the southeastern sky. The wind rose again. The scent of ethanol filled Kali's nose and the Reverend's robe rippled like a flag. Across the square, the Procurator was leaning on the balcony railing, yelling something to a small squad of Regs on the cobblestones. Beside him, the General looked cool and amused. And she noticed the tall Reverend, pushing through the shouting strangers in a diagonal path that would intersect with the plywood stairs. The hat was gone and the dark hair was whipping across angular features. All at once, the head lifted up and the eyes looked right at her, and with a stifled breath, Kali recognized the gloriously singular planes of that face. The grim set of the jaw. The long aquiline nose. The gray-eyed stare that told Kali how close to losing her self-control Whit really was.

As if to emphasize that point, Whit's gaze shifted to the Reverend, and her eyes were filled with murderous intent.

Time to get serious about getting out of here before Tomyris takes that man apart with her bare hands.

Kali took a deep breath and concentrated, drawing her power together. In the back of her mind, she remembered Tor's joke, made several days ago as they were preparing to take off from Isis. "Sure will teach them all not to mess with a hormonal mage!"

Yeah. Time for a lesson.

Chapter 11

With a decisive flex of power, Kali released a burst of force at her wrists. Instantly, the chains on her wrists exploded in a shower of molten metal. Filled with vitality, she shoved herself away from the stake and strode to the edge of the platform. The roaring crowd fell abruptly silent.

The Reverend saw them all gaping, looking past him, and in mid-swing, ceased waving his torch. He turned to see her standing free and defiant at the edge of the platform.

A long roll of thunder rumbled, growing ever louder, lending to the suspense.

The voice of the Procurator came. "Burn her, dammit!"

Kali shook her closed fist a few times, then threw a glowing, yellow ball of lightning across the square. The power charge grew as it traveled, throwing a shower of sparks in a terrifying and graphic display. People in the square ran. The charge arced down, impacting the balcony with a loud crack, sending the Procurator and the General flying five meters into the air. They smashed onto the cobblestones below, disjointed limbs splayed. Their bodies were on fire.

Horrified, Kali stepped back, then stared at her hand.

Everyone was shouting and running. The Reverend drew back his arm to heave the torch beneath the platform, and before Kali could react, she saw Miles Macowmber break through a mass of people moving the opposite way. The mild-mannered boy tackled the Reverend to the ground, wrestling away the torch.

From the corner of her eye, Kali saw Whit reach the stairs, taking the steps in bounding leaps. Giving a small cry, Kali ran to her, closing the short space that separated them. They landed in each other's arms with a thump, but Whit held on for only a few seconds before jumping back. "You're . . . hot!" Whit said, shaking out her hands.

More than that, Kali also knew the bullet wound in her shoulder was completely gone.

Kali knew it was the power, accelerating molecules within her body, healing her and simultaneously heating her like nothing she had ever experienced. But this was beyond her usual capacity for magic. It felt unbalanced and frantic and so much more than she was used to manipulating.

She had indulged in a fit of temper just now, and two men were dead when she had only meant to scare them. One of those men was the father of the young man fighting down below, a young man who had done all he could to save her life. How would she explain to Miles what she had done?

"Are you okay?" Whit asked. "We have to move."

Kali couldn't answer. Her mind was churning with anxiety. She could see close to three hundred Regs waiting at the periphery of the frenzied crowd. Between the Regs and the spectacle-maddened citizens, how were she and Whit ever going to get out of Buckhannon? And the power pinging around inside of her was barely under her control. Kali could feel it growing exponentially.

Gaea, I hope it doesn't hurt our baby, she thought, and suddenly of all the worries in her mind, this was the greatest. Overwhelmed, Kali could only gaze up at Whit and confess, "I don't know what to do."

As if she understood that her partner was close to collapse, Whit urged, "C'mon," and took over completely. Mute, Kali followed Whit's directing gesture. They ran to the other side of the platform, to the opposite side of the big column. Whit vaulted over the side, then reached back for Kali to help her negotiate the height. Kali knelt down, preparing to slip over the plywood rim.

"Die!" Shockingly, the Reverend was there, on his knees, grabbing Kali and hauling her back toward him, then hitting her with his fist. Her head rang with the first blow, then with a shrill cry, he let her go. He wailed with panic, holding his hands up before his face. Both of them were smoldering and the stench of burned flesh hung in the air.

"What kind of demon are you! This didn't happen with the others!" His face twisting with revulsion, the Reverend stood up and raised his leg, readying to stomp Kali with his boot.

A laser blast seared past Kali and took most of the Reverend's left leg out from under him. He fell to the plywood planks, screaming and writhing.

Whit held the laser gun in her left hand as she reached again for Kali, coaxing her into her arms. "You're okay. I have you now. We're going home."

"I'll burn you," Kali whispered, trying to resist the compelling desire to just bury her head in Whit's chest and disappear.

"You've had me burning for a couple of years now," Whit teased. "You can't hurt me, little wizard. Now c'mon down."

Kali was crying as she slid from the platform and was caught in Whit's strong arms. The heat in her seemed to ease, either over the worst of the power surge that had occurred at the stake, or already phasing into a natural reduction due to Whit's grounding presence. Whit held her just a few seconds longer, then kissed her on the top of the head.

"C'mon," Whit said again. Taking her by the hand, Whit headed for the main gate.

"Where are we going?"

As Whit turned to answer her, a powerful detonation punched through the air. The compression shock knocked them both to the ground.

Kali looked up to see that the entire southeastern wall was gone.

"You okay?" Whit was yelling close to her ear and Kali could barely hear her.

Feeling as if the world had become an unpredictable and surreal nightmare, she bit her lip and managed a brief nod.

Whit helped her up, pulled Kali's arm across her shoulders, and then half-carried her to a sheltered corner by the main gate. The Regs who should have been there standing guard were nowhere to be seen. Whit ran to an overturned pushcart a short distance away, righted it, and trundled it over to the corner where Kali was. She sent the cart to its side again, obviously determined to build them some cover. To the cart, she quickly added several large barrels that were sitting by the sentry's post, rolling the barrels in front of the cart.

Several bullets whined by their shelter, and Kali yelled, "That's enough! Get in here!"

Convinced, Whit climbed over the impromptu barricade and dropped down to the cobblestones. Using an embrace, she maneuvered Kali lengthwise, up against the wall, then positioned herself so that her body was the last protection.

Kali wriggled, using her hands to push herself up Whit's body.

"Are you trying to tickle me?"

"No!"

"Then what on Gaea's sweet earth are you doing?"

"Want to see," Kali answered breathlessly.

She reached the point where she could peer over Whit's shoulder. There was an uneven crack between the floorboards of the cart, and it was spaced perfectly between the barrels, allowing Kali a narrow but serviceable view.

In the distance, huge groups of raiders were pouring through the rubble of the destroyed wall. They raced across the square, some of them moving off through the town, others running up the steps of the Procurator's palace.

Hearing Kali's gasp, curiosity overcame Whit. She rolled over and watched, too. Another enormous boom sounded, shaking the ground. Kali clutched Whit, willing the explosions to stop.

A Reg dashed by, yelling up to some Regs trying to assemble on the heights of the wall. "They took down the northern wall! There must be a hundred cannon out there!"

"Maybe we should move," Kali whispered, looking back uneasily at the wall behind her.

"No. We're by the gate. The assault has bypassed this option. Just hang tight."

Returning her attention to the square, Kali heard the cries of the attacking force growing steadily louder. Then through clouds of billowing dust, more raiders emerged on the far side of the square. She squinted, trying to make out who they were. Gradually, she saw men in homespun, carrying crossbows and ancient hunting rifles. Running alongside them were women in deerskins, carrying M-28s. And then, through the rubble, came the dirt bikes, churning over stones and heading straight for the Regs scrambling out to meet them.

Freeland Warriors.

Kali felt a great core of tension slacken. They weren't alone any longer. Help had arrived in the form of a whole troop of warriors, no doubt sent to round her up, just as Tor had joked when they were first flying into Elysium.

Tor . . . at the memory, Kali's heart sank. *Oh, Tor. You paid the price for my willfulness, my impatience . . .*

And there was nothing she could do to rectify that. She would carry the pain of this folly all the rest of her life.

She was shivering now, her eyes closing against her will as she felt the effects of everything that had happened to her.

Concerned, Whit kissed her cheek and smoothed her hair, trying to comfort her. "Looks like our ride is here," she joked.

Kali lowered her head to Whit's shoulder. She knew Whit was trying to help her put some distance between herself and the ordeal by keeping things light. She kissed the shoulder she rested upon, thanking Gaea they were both alive and whole.

"Did you see her, Whit? Is that why you knew to come get me?" Kali looked up at her partner. "Just at the end, Tor was there with me on the platform . . ."

Whit was carefully controlling her expression. Kali saw it and instantly knew something was amiss. Another explosion sounded, farther off this time, and when Kali started, Whit cradled her. "We'll talk about it later. You look exhausted. Let me just hold you, while you try to get some rest."

Kali let it go.

The battle raged for the next few hours. For Whit, worried about Kali's lack of color and increasing lethargy, it seemed like an eternity.

Once, when a group of three Regs came at them to steal their makeshift shelter, Whit used the laser pistol to convince them to move on. Otherwise, to Whit's relief, their part in the Battle of Buckhannon was a nonevent. For both of them, the battle for the city was a postscript to Kali's near execution.

Something set the pyre afire, some spark from a detonation grenade or a stray bullet ricocheting off the ethanol-soaked logs. Whit couldn't see if the Reverend was still on the plywood platform because they were too far away. Much as she would like to have scored saint-like karma by overlooking his cruelty to her partner, she found she could not. She thought it would be sweet justice if he perished in the manner he had so heartlessly planned for Kali.

There was some house-to-house fighting for a while, but eventually in the late afternoon, outmanned, and outgunned by the Freeland weapons, the remaining Regs surrendered. Freeland warriors organized the columns of weaponless men, sitting them down in the square and binding their hands. Then those same Freeland warriors coolly and effectively imposed order on the furious clansmen and Amazons who gathered there, wanting to fight the Regs whether they were armed or not.

The storm that had threatened all morning never did break, but the dark clouds didn't leave either. Instead, the storm seemed to circle the city, rotating above it in a slow boil, lending an atmosphere of peril.

As the first line of Freeland support personnel came through, Whit hailed a healer that came running through the gate. Recognizing Whit and then Kali, the young woman immediately radioed their position to the operations base set up in the woods beyond the walls. Then, while Whit leaned against the wall, with Kali half asleep in her lap, the healer pulled a biometric scanner from her med kit and checked Kali out thoroughly. Whit couldn't seem to fill her lungs with air until the healer told her all the readings were normal, including those for the baby.

Kali took Whit's hand and murmured, "Did you see her, Tomyris? Did you see Tor there beside me?"

Whit looked down at her, debating whether to answer truthfully or not.

However, no one knew her the way Kali did. She read Whit's hesitation for what it was. "What did you see, Tomyris? Tell me."

Whit ran her hand through her dark hair, nervous under Kali's suddenly keen regard. "Kal, I didn't see Tor. But I did see Arinna Sojourner."

"No," Kali whispered, reaching up and gripping the waist of Whit's black robe.

"She spoke to you and touched your cheek, and when she touched you, you glowed like she had switched on some inner light."

"It doesn't make sense. How could she be here?" Kali asked, trying not to show her fear, and failing.

She moved to sit up, and Whit placed a gentle hand on her

shoulder, staying her. "Relax, love. It's a mystery that will take more than today to unravel. I think I already have some leads, though, if that helps."

"Like what?"

"Like there's a village about twenty-five kilometers west of here that has its own personal witch. A witch that created a photo-electromagnetic screen—similar to our Border—but much smaller." Whit smiled. "I've made friends with the militia colonel, a woman named Jamie Rexrode. I'll leave it to you to make friends with her mother and clan Chief, Irene. You always seem to get on so well with the elder butches."

A West Virginia drawl spoke up, then. "Such as yerself, Freelander?"

Whit looked up to see Jamie Rexrode and Danu Sullivan, standing together, battle weary, but alert. Beyond them she could see Nakotah Berry wearing a Freeland Warrior's uniform with a colonel's insignia of her own. With Colonel Berry, at least a hundred Freeland Warriors were marching through Buckhannon, side by side with clansmen and Amazons.

"Happy Independence Day," Whit offered to Jamie.

Jamie broke into a wide grin, then nodded at Kali. "This yer lady, then?"

As Whit introduced them, she cast a quick assessing gaze at Danu. Jamie knelt down to speak with Kali, and Whit took the opportunity to move out from under her partner's head and slip in her place a wadded-up blanket from the healer. "Be right back," she told Kali, and then took Danu aside.

They looked at each other, tears welling, then looked away, fidgeting. Neither one could find any words. Working on some inner knowledge, Whit led Danu farther away from the group of celebrating allies gathering around Kali and the healer at the gate.

When they stopped, Whit reached out for her friend and drew her into an embrace. With a sharp, bitter moan, Danu leaned into her and gripped Whit's shoulders, as if Whit's solid form was all that tied her to this earth. And then Danu wept with an abandonment that demonstrated how shattered her heart was, and how deep this loss rent her heart.

Whit wept with her.

After a long while, they separated. They repeatedly wiped their faces on their sleeves and tried to regain a tenuous control, each of them still unable to completely stop the flow of tears.

"Thanks," Danu finally mumbled. "I won't forget that."

"Ah, you'd do the same for me," Whit replied, then added softly, "Kali's blaming herself."

"Figured she'd take it like that," Danu said, sniffling. "Tell her that Tor was doing what she thought was right. She lived her life that way. And she really got a kick out of taking risks." Danu grinned a little. "That's why I loved her."

"Just as they were getting all set to burn Kali for witchcraft, Kali says she saw Tor there by the big stake." When Danu looked at her, hurting and hopeful, Whit hastened to add, "But I saw Arinna."

Stricken, Danu looked away, and a new rush of tears glided down her face.

"I'm sorry. I had to fill you in," Whit elaborated quietly. "There's something going on here, and I'm not sure we can just say goodbye and go home now."

"I volunteer to stay," Danu said.

"Danu," Whit began carefully. "Maybe you should get a little counseling. This was a tough mission."

"It'll be worse for me to go home. I . . . can't, Whit." The young redhead wiped her face on her sleeve again. "At Colonel Rexrode's request, Colonel Berry had me acting as military liaison during the preparation for this assault. Seemed to work out okay. Maybe I could continue to do that while we search for Sojourner."

"Yeah. I guess when Kal and I get back home, we'll talk with Warrior Command about a beefed-up recon of this area. I'm thinking about asking Lilith to cover for me and remain Acting Leader for a while longer so I can come back—alone. I don't want Kali out of Freeland again before that baby arrives—but you know Kali."

They both laughed softly.

Danu warned, "She'd whack you one if she ever heard you talking like that about her."

"Yeah, she would," Whit agreed. "I sound like one of those twentieth century male chauvinists." She was sheepish, then. "I'll have to talk to Kal. Maybe we can figure something out. I guess we could do the technology setup, or even the actual search of West Virginia together, you know . . . track down Arinna. But then keep Kali largely out of whatever action might develop when we move on apprehending our friend Sojourner."

"Good luck," Danu offered, laughing a little.

"I think I'll let that be a worry for another day. In the meantime, I don't think anyone will go nuts if you stay in Seneca for awhile with a detachment of ten or so warriors. Just don't meet with the witch until you've got a helluva lot more backup."

Danu frowned. "You think Arinna would hang around once she knows we're onto her? I don't. I think she has another cave and another village, all set up and waiting, just like she seems to have had Seneca ready for her arrival when we flushed her out of that SAC missile site in the North Cascades. Could be she's in another state by now."

"Damn," Whit muttered, realizing how accurate the supposition probably was.

"But I bet I can find her," Danu said, a slight suggestion of smile in her red-rimmed eyes. "After all, I'm the one that found her last time."

"And don't think she doesn't remember that, little sister," Whit replied, tugging Danu into her arms again. "Be careful."

At the endearment, Danu was crying once more, but it was a more serene display this time and brief. They held each other for a little while longer, and put their arms around each other's shoulders, ambling slowly back to their friends.

Through the warriors and Amazons, Whit could see Kali standing on her own feet, and personally taking the bonds from Miles Macowmber's hands. The boy stood there, his face crimson with embarrassment, as Kali hugged him and then began enthusiastically describing for everyone his part in her narrow escape.

"Hey—how about this?" Kali asserted as she finished the tale. "Miles, why don't you come back with us to Freeland!"

Nakotah Berry sidled up to Whit and said from the corner of her mouth, "Looks like you just got yourself a ward."

Whit shook her head. She spent some time congratulating Nakotah on both her Colonel's oak leaves and the masterful assault, then gradually eased away from the group, walking alone into the square.

As she moved, she let her eyes drift over Buckhannon.

While huge sections of the city walls were now only rock and concrete debris, the brick and wooden clapboard buildings that made up much of the town were still standing unharmed, the Procurator's Palace among them. Bodies lay in the square and the streets farther away, mostly Regs, but clansmen, Amazons, and Freelanders as well. Allied troops were working together, tenderly collecting the fallen, and lining them up in rows.

Something started here today, Whit thought. *Something remarkable. And despite all the death and destruction and sorrow, I think something incredible is going to come of it.*

A hand touched her back and then Kali was there, slipping an arm around her waist and squeezing, in that inimitable way Kali had of using touch to convey all she felt.

In a rush of gratitude and relief, Whit gathered her in and kissed her. Kissed her the way people who have loved and almost lost kissed—with a fine edge of despair racing beside the sheer erotic joy.

When they at last broke for air, they leaned the top of their foreheads together, gazing at each other and breathing fast.

"I love you," Whit said, her voice low and urgent.

"Same," Kali whispered. She trembled as she moved her head to

Whit's shoulder, and eased back into Whit's arms. "Even as wrong as it went, I'd do it all again—Gaea help me—I'd do it all again."

They stood there holding one another, offering comfort, until they heard their friends by the gate, calling them.

They joined hands and walked back together.

There was, after all, much to do.

ABOUT THE AUTHOR

Jean Stewart was born and raised in the suburbs of Philadelphia. She loves books, music, movies, dogs, and people who laugh. She was a teacher and coach for a while, but now she writes. She lives near Seattle, with her partner, Susie, three badly behaved dogs, and a reclusive Maine Coon cat named Emily Dickinson.

Glossary

AGH. AIDS Genital Herpes. Ignored in its formative years, the plague spread silently through the American populace in the early twenty-first century. By 2013 mass death and a civil war had erupted as a result. Most lethal to men, the plague killed two-thirds of the people driven out of Elysium (eastern U.S.). Freeland (western U.S.) found a vaccine and the plague no longer exists there. In Elysium, a milder version of the plague still kills two in ten.

Arinna (Ah-RIN-ah). Hittite name for the Great Goddess, Mother of the Sun. Worshiped by the Amazons who resided around the Black Sea (once called the Amazon Sea) until the fifth century.

Arinna Sojourner was a Think Tank innovation, created at the same time as Kali, by Kali's mother Maat. Arinna came to Isis during its re-founding as a systems director. Later, as a means of creating a power base, she tried to take control of both Isis and Kali. Arinna shocked everyone with a display of mage power never before witnessed. The mage power was a byproduct of Maat's recombinant DNA engineering. It is generally thought that Whit destroyed Arinna by deflecting back onto Arinna a burst of electricity Arinna unleashed against Kali.

Baubo (BAW-bo). The belly goddess, or "goddess of obscenity" of ancient Greece. Headless, she was a short, squatty torso with arms and legs. Her nipples served as her eyes and her vulva was her mouth. When Demeter was in despair during her long sad search for Persephone, Baubo told Demeter dirty jokes and made her laugh; it gave Demeter the energy to continue her search and eventually find her daughter.

Baubo was an Elder of Artemis, renowned for her scholarship in Wiccan Arts. She trained Styx in the craft before disappearing on a retreat into The Wilderness. Later, it was learned that Baubo had in reality gone into Elysium, spreading an herbal vaccination for AGH and basic medical, agricultural, and mechanical engineering information. While in Elysium, she found Kali Tyler after Kali's escape from a Breeding Pen, and sheltered her for five years.

Border. The photo-electromagnetic dome-like screen that is beamed from satellites suspended in the Earth's atmosphere. Constructed originally by Elysian scientists to keep AGH victims out of Elysium, it became too complex for their scientists to manage. Later, Maat Tyler broke the operating code and rewrote the software that controlled the screen. The Border rises from the Atlantic Ocean in the east and falls in an oval over the American continent, all the way to just past the Mississippi river in the west. A micro-mesh, the Border cannot be penetrated by pollutants or particles larger than a predetermined molecular size.

Bordergate. The photo-electromagnetic screen can be interrupted at various locations to create a door. There are Bordergates in the northwest and southwest sections. To open the gate, one must key the operational commands to the specific satellite controlling the beams in that section.

comline. Freeland's satellite-based communications system. The melding of telephone, computer, and television functions into one system with many diverse uses. Wrist chronometers (wrist coms), desktop computers, computer slates, palm computers are all on the comline.

Danu (dah-NEW). Celtic name for their Great Mother Goddess, often associated with rivers such as the Danube in Germany, the Don in both Russia and Ireland, as the Goddess of "waters of life." Also, the leader of the Irish trinity of Fates. The other two are called Bobd and Macha; collectively they are called the Morrighan.

Danu Sullivan is a Think Tank innovation created approximately nine years after Arinna and Kali were in the final weeks of the program. Her enhancements are in mathematics and architectural design. She possesses a photographic memory. She first came to Isis as architectural director when she was seventeen, after submitting her designs on the comline to the Seven Leaders Council. After assisting in the building of Isis, she tracked Arinna Sojourner to her hiding place in the North Cascades and went there to seek vengeance for the death of a friend. Instead, she was captured and tortured. Tor rescued Danu, while Kali fought Arinna in a duel of mage power.

Delphi Clinic. Medical facility where parthenogenic procedures are conducted and a Delphi unit is housed.

Delphi Unit. Supportive, artificial womb where a newly created being is able to grow from mitosis, through embryo to fetus stages. The units were created to free women to continue vital community work during the initial depopulation crisis that followed the AGH plague.

electrobile. Motor vehicle powered by fuel cell. Commonly called a "beel" in most city-colonies. The fuel cell is charged approximately once a month by an electrical unit.

Elysium (ill-LIZ-ee-em). Greek name for the plain of the departed, the dwelling place for virtuous people after death. Also known as "paradise," it was thought to be located in the underworld, or in the far west. A place of ideal bliss or perfect happiness.

Elysium is what the Procurators and Reverends of the New Order decided to call the nation they carved from the eastern United States during the Great Rift or civil war of 2013. Elysium is a fascist dictatorship ruled by the Procurators and Reverends and holds to the beliefs of the Aryan Nation and the Fundamentalist Christian Church.

Freeland (FREE-land). The name of a town on Whidbey Island, in Washington state. Settled by former slaves and wandering idealists who were looking for peace and brotherhood following the War Between the States (1861–1864), the town still exists in Washington today.

Freeland is the name the Mothers decided to call the western half of the former United States. The Mothers is what herstory calls the matriarchs who ended up leading small bands of villages after most of the men died in the AGH plague. Freeland consists of eight city-colonies and is a democracy, multicultural by necessity of survival; diversity is cherished and encouraged.

Gaea (GAY-ah). The Primeval Prophetess, our most ancient Earth. She came before everything else and brought the world into being. Fires were lit to Her on mountaintops. Believers went into oracular caverns deep in the ground to hear what she would reveal of the future. She created heaven (Uranus) and she created the sea (Pontus) and took both as lovers. The Greek name for Mother Earth. Also known as "Gaia," the Great Earth Mother, one of the earliest of humanity's deities.

GPS. Global Positioning System. A worldwide radio-navigation system formed from a constellation of space satellites and their ground stations. GPS uses satellites to calculate positions accurate to a few meters, if not centimeters.

herstory. Because the vast majority of people in Freeland were women, this word gradually replaced the term "history," as it was felt to be more applicable.

Isis (EYE-sis). Egyptian Goddess of Fertility, generally thought to be the oldest of the old goddesses. Her name means "throne." Cleopatra wore her crescent mantle as warrior-queen. She was a creating and destroying goddess. She was worshiped throughout the ancient world, including Rome, where many aspects of the Isis cult were absorbed into legends of Mary, the Madonna, Mother of Christ.

Kali (KAH-lee). Hindu Goddess, born fully armed from the brow of her mother, the goddess in one of her earliest aspects, before fathers were recognized. She is also known as "Dark Mother," a triple goddess of creation, preservation, and destruction. Kali the Destroyer is the reality that as death cannot exist without life, so life cannot exist without death. She is Virgin, Mother, and Crone. She is a blood-smeared face with a lolling tongue, the devourer of all existence. She is the ocean of blood at the beginning and end of the world. She is terrifying to Western man.

Kali Tyler is Maat Tyler's daughter, a Think Tank innovation engineered with abilities in mathematics and science. She possesses a photographic memory. She was fourteen when Isis was attacked and burned to the ground by invading Elysians. Her mother was burned at the stake before her eyes, and Kali was taken into Elysium as a prize of war. She killed the Tribune who had ordered her mother's death and escaped. Following an emotional breakdown and a complete loss of memory, she spent the next ten years in Elysium masquerading as an AGH serf. She met Whit when Whit was evading Regulators on her way out of Elysium following two years of undercover activity as a spy. After Kali was wounded while helping Whit escape, Whit took her out of Elysium and back to Whit's home colony of Artemis. Kali and Whit fell in love, became partners, and returned to re-found Isis. Later, Kali ended up fighting Arinna Sojourner when Arinna decided to use Isis as a power base and Kali as an acolyte. In resisting Arinna, Kali discovered she had many of the same mage powers Arinna had developed: bursts of electric energy which can be directed in pinpoint blasts, psychic awareness of where others are and what they are doing, the ability to mind-read, to mind-bond, and a tenuous ability at foresight. Kali still bears the effects of her captivity in Elysium: She is deathly afraid of the Regs, and she has difficulty being in a closed room.

Lilith (LIL-lith). Sumero-Babylonian Goddess "Belili." Early Jewish rabbis tried to assimilate the strong and independent agricultural Goddess by incorporating her into Jewish mythology as Adam's first wife, Lilith. As such, she was created at the same time and in the same way as Adam—from the dust of the earth. Lilith was Adam's equal. She would not be subservient to Adam. She would not lie beneath Adam in the "missionary position," instead preferring being on top and participating in a marriage based on mutual respect. When Adam tried to force her to his way, she damned him and left him, going to make her home by the Red Sea. The Hebrew God then created Eve as a more compliant mate for Adam. The story of Lilith was later removed from the canonical Bible.

Lilith is Kali's biological mother, having donated an ovum to her partner, Maat Tyler, which Maat joined with an ovum of her own and then used in a Recombinant DNA engineering experiment. Kali was incubated and born from a Delphi Unit in Artemis. Lilith was part of a happy family with Kali and Maat for twelve years until Maat separated from Lilith and took Kali with her to participate in the founding of Isis. Lilith, a grain trader, was elected as Leader of Artemis (rather like a city mayor, except for additional senator-like representation on the Seven Leaders Council). She served in Artemis, re-elected as Leader for three consecutive five-year terms. She retired from the post to settle down with her new partner, Styx, then ended up being asked to take on the position of Deputy Leader in Isis, when the elected Deputy Leader, Kali, had to step out of that role. Lilith is also Whit's adopted mother, having taken the grief-stricken, nineteen-year-old Whit in when Whit's family was killed in the Fall of Isis.

Maat (MAH-aht or maht). "Mother." A very early Egyptian goddess, the personification of "truth" or "justice." She was the lion-headed goddess of both law and revenge. She was the original Eye of Heaven (before Hathor). She was also associated with the heart, as that is the place where judgments are made. She was the lawgiver in archaic Egypt, giving rules of behavior. She was the All-Mother. She is depicted as a woman, with an ostrich feather upon her head, a scepter in one hand, the life symbol of the ankh in the other. The same feathers of truth are worn by other aspects of the Goddess, such as Isis, who was the same sort of law-giving Mother. All other gods were required to "live by Maat." She was the manifestation of truth, justice, moral law, and cosmic balance.

Maat Tyler was Kali Tyler's mother. Maat used an ovum donated by Lilith to fertilize her own egg in a parthenogenic procedure, then employed recombinant DNA engineering to enhance Kali's intellect. After Kali was born from a Delphi Unit, Maat, Lilith, and Kali formed a happy family unit in Artemis for twelve years. Earlier, as a very young woman, Maat developed the computerized manufacturing program that mass-produced the AGH vaccine she and other medical scientists had discovered. The vaccine eradicated AGH in Freeland and allowed them to survive. Later, Maat created the Border software, which reprogrammed the electromagnetic shield the Elysians had put in place in 2013. In doing this, Maat allowed Freeland to gain control of the Border and use it to keep contained the violent medieval culture Elysium had become. Courted by dynamic younger women, Maat grew restless in her settled family life with Lilith. She ended their partnership and struck out for new experiences. Maat led the initial founding of Isis and was elected the city-colony's first Leader. She was burned at the stake there as a witch during an Elysian invasion. Her ghost has since been seen in various parts of the city-colony.

mage. Magician. Wizard. Person who is able to able to employ the sixth sense or engage in supernatural feats.

MRE. Meals ready to eat. Also know as k-rations. Supplied to Freeland Warriors for quick and easy consumption in the field, this is a biodegradable pouch filled with a nutritionally balanced meal portion.

Parthenogenesis. Process by which a woman's ovum or egg shell is sliced open by a microlaser. Using an electron microscope, chromosomes from a donor's egg are removed and placed in the ovum of the mother-to-be. The fertilized egg is placed in a test tube and allowed to become mitotic.

Regulators. A group in charge of regulations.

Elysian Regulators are the storm troopers of the New Order. They wear green uniform jackets, small caps, dark pants, and knee-high boots. They are allowed little initiative and follow orders to the smallest detail. They are known for enjoying the violence and terror they are enlisted to inflict.

Sight. Inner eye, sixth sense. Mage vision. Precognitive awareness.

Styx (sticks). Name for the mythological Roman river which led into the underworld.

Styx is city-colony Herstorian, first for Artemis and later for Isis. Her overwhelming mission is to save as many printed paper books and other artifacts from Old America as possible. She studied Wicca with Baubo as a young woman and has mastered some minor psychic skills. She was an early product of Think Tank experimentation when a cystic fibrosis gene was engineered out of her DNA chain during mitosis. She was also given minor psychic gifts during that same genetic work. She is Lilith's partner.

Tamatori (tama-TOR-ee). A Japanese legend, Tamatori was an ama (nun). Under the sea, she battled a giant octopus and the Dragon lord, while trying to recover a sacred jewel. When she realized she would be unable to make it back to the surface of the sea, she ripped her stomach open with her sword, and pushed the jewel deep within herself. Her corpse washed ashore and the sacred jewel was recovered.

Tor Yakami came to Isis as a lieutenant to assist Kali in readying to battle Arinna Sojourner. An expert martial arts champion, Tor was also gifted in channeling ki and the intricacies of Zen. While sharing quarters in the warrior barracks, Tor and Danu fell in love and are now deeply involved. Tor went into Arinna's mountain bastion with Kali. She rescued Danu and Loy, but was slain by Arinna's death spell. Kali sought Tor's spirit in the netherworld and brought her back. Her body has never fully recovered from the trauma, and she is on extended medical leave from the warriors.

Think Tank. Nickname given to a Freeland program in genetic engineering. Recombinant DNA technology used specialized enzymes to snip a gene from one organism and splice it to another. Developed by Maat Tyler in an effort to improve Freeland's chances of surviving the severe depopulation effects of AGH, Think Tank creations are enhanced intellects. They also meet fierce prejudice and suspicion because they are different.

Tomyris (toe-MY-ris). Queen of the Massagetae (Celtish origins) in Central Asia (now part of Iran) in the sixth century. She was a brilliant military tactician and founded the city of Tomis. When her nation was invaded by Cyrus the Great and his huge Persian army, she promised him "enough blood to sate your gluttony." In a savage battle, she and her warriors slaughtered 200,000 Persians; not even a messenger escaped to take news of the defeat back to Persia. Tomyris personally decapitated the captured Cyrus and tossed his head in a skin filled like a bucket with human blood, saying, "I have fulfilled my promise. You have your fill of blood."

Tomyris Whitaker, nicknamed "Whit" by her friends, has spent most of her life as a Freeland Warrior. Following the loss of her friends and family in the Fall of Isis, she was taken in by Lilith, the Leader of Artemis, in an informal adoption. Lilith has acted as a mentor and mother-figure as Whit made her way through the ranks. While a major, after a frustrating involvement with the healer Cimbri Braun, Whit went into Elysium and spent two years there on an undercover spying mission. She worked as a computer technician, enduring the open misogyny and casual brutality of that primitive culture and developed a hatred of all things Elysian, especially men. Eventually, while making a repair to the Procurator's computer, she accessed the Regulator's mainframe and downloaded every file stored there into a satellite transmission to Freeland. On the run from Regulators, Whit's stolen Elysian jet malfunctioned and she had to ditch in Kali's potato field, near the Northern Bordergate. In a fight with two pursuing Regs, Kali saved Whit's life and was badly wounded. Unable to leave her, Whit broke a Freeland law that prohibited bringing Elysians through the Border and brought Kali into Freeland. Together, they crossed the Wilderness, the huge abandoned section of the West, until they were found by a search party. Whit and Kali were taken to Artemis. Gradually, they had been falling in love with each other. Kali eventually recovered her memory of the Fall of Isis, and with it, she remembered enough to incriminate the unsuspected person responsible for the disaster. In a fight to the death, Whit saved Kali from the traitor.

Declaring themselves partners, Kali and Whit went into the ruins of Isis and began building a country home on Whit's family land. Other women from all over Freeland followed their example, and Isis was once again opened as a city-colony. Whit was made military governor, overseeing three directors (Loy, Arinna, and Danu). Kali worked on a construction team and took school courses on the comline in an effort to catch up on ten years of missed education. When accidents around the half-built colony escalated into catastrophe, no one knew what to think. Meanwhile, Kali was dealing with a discomfiting ability to read minds and influence others to do her will. Styx, Lilith's partner, informed Kali that her psychic gifts might be a byproduct of her Think Tank origins. Eventually, the accidents and deaths that had occurred in Isis were explained when it was revealed that Arinna Sojourner had been operating on an agenda all her own. When her plans to take control of Isis and Kali were thwarted, Arinna fled Isis, taking an unwilling Loy Yin Chen with her. Isis was saved, but everyone knew it was only a temporary reprieve. Whit was elected Leader of Isis.

Publications from
BELLA BOOKS, INC.
The best in contemporary lesbian fiction

P.O. Box 10543, Tallahassee, FL 32302
Phone: 800-729-4992
www.bellabooks.com

A MOMENT'S INDISCRETION by Peggy J. Herring. 154 pp. Jackie is torn between her better judgment and the overwhelming attraction she feels for Valerie.
ISBN 1-931513-59-7 $12.95

IN EVERY PORT by Karin Kallmaker. 224 pp. Jessica's sexy, adventuresome travels.
ISBN 1-931513-36-8 $12.95

TOUCHWOOD by Karin Kallmaker. 240 pp. Loving May/December romance.
ISBN 1-931513-37-6 $12.95

WATERMARK by Karin Kallmaker. 248 pp. One burning question . . . how to lead her back to love?
ISBN 1-931513-38-4 $12.95

EMBRACE IN MOTION by Karin Kallmaker. 240 pp. A whirlwind love affair.
ISBN 1-931513-39-2 $12.95

ONE DEGREE OF SEPARATION by Karin Kallmaker. 232 pp. Can an Iowa City librarian find love and passion when a California girl surfs into the close-knit dyke capital of the Midwest?
ISBN 1-931513-30-9 $12.95

CRY HAVOC A Detective Franco Mystery by Baxter Clare. 240 pp. A dead hustler with a headless rooster in his lap sends Lt. L.A. Franco headfirst against Mother Love.
ISBN 1-931513931-7 $12.95

DISTANT THUNDER by Peggy J. Herring. 294 pp. Bankrobbing drifter Cordy awakens strange new feelings in Leo in this romantic tale set in the Old West.
ISBN 1-931513-28-7 $12.95

COP OUT by Claire McNab. 216 pp. 4th Detective Inspector Carol Ashton Mystery.
ISBN 1-931513-29-5 $12.95

BLOOD LINK by Claire McNab. 159 pp. 15th Detective Inspector Carol Ashton Mystery. Is Carol unwittingly playing into a deadly plan?
ISBN 1-931513-27-9 $12.95

TALK OF THE TOWN by Saxon Bennett. 239 pp. With enough beer, barbecue and B.S., anything is possible!
ISBN 1-931513-18-X $12.95

MAYBE NEXT TIME by Karin Kallmaker. 256 pp. Sabrina Starling has it all: fame, money, women—and pain. Nothing hurts like the one that got away.
ISBN 1-931513-26-0 $12.95

WHEN GOOD GIRLS GO BAD: A Motor City Thriller by Therese Szymanski. 230 pp. Brett, Randi, and Allie join forces to stop a serial killer.
ISBN 1-931513-11-2 $12.95

A DAY TOO LONG: A Helen Black Mystery by Pat Welch. 328 pp. This time Helen's fate is in her own hands.
ISBN 1-931513-22-8 $12.95

THE RED LINE OF YARMALD by Diana Rivers. 256 pp. The Hadra's only hope lies in a magical red line . . . climactic sequel to *Clouds of War*.
ISBN 1-931513-23-6 $12.95

OUTSIDE THE FLOCK by Jackie Calhoun. 224 pp. Jo embraces her new love and life.
ISBN 1-931513-13-9 $12.95

LEGACY OF LOVE by Marianne K. Martin. 224 pp. Read the whole Sage Bristo story.
ISBN 1-931513-15-5 $12.95

STREET RULES: A Detective Franco Mystery by Baxter Clare. 304 pp. Gritty, fast-paced mystery with compelling Detective L.A. Franco
ISBN 1-931513-14-7 $12.95

RECOGNITION FACTOR: 4th Denise Cleever Thriller by Claire McNab. 176 pp. Denise Cleever tracks a notorious terrorist to America.   ISBN 1-931513-24-4 $12.95

NORA AND LIZ by Nancy Garden. 296 pp. Lesbian romance by the author of *Annie on My Mind*.   ISBN 1931513-20-1 $12.95

MIDAS TOUCH by Frankie J. Jones. 208 pp. Sandra had everything but love.
ISBN 1-931513-21-X $12.95

BEYOND ALL REASON by Peggy J. Herring. 240 pp. A romance hotter than Texas.
ISBN 1-9513-25-2 $12.95

ACCIDENTAL MURDER: 14th Detective Inspector Carol Ashton Mystery by Claire McNab. 208 pp. Carol Ashton tracks an elusive killer.   ISBN 1-931513-16-3 $12.95

SEEDS OF FIRE: Tunnel of Light Trilogy, Book 2 by Karin Kallmaker writing as Laura Adams. 274 pp. Intriguing sequel to *Sleight of Hand*.   ISBN 1-931513-19-8 $12.95

DRIFTING AT THE BOTTOM OF THE WORLD by Auden Bailey. 288 pp. Beautifully written first novel set in Antarctica.   ISBN 1-931513-17-1 $12.95

CLOUDS OF WAR by Diana Rivers. 288 pp. Women unite to defend Zelindar!
ISBN 1-931513-12-0 $12.95

DEATHS OF JOCASTA: 2nd Micky Knight Mystery by J.M. Redmann. 408 pp. Sexy and intriguing Lambda Literary Award-nominated mystery.   ISBN 1-931513-10-4 $12.95

LOVE IN THE BALANCE by Marianne K. Martin. 256 pp. The classic lesbian love story, back in print!   ISBN 1-931513-08-2 $12.95

THE COMFORT OF STRANGERS by Peggy J. Herring. 272 pp. Lela's work was her passion . . . until now.   ISBN 1-931513-09-0 $12.95

CHICKEN by Paula Martinac. 208 pp. Lynn finds that the only thing harder than being in a lesbian relationship is ending one.   ISBN 1-931513-07-4 $11.95

TAMARACK CREEK by Jackie Calhoun. 208 pp. An intriguing story of love and danger.
ISBN 1-931513-06-6 $11.95

DEATH BY THE RIVERSIDE: 1st Micky Knight Mystery by J.M. Redmann. 320 pp. Finally back in print, the book that launched the Lambda Literary Award–winning Micky Knight mystery series.   ISBN 1-931513-05-8 $11.95

EIGHTH DAY: A Cassidy James Mystery by Kate Calloway. 272 pp. In the eighth installment of the Cassidy James mystery series, Cassidy goes undercover at a camp for troubled teens.   ISBN 1-931513-04-X $11.95

MIRRORS by Marianne K. Martin. 208 pp. Jean Carson and Shayna Bradley fight for a future together.   ISBN 1-931513-02-3 $11.95

THE ULTIMATE EXIT STRATEGY: A Virginia Kelly Mystery by Nikki Baker. 240 pp. The long-awaited return of the wickedly observant Virginia Kelly.
ISBN 1-931513-03-1 $11.95

FOREVER AND THE NIGHT by Laura DeHart Young. 224 pp. Desire and passion ignite the frozen Arctic in this exciting sequel to the classic romantic adventure *Love on the Line*.
ISBN 0-931513-00-7 $11.95

WINGED ISIS by Jean Stewart. 240 pp. The long-awaited sequel to *Warriors of Isis* and the fourth in the exciting Isis series. ISBN 1-931513-01-5 $11.95

ROOM FOR LOVE by Frankie J. Jones. 192 pp. Jo and Beth must overcome the past in order to have a future together. ISBN 0-9677753-9-6 $11.95

THE QUESTION OF SABOTAGE by Bonnie J. Morris. 144 pp. A charming, sexy tale of romance, intrigue, and coming of age. ISBN 0-9677753-8-8 $11.95

SLEIGHT OF HAND by Karin Kallmaker writing as Laura Adams. 256 pp. A journey of passion, heartbreak, and triumph that reunites two women for a final chance at their destiny. ISBN 0-9677753-7-X $11.95

MOVING TARGETS: A Helen Black Mystery by Pat Welch. 240 pp. Helen must decide if getting to the bottom of a mystery is worth hitting bottom. ISBN 0-9677753-6-1 $11.95

CALM BEFORE THE STORM by Peggy J. Herring. 208 pp. Colonel Robicheaux retires from the military and comes out of the closet. ISBN 0-9677753-1-0 $11.95

OFF SEASON by Jackie Calhoun. 208 pp. Pam threatens Jenny and Rita's fledgling relationship. ISBN 0-9677753-0-2 $11.95

WHEN EVIL CHANGES FACE: A Motor City Thriller by Therese Szymanski. 240 pp. Brett Higgins is back in another heart-pounding thriller. ISBN 0-9677753-3-7 $11.95

BOLD COAST LOVE by Diana Tremain Braund. 208 pp. Jackie Claymont fights for her reputation and the right to love the woman she chooses. ISBN 0-9677753-2-9 $11.95

THE WILD ONE by Lyn Denison. 176 pp. Rachel never expected that Quinn's wild yearnings would change her life forever. ISBN 0-9677753-4-5 $11.95

SWEET FIRE by Saxon Bennett. 224 pp. Welcome to Heroy—the town with more lesbians per capita than any other place on the planet! ISBN 0-9677753-5-3 $11.95

Visit

Bella Books

at

BellaBooks.com

or call our toll-free number

1-800-729-4992